Time To Grow

Nature's Crossing Series

Interior Format

Books by CLAUDIA SHELTON...

CONTEMPORARY ROMANCE

Nature's Crossing Series
A Week at Most
Time to Grow

An Awesome Christmas Book
Cocoa for Two

ROMANTIC SUSPENSE

Shades of Leverage Series
Slater's Revenge
Dangerous Lies

Risk Series
Risk of a Lifetime

Time To Grow

Nature's Crossing Series

CLAUDIA SHELTON

CCS Writings, LLC

Dedicated to love's sunshine and rain…
Laughter and tears…
Moments and memories…
And to anyone who has ever lost their soulmate.

CHAPTER ONE

A FEW THINGS NEW York CEO Taylor Randolph had learned during the time he'd spent serving as an Army Ranger were how to hear the lies. See the trepidation. Smell the fear. Long since out of the military, those same instincts now guided him in his position as head of T-Randolph Environmental Development (TRED). And the man he'd just fired had dinged every one of those tells.

Taylor walked to the door of his office and braced his hands against the side doorjamb. Watching the hastily retreating back of the ex-employee charging down the hallway, he briefly glanced in the direction of his executive assistant's desk located outside his office.

"Mrs. Parker, call front door security. Tell them Chase Andrews no longer works here. Have them relieve him of his company credit card, phone, keys, and anything else he was issued when he came on board."

"Should I also contact our site in Nature's Crossing?" She reached for the phone.

"Yes. Jake will know what to do on that end."

He turned his attention back to Chase just in time to see the angry man shoulder-shove a woman out of his way.

She stumbled, slamming against the wall before bumping her head. Her arm collided with the table lamp, knocking it to the floor as her briefcase fell from her fingers. The satchel landed with a thud, spewing pens, notebooks, and a pink cell phone across the carpet.

Reactively, Taylor rushed to help the blonde-haired woman trying to regain her balance. She rubbed her shoulder as she kicked her phone from beneath a chair, then grimaced with the move. Hurt? That was all he needed to make this day one perfect disaster.

"Darn it, darn it," she mumbled in clear exasperation. "Double dang darn it!"

"I'm sorry. What did you say?" Taylor asked.

Kneeling on both knees now, she reached under the side chair, trying to grab her pens. "I said darn it." She glanced up at him. "Got a problem with that?"

"Nope. No problem." The touch of a Southern accent made him inwardly smile. And her eyes— the color of melted caramel—took his breath away.

He prided himself on trying to know every employee in the office, but he'd never seen this woman before. Maybe she was a new hire or lost on her way to Human Resources. Moving closer, he offered his hand to assist her in standing. "Here, let me help you up. Are you okay?"

"Yes, I'm fine. Thank you kindly." She barely

glanced at his offer of assistance. "I don't need any help."

In one fluid motion, she nudged back on her high heels and flexed upward. Trying to avoid contact, he stepped to the side as she tugged her suit into place. Brushing her skirt smooth, she blew out a soft sigh and lifted the corners of her mouth in a half-smile.

He took in the trim navy suit cropped above the knees, showing only the business-proper amount of skin. Long legs that flowed into conservative heels. And what looked like blonde hair. Hard to tell with the way her hair was twisted up tight on her head like some high fashion model.

"Human Resources is down the hall." Taylor jerked his hand to the left and pointed. He'd had enough disruption to his day. "Be sure to tell them you fell after being pushed by Chase Andrews. They can help you fill out the proper paperwork. Get you medical attention."

"There's no need for that. I'm fine. I just—"

"Fine now, but you could wake up tomorrow with a concussion." Yeah, he knew he sounded over-reactive. But, damn it, he didn't like anyone getting hurt on his watch.

She didn't budge. "I don't need to fill out paperwork."

"Human Resources." He pointed to the left again. "Fill out the paperwork. See the nurse."

"Oh, excuse me." She stooped to pick up a pen lying by his foot. Her fingers lightly touched the side of his arm as she steadied herself when she rose, then blushed and stepped back. "Sorry."

His mouth dried like sand in a high noon desert sun. The warmth of her touch lingered on his skin, shocking him with the unexpected sensation. He glanced at his forearm then felt the heat travel all the way to his core.

He needed this reaction like he needed to be called up on active duty again. Thankfully, he'd never been attracted to an employee, and he sure as hell didn't plan to start now. He gulped in a breath of air a moment before he focused on her face and opened his mouth to speak.

She stop-signed him with the palm of her hand. "Okay…okay…okay. If it makes you happy, I'll fill out paperwork."

"Good." He had things to do. People to see. The past to get past. He half-turned away. "Keep a copy for yourself, too."

"Why not? In fact, maybe there'll be a hundred pages." The woman pushed wisps of her hair that had loosened in the altercation back in place. "I'm sure the world won't mind losing a tree for the tiny bump on my head."

Sass? She'd sassed him? "Do you know who I am?"

"Does it matter?"

"Yes, it matters."

"Why?" She stared into his eyes. Didn't blink. Didn't smile. Didn't appear intimidated in the least. "Why is knowing who you are so important?"

"Because…because I said so." That even sounded childish to himself. He inwardly winced at the wrinkling of his forehead as his eyebrows pinched together. The woman had turned him into a babbling idiot. Exasperating. That's what she was.

Struggling to keep his reactions in check, he braced his hands on his waist. "As I was saying. Do you know—"

Behind him, he heard Mrs. Parker laugh along with a fake clearing of her throat.

He knew full well her cleared throat was his clue to calm down. Don't overreact. They'd worked together long enough to have their signals. But the laugh? The laugh was new. "Mrs. Parker, is there something funny?"

"No, sir." The middle-aged woman shuffled papers on her desk. "Not a thing."

He focused back on the long-legged blonde who'd defied him. She met his gaze, confident and unapologetic. Then, as if everything was her idea, she turned and walked down the hallway toward Human Resources.

Unable to drag his eyes away, he watched the way her jacket hugged her waist. The glide of the skirt skimming her hips. Her slender ankles as they balanced safe and secure with every step she took until she turned the corner. With any luck, he wouldn't run into her again.

Although, if he wanted to, he could find out her name from Human Resources. See which department she worked in. Check on her progress and… Nope, one of his rules was don't mix business and pleasure.

Besides, this was the first woman in a very long time who'd stoked his fire the moment he laid eyes on her. Didn't mean a thing. Just an already rough day, sharpening a dull edge.

He'd made himself a promise years ago. The day his life had shattered in a barrage of bullets halfway around the world. Loss was always hard. But failing so many people he'd cared about, all in one day, had changed his outlook on life forever. Some days he wished he could just move to Nature's Crossing permanently, instead of being stuck here at his office in Kansas City part of the week. At least this setup had allowed him to move out of New York.

He rolled his shirtsleeves down and buttoned the cuffs before turning toward his own office. Time to focus on his next appointment. He lifted a couple of butterscotch candies from the dish on the corner of his assistant's desk. "Guess I got a little absorbed for a second."

"I don't know what you're talking about, Mr. Randolph." Mrs. Parker held out a folder. "Here's the extra info you requested earlier today."

Some days, Mrs. Parker knew him better than he knew himself even if she did try to mother him, telling him what she thought he should do. How he should move on with his life. He let her. Only her. Others knew to keep their thoughts to themselves.

"Thanks. You know, I think I'll keep you around." Taylor grinned and tossed a candy in his mouth, remembering the day almost three years ago that he'd inherited Mrs. Parker along with the chair his dad used to sit in as the head of TRED.

"Oh, that's such a relief, sir." She patted her heart in mock thankfulness at his remark. "You don't know how worried I was about that."

Trim, professional, and somewhere in her late fifties, she'd let him know she expected to be treated with the same respect that she'd always garnered from his father. Part of which meant he'd call her Mrs. Parker, and she'd call him Mr. Randolph. He smiled to himself. And any comments about her prematurely gray hair or dangly earrings would not be tolerated. That part he'd learned the hard way.

He pocketed another piece of candy, then walked across the hall to the executive conference room. The room and the view always seemed to center him. Today was no different.

Thinking about his upcoming meeting with Crawford Enterprises, he wished his old college buddy Mathew Crawford was the one coming. But today's meeting would be with a company representative instead. Years ago, Mathew had mentioned his brother and him planning a business after college. Maybe that's who was coming. But for the life of him, he couldn't remember the brother's name.

If today's deal worked out the way he hoped, he and Mathew would have plenty of time to hash over college times. They'd only been friends in passing, but they'd kept in touch occasionally after graduation, then less and less. In fact, he hadn't heard from him since about the time his own life had been hurtling out of control. Life had been one giant blur of business since then.

Taylor left the calming atmosphere of the conference room and headed back to his office. The image of the long-legged blonde flitted through his thoughts. Had she found her way to Human Resources? Before he left for the day, he'd make a call to see if she filled out the paperwork or if she'd simply ignored him once she turned out of sight.

"Anything else you need for your meeting?" Mrs. Parker asked as he passed her desk.

"Yeah. I can't believe I'm saying this, but…" he laughed at himself, "I've completely forgotten the name of the man I'm meeting from Crawford Enterprises."

"Rylie…Rylie Crawford."

CHAPTER TWO

BRIDGETTE RYLIE CRAWFORD walked a few steps down the hall toward Human Resources and pretended to be rummaging in the side of her briefcase. She didn't need to fill out paperwork. She wasn't hurt. Sooner or later, Taylor Randolph would go back in his office, then she could introduce herself to his assistant. She'd already swallowed a ton of nerves when he reached out to help her up from the floor.

Then he'd asked if she knew who he was. Of course, she knew. But right then had not seemed like a good time to introduce herself. Especially when less than a minute before she'd been kneeling on the floor in front of him, searching for pens and her composure.

He was every bit as handsome as his photos on the Internet, where articles declared him to be a thirty-eight-year-old mastermind in leadership. Of course, his dark-brown hair was a bit longer than what she would have imagined for a businessman of his magnitude. Plus, the flash of sunburst amber in his intense hazel-green eyes had been completely unexpected.

At least six-two, clean-shaved and broad-shouldered, he'd more than fill her dream of the ideal man. When she touched him to steady herself, his rock-solid forearms had sizzled with energy beneath her fingers.

From the impatient look on Taylor's face and the instructions he'd given his assistant, the man who'd charged out of his office had evidently crossed an invisible line. Was this what she had to contend with in her negotiations? An invisible line she might stumble over? In fact, she might have just crossed that line with her saving a tree remark. She sighed. Only time would tell on that front, but nothing would sidetrack her goal—a contract with TRED.

After what seemed like forever instead of five minutes, the muffled voices of the CEO and his assistant ended with the closing of a door. His office door, Rylie hoped.

She'd used the Crawford Enterprises stationery that listed her deceased husband Mathew and herself as owners when she answered the ad for a consulting contract a few months ago. Her company was desperate for this business, and she'd used the only leverage she might have… Mathew and Taylor's history as college classmates. But when the request for the proposal had come, she'd submitted that on the company's new stationery listing her as the CEO/Owner.

Glancing around the corner, Rylie once again smoothed the short skirt of her four-year-old navy suit, then tugged the worn jacket into place. She tightened her fingers around the handle of her six-year-old Coach briefcase. It might be scuffed, but this was her lucky case. The one Mathew bought her when a dollar meant the world to them.

Rylie's cell phone vibrated, and caller ID displayed her sister's name. She knew about the meeting and probably wouldn't have phoned if it weren't important.

Hoping no one would be there, Rylie stepped into the women's restroom across the hall. "Yes, Gwen. What do you need?"

"I know you're busy, but… Well, like it or not, I don't think you should go through with your plan." Rapid and to the point was one of her sister's qualities.

"Of course, I'm going to meet with Taylor Randolph. I flew all the way to Missouri for this opportunity." Rylie checked the stalls in the bathroom. All clear. "What would possibly make you think I wouldn't?"

"That's not what I meant." Gwen sighed. "Yes, you should meet him. Let him see what a fool he'd be not to hire you on the spot." Gwen paused, inhaled deep, and exhaled long. "Just remember, you were the one who built the business plan for the company when you and Mathew first started out. The one who always saw the growth potential every year. Crawford Enterprises is an A-one company because of the original footing you built. You don't need to beg for the contract."

Before today, Rylie had never resorted to anything but good honest truth in her business dealings. And that's what she planned to do now.

But the employees had put their faith in her when they agreed to stay on without any raises last year. This year had hit an even bigger financial loss. She needed this contract and would do whatever it took to come out with something. Even if she had to remind Taylor that she was the widow of an old acquaintance.

"Are you still there?" Gwen asked.

"Yes, I'm here." Rylie stared at herself in the mirror. "Do you think I haven't thought about what I'm doing? This isn't easy for me, you know."

"That's what I mean. Don't go in begging. Don't downplay your place in Crawford's success."

"You seem to forget, the company's in the red."

"And you seem to forget that the accountant's embezzlement didn't happen on your watch. Happened on Mathew's. You're the one who discovered it during an audit, once you took complete control of the company, after his death," Gwen mumbled under her breath. "Listen to me, sis. You are great at what you do. And whether you get the contract or not, don't go in there begging. You'll hate yourself in the end."

Rylie already hated herself, but if there was no other way, then there was no other way. "Thanks for calling, but it's time for the appointment. I've got to go."

"Mathew wouldn't want you to be untrue to yourself. Not this way. He would—"

"Mathew's not here, Gwen. He's gone." Rylie's voice cracked. "I'm here. And I'm in charge. Good-bye."

Glancing in the restroom mirror, she dampened

a paper towel with cold water and lightly blotted her neck. Staring back at her was the doubt in her expression, the slump of her shoulders, and the red blotches threatening to shine forth on her cheeks.

Quickly, she dabbed on a bit of concealer, but there was nothing she could do about the nervous queasiness that had taken hold inside her stomach. She freshened her lipstick and smiled at the reflection. Still not good enough. Again, she applied her lipstick, smiled, and added in a shoulder straightening this time. Better...lots better.

Bottom line, Crawford Enterprises needed the TRED contract to stay afloat. By the time she walked out the front door of the building later today, she'd have that contract. And, if not, then she'd know she'd given everything she had, and her everything just hadn't been good enough to impress Taylor Randolph.

Alive with confidence, Rylie left the restroom and walked to the executive assistant's desk. "Mrs. Parker, I'm Rylie Crawford." She handed her business card to the woman. "I have an appointment with Mr. Randolph."

The assistant shot her a you're-kidding-me glance along with the arch of her eyebrows, then pushed the button on her intercom phone. "Sir, Rylie Crawford is here for your appointment."

"Got it." His voice echoed through the speaker. "I'm finishing up a call, but go ahead and send Mr. Crawford in."

Mister? The assumption tweaked a well-known

reaction in Rylie, one she'd faced many times in her business career. The assistant reached for the intercom button once again, but Rylie waved her off.

"Let's make this a surprise. Maybe he'll get a laugh out of my being a woman."

Mrs. Parker looked unsure for a moment, then brushed her finger across the date on the desk calendar. Smiling, the assistant motioned her toward the meeting. "Give it a try. He could probably use a laugh today."

CHAPTER THREE

RYLIE PUSHED AGAINST one of the heavy double doors leading into Taylor's office, and it slid open with the ease and quiet of money well spent. Instantly, a panorama of the Kansas City skyline filled her view. The vista of skyscrapers mingled among vintage buildings in numerous styles of architecture and windows and facades. The Missouri River, marking the division between Missouri and Kansas, in the background.

Her breath caught. She never ceased to be amazed when overlooking a panorama, city or urban, from a higher vantage. "Unbelievable. Truly unbelievable."

Taylor's oversized mahogany desk sat centered in front of the view. The back of a black leather high-back chair, currently swiveled toward the skyline, revealed nothing of the man on the other side except the back of his head. His oversized office, furnished with greens and browns, woods and granite, polished brass and supple leather, felt professional. Yet, the ambiance pulled her in with the feel and slight scent of the great outdoors. Pots of saplings to tall trees accented the space, along with the slash of gold letters along the sidewall—TRED.

Quietly, Taylor turned the chair around to face her, and for a brief moment, confusion blanketed his face. Then the corners of his mouth quirked as he placed the phone in its cradle. Eyeing her with the intensity of a lion questioning why his prey had walked into his realm, he rolled back into control with ease. "We meet again."

"Yes, we meet again." She held out her hand. "I'm Rylie Crawford. It's nice to officially meet you, Mr. Randolph."

"Please have a seat. You'll have to excuse me for saying so, Ms. Crawford, but you're not exactly what I expected." He offered a secure business handshake along with an unmoving expression that said he didn't let the world know his thoughts.

"Which was?" The warmth of his touch lingered on her hand, folding around her like heat from a crackling fire after a cold day on the slopes.

"A man." Never missing a beat in his outward demeanor, he retrieved his suit coat from a small closet at the side of the office. With the ease of born style, he slid into the jacket as he walked back to his desk.

"When Mathew and I were in college, he talked about him and his brother starting a company together. I thought Rylie might be his brother's name." Taylor eased into his chair, not one bit flustered by his blunder. "Doesn't matter. My mistake. I hope you'll accept my apology for the wrong assumption."

Nodding, she sat down in the chair across the desk from him. "Mathew's brother was part of the business, but it was Mathew and I that started Crawford Enterprises as a design and engineering company in the real estate field."

She knew these words by heart after all the recitations she'd made over the past few years. In fact, she could almost hear Mathew telling her to watch her tone. "Once I finished my MBA, we decided to expand the company into commercial and developer real estate sales as well. We deliberately remained small to retain the personal level, but have a contingent of trusted, repeat contractors at the call. There may be less than thirty Crawford Enterprise employees, but I have access to hundreds of contractors on a moment's notice."

What was she bragging about? He probably had ten times that many people working for him worldwide. TRED was known to be a family business. One Taylor's father started over two decades ago. One that was now had a worldwide reputation for excellent work.

Heart racing, she fidgeted in the chair, biting her lip. This meeting would go nowhere if she couldn't regain her composure. Think of him as a friend of the family. She stilled. Her heart slowed. Think of him as Mathew's friend. Her breathing shallowed back to normal.

"As far as the name goes, I'm named after someone who saved my dad's life in Vietnam. My given name is Bridgette Rylie Crawford." She smiled as she felt the ease of conversation filter into her mind. "When I was little, my dad always called me Rylie, and it stuck."

Taylor crossed his hands in front of him, nodding. "I assure you there was no offense intended. Man or woman, it doesn't matter to me as long as the work gets done."

"Is that so? Would you have put your suit coat on for Mathew?"

As the words escaped her lips, she realized he hadn't been patronizing. He'd been businesslike and confident. She was the one playing a part. Trying to be strong enough to outwit a millionaire was harder than she'd imagined.

He stared at her as his brow furrowed along with the clench of his jaw, then he cleared his throat. "I was tied up this morning and didn't get a chance to review the Crawford proposal again. Why don't we get right to the point and discuss the reason you're here?"

Her insides shouted at her stupidity, but she didn't withdraw her question. From the way he'd moved on with their meeting, she knew he didn't plan to answer either. But if those few words lost her company's chance, she had no one to blame but herself.

She felt him watching her from the corner of his eye as he leaned back in his chair as if he had all the time in the world. As for her, she'd never been so nervous in all her life. Must be why she'd spoke before she thought. Previously, she'd always felt comfortable in her presentations, but not this time.

Pulling two copies of her proposal from her

briefcase, she laid one in front of him and one on her side of the desk. He moved forward in his chair and looked down at the first page of her proposal as she exhaled, ready for the biggest negotiation of her life. Quickly, she delved into her presentation. No games. No sass. No nerves. She just focused on her pure professional business knowledge.

For the next hour, the two of them discussed costs and plat layout for the new housing development in Nature's Crossing. Parcels and expectations. Percentages and bonuses. He offered, she countered, he questioned, she responded.

She knew her company inside and out. Knew she had all the licenses necessary. And, without a doubt, she knew how to sell good property investments to builders. To see their visions. To know the limits of the overall development. Her nerves evaporated, and she quickly fell into the ease she had in quoting figures and stats in a nanosecond.

Ultimately, he contemplated, made notes, drew diagrams, and made more notes. In a purely professional manner, he looked her up and down as if assessing her strength and reliability. Glanced at her briefcase, the sleeves of her suit coat.

"Nice. You made some good points on those suggestions for increasing sale options. Do you have any questions for me?" Taylor leaned forward in his chair.

"How many builder sections have you divided your acreage into?"

"Six. Plus, I've kept one section to build houses

I've designed." He reached into his desk, pulled out a sheet of paper, and handed her the list of specifics on the Peaceful Lake Acres development. "As you already know, there are minimum lot sizes for each builder section. All infrastructure, including street lighting, signs, flower beds, and other aesthetics of the development, will all be installed per TRED specifications. Roads are already in the works, as are the main lines for utilities."

"Will builders be required to pay the cost of their portion of infrastructure at closing?"

"Negotiable." Taylor semi-smiled.

She nodded in agreement. "That can be a good asset when it comes to my working to get the top price for the builder section."

"Exactly. You need to have a chip to play on your side, too." Taylor leaned back, pushing aside her proposal. "Now, in one concise, simply worded statement, tell me the basics of what you'll do for TRED and Peaceful Lake Acres."

This she knew by heart and knew how to make things happen. "My job is to become familiar with the overall layout and plans for the development. To research builders interested in the location or the idea of building with nature in mind, and get a feel of what other developments within the state will offer the same amenities. And even though I'm sure you stay on top of codes and pricing, I will do the same just to make sure builders don't try to take shortcuts in building plans, quality, or price points.

"Bottom line, I'm there to get the builder

sections sold while keeping the reputation of
TRED. I'm not there to sell individual lots or give
advice on the pricing of such. And just because
a builder is the first to show interest in a section
doesn't mean they are first in line. Negotiations
are fluid. You—meaning TRED—have the final
say. I make sure the paperwork is signed, sealed,
and delivered. Is that enough?"

"That's enough." He picked up her proposal
and walked to the windows. Whether it had been
enough or not, she'd done her best, and it was
damn good, if she did say so herself. Gwen had
been right after all. Now it was up to the man at
the window. The one with his back to her once
again.

"If you have further questions, I'd be happy to
answer them."

"No, I've got what I need."

He braced one hand against the window
bracket, staring out. The papers in his other hand
hung at his side. After a bit, he glanced over his
shoulder at her, then back at the skyline, but she
could feel he wasn't being rude. Rather, this was
his way of making a decision. Unable to gauge
his reaction, she repacked her briefcase as her
mind skimmed through her presentation. Things
had gone well except for that one outburst about
the suit coat.

"I like your ideas. Your commission breakdown."
Taylor eased into the black leather sanctuary of
his chair and reviewed the stack of papers again,
then laid them aside as he leaned back and looked
her in the eye. "From what I see, I think we can

make this work. What do you think?"

"Yes. Definitely yes." She quivered on a sigh of relief. She had the contract. She had the money to keep Crawford Enterprises alive. She still had a piece of Mathew.

If Taylor noticed her elation, he didn't show it. "You know it means someone in your company will be spending a lot of time in Nature's Crossing, right? I plan to be hands-on with this project, and I expect a representative from Crawford Enterprises to be onsite, too. Agreed?"

A representative? No, she wouldn't trust this job to anyone else. Commute? Too expensive. Rylie's world shifted with the only solution. "I'll be happy to move to Nature's Crossing. That way, I'll be onsite, and you won't be bothered with a move. I assure you, I can handle the job by myself."

"Trust me, I wouldn't have hired you if I didn't think you could do the job. Maybe I should explain. You see…" Taylor blinked a couple of times. "Never mind."

"No, I'd like to hear what you have to say."

He took a deep breath, and his shoulders eased just a bit as he turned to look at her again. "You see, when I was a kid, my dad worked forty-hour weeks at his job, then he started this company from the back of his pickup on weekends. Those first couple of years, I worked side-by-side with him, weekends and after school. Sunup to sundown during summer break. Hard work, but a lot of good times, too." He glanced away. "I miss those days."

She didn't know where he was headed with this explanation, but she knew to pay close attention. His casual, trusting tone spoke more about their future work relationship than the words he was saying.

"What has that got to do with you packing up and moving to Nature's Crossing?"

"Oh, I'm not moving there for good. Just for this project. In fact, I've kept a large tract of land to develop eco-friendly homes under my personal division of TRED." His shoulders straightened along with a quick nod, looking as if he'd made his point. "And my crew will be comprised of at least fifty percent military veterans."

"You sound excited."

"Been a long time since I was part of a work crew. Or the military." He raked his finger through his hair. "I need those feelings in my life again. Even if I'll actually be stuck running the KC office from the local construction office most of the time, I'll still be able to feel that surge of onsite adrenaline. So, since I run the company now, I get to say where I go. Right now, I want to be in Nature's Crossing." He cocked his head at her, quirking the corner of his mouth. "Does that make sense?"

"Makes perfect sense to me." From the research she'd done on Nature's Crossing, she had to agree it sounded like a peaceful location just waiting for this new infusion of nature-inclusive development and people. "Honestly, I'm excited by the prospect of reviving the community, too."

"Okay then. I was beginning to think I was

the only one who could understand where I'm coming from on this project." Taylor stood and extended his hand across the desk. "My assistant will have the contract drawn up for your signature and put in overnight mail today."

"Sounds good. Thank you so very much." Her insides were binging on energy. All by herself, she'd negotiated the biggest deal of her life. She glanced at her watch, making sure she still had time to make her flight back to her parents' home in South Carolina.

As if her hand had a mind of its own, she found herself accepting his handshake. The heat notched upward. "Thank you for the opportunity. I won't let you down."

"I'm sure you won't."

She glanced at her watch. Then nervously looked back up and smiled. "I'm sorry, it's just that I have a flight to catch, and I'm not sure how hard it will be to get a taxi at this hour. My plane leaves in a couple of hours. And I don't know how long getting thru security takes at this airport."

"No problem. But we better get you out the door and on the way to the airport now." Using the intercom, he instructed Mrs. Parker to have a limo waiting in front of the office building. He pointed toward the door rapidly. "We need to get you on the way, now."

Quickly bundling everything into her lucky briefcase, she followed his directions to get going.

Taylor's footsteps closed behind her as he walked her out of his office, over to Mrs. Parker's desk.

She stopped and turned. His towering presence invaded her personal space, but she didn't back away. "Is there anything else for the moment?"

From his pocket, the ringtone of a cell phone filled the air with "Airborne Cadence." She knew that song. One filled with soldiers, training, and jumping out of planes.

"Excuse me." Taylor checked the caller ID on the cell phone, then smiled and let it go to voice mail. The man looked happy. The happiest she'd seen him since she first laid eyes on him.

Heat raced to fill her entire being, and she parted her lips. The mere action of his movements, his expression, his momentary smile had set her core in motion. She smoothed her palms across her skirt once again.

"Sorry about that." He returned to her side.

"'Airborne Cadence', that was great!" Rylie couldn't stop the smile that filled her lips. "My dad is retired military, but he used to sing that to my mom. In fact, he uses that same ring tone sometimes. Maybe you two know each other?"

"Doubtful. I've been out of the Army for quite a while."

She felt him in her personal space. A nearness that she'd missed the past few years, but she pushed the thought aside. "You were about to say something before the phone rang."

"Yes, about the suit coat." For a moment, he seemed to sense their closeness, too. Almost imperceptible, he leaned away. "When a person comes in this office for a meeting with me, and they're dressed in a suit, I give them the respect of wearing my suit coat. I may not always give them the job, but I give them respect for showing up in a professional manner."

"Thank you." She smiled. There he was, being nice…respectful…thoughtful, again. "By the way, since we'll be working together, please call me Rylie. May I call you Taylor?"

"Okay."

Mrs. Parker motioned toward the elevator bank. "Hurry, or you'll miss your flight. The limo service said they'd be here between ten and twenty minutes, but that was five minutes ago."

She started down the hall. "Thank you both for everything. I'll call when I—"

"Hurry. Hurry!" Taylor said. "I sure don't want Mathew mad at me the first day of our new working arrangement. In fact, I'll give him a call to let him know you're headed home."

She stopped. And the hole in her heart ripped open again. A chill pulsed through her body. Her hand trembled as she fist-clutched it against her stomach. She slowly turned to face him. He didn't know. How was that possible?

"Is there something wrong, Ms. Crawford?" Taylor stared into her eyes as though reading the panic coursing through her brain.

"I…I thought you knew. Mathew…" Her words froze in her throat.

"Knew what?"

Stretching her neck upward just a bit, she lifted her face to look into Taylor's eyes. "Mathew and his brother were killed in a plane crash three years ago."

Rylie watched Taylor's expression change from business to disbelief. His face paled along with the twitch of his eye as he took a few steps backward. He was visibly shaken, and she wanted to reach out to him but couldn't bring herself to move.

"I'm sorry for your loss, Ms. Crawford. I…I didn't…I…mean…" His voice hoarsened with the words. "Sorry."

"Thank you." When Mathew died, she'd asked her father to call all the names in her husband's address book to let them know of his passing. In fact, in the column next to Taylor's name had been written that two calls had been made, two voice messages left.

She noticed Mrs. Parker discreetly watching him as he heaved in a couple of deep, ragged breaths. He seemed to lose himself as he stared at the bowl of candy on the corner of her desk. The assistant pressed her hand against his shoulder, tapped a couple of times.

Mrs. Parker cleared her throat. "Sir, the call you've been expecting is on the line. Press number eight. Do you have your phone?"

Rummaging in his pocket, he nodded and headed into his office. "Sorry, Ms. Crawford. I need to take this call."

"Number eight, Mr. Randolph."

Every time Rylie faced telling someone about Mathew's death, she felt an overwhelming reliving of that day. Most people gave a word of condolence, she thanked them, and they moved on with life. This had felt different. He'd been shaken.

"Is he okay?" Rylie asked Mrs. Parker.

"Yes, of course. I'm sure the news was a shock, but he'll be fine. He really does have a lot of phone calls to take care of today."

"That had to be horrible, learning of Mathew's death so abruptly." Rylie lightly shook her head. "I truly thought he knew."

"I'm sure you did." Mrs. Parker pointed toward the elevator bank and walked alongside her. "Now, let's get you on that plane."

CHAPTER FOUR

RYLIE DASHED ACROSS the front lobby and thru the revolving doors. Something about being outside made her feel as if her contract was real. Taylor's reaction to Mathew's death had been unexpected. Distressing. She struggled to pull herself together before she hyperventilated and collapsed. The last thing she needed was for Taylor to find her passed out in front of the building.

At least she had some time to compose herself before the limo arrived. She walked over to the central fountain and sat on the edge of the concrete, dragging her fingers in the water before patting them against her cheeks and forehead. With a quick flick of her fingers, she released her hair from the clip and shook her long, straight hair free. The cool breeze fluttered the strands wildly about her face, eliciting a soothing sigh along with a smile to herself. She loved the wind and its promise to bring a change no matter which way it blew.

Except for signing the paperwork, she had a contract with T-Randolph Environmental

Development. Unable to contain herself anymore, she fisted her hand high above her head, then pumped her arm up and down, hard and fast. "Yes. Yes. Yes!"

Changing to a pair of pink tennis shoes, Rylie powered on her cell phone and dialed her temporary office number. She told herself she'd cut back on staff because she was between commitments and had no base of operations. True. Partly true. The bigger part was the money. She'd saved even more by asking her sister to fill in as her assistant for a few weeks.

"Crawford Enterprises. How may I help you, mate?" Gwen answered in an exaggerated Cockney accent.

Rylie released a loud moan and shook the phone, eyes crossing as she held the cell in front of her face for a microphone. "You've got to stop doing that."

"Oh, 'ello dearie. Stop doing what?"

"Today you're British. Yesterday you were Western, and I never figured out what it was the day before."

Gwen giggled. "It was you. No, actually, it was a cross between you and Bernadette Peters. Don't you just love the way she talks? And her hair. I'm thinking of doing my hair like hers. What do you think?"

Rylie did a slow count to ten before she answered. "Gwen?"

"Yes?"

"Be a little more professional when you answer the phone. Please."

"I'll try." Gwen's voice lost its excitement.

"Do more than try. Understand?" Rylie snapped.

"Understood loud and clear, your highness." Gwen's tone snapped even louder. "Now you understand this, Bridgette Rylie Crawford. Either pay me a salary or find someone else to take your messages. And your attitude."

Rylie slumped inside and out. Her sister only used her full name when she was good and mad or when she knew she was right. This outburst seemed to be about both. "I'm sorry. I shouldn't have… Gwen? Gwen, are you there?"

Her sister had hung up. Who could blame her when she had financial problems of her own to worry about?

Frustrated, Rylie pushed the phone into her jacket pocket and made her way toward the driver motioning her to the black SUV. She slid inside, glad to be heading home. "I'm in a hurry to get to the airport."

"Yes, ma'am. We've got plenty of time." The chauffeur offered her a bottled water and tucked another into the cup holder for the seat beside her. "I got a call to wait an extra five minutes for one other passenger."

She buckled her seatbelt and lifted the water in acknowledgment before placing it in the cup holder next to the other one. "Thanks."

Famished because she'd been too nervous to eat before her meeting, she pulled a napkin and orange from her briefcase along with a baggie before easing back in the seat. She could relax now that she had the contract, so she closed her eyes for a moment, relishing the thought that she had held on to her and Mathew's dream a bit longer.

At least five minutes passed, and she noticed the driver texting. Finished, he glanced at his watch and walked to the driver's side door, slid behind the wheel. "The other passenger is just finishing a meeting. I'll give him five more minutes. No more."

True to his word, the limo driver started the SUV and moved forward at the deadline. A second later, the driver slammed on the brakes. The car ricocheted once, then stilled. All she saw as she made an unsuccessful grab for her runaway orange was a man's hand waving two hundred-dollar bills in front of the windshield.

The driver powered down the passenger window. "Hop in. We've got to get going."

Before Rylie could react, the back-seat passenger door was yanked open, and a suit coat flew through the air, landing in her lap. Next, a carry-on suitcase was rammed across the seat and crashed into her side.

"Ouch. What the heck do you think you're doing?" Rylie glared at the man who filled the doorway before he slid into the seat next to her—Taylor Randolph. Plopping her head back against the seat, she cringed at her own mistake.

Taylor turned the luggage sideways, squeezed himself into the empty space, and slammed the door, tossing the money to the driver. "Thanks for waiting. You can just drop me at the airport's main entrance today."

She pushed his jacket off her lap, but his scent lingered on her senses. "We're already on our way to the airport."

"I know, but seeing this is my usual driver, he would have taken me all the way to the side terminal. This saves him a stop this time. Gets you there faster." His gaze lingered on her face, and his lips turned up ever so slightly. "You let your hair down. Looks better that way."

The heat from her blush reached all the way to her brain. And to another little part of her body she'd refused to free the past few years. She caught the attention of the cab driver. "It's a little warm in here. Could you turn the A/C up a bit, please?"

The cabbie nodded. "Sure thing."

Taylor bent to retrieve his coat from the floor bed along with her still unpeeled orange.

"Mine," she said.

"You gonna eat this?"

"That's the plan."

"Look, it's going on three thirty, and I haven't eaten since five this morning. How about half?" He tore the orange open with one quick motion, then held the two pieces out to her in his hands.

Rylie took half. The smaller half. Of her own orange. Something about that didn't seem right. "Do you always barge right in and take control?"

"You'll find I'm full of bad habits. Do you happen to have another napkin?"

"No, I don't." Next, he'd want half of her napkin. She swallowed the catch in her throat and tried to focus on the back of the seat ahead of her. His pure masculinity mixed with a store-bought outdoor scent of sandalwood, cedar, and musk pulled her in, playing pitter-pat with her senses. Nice. Very, very nice. "Ummm."

"Did you say something?" Taylor asked.

"Me? No."

He yanked a handkerchief from his inside breast pocket and stacked the pieces of orange rind in the center. "By the way, Ms. Crawford, why did you feel the need to lie to me in your company's proposal?"

"I didn't lie." She also didn't give him the satisfaction of looking at him, even though she felt his non-wavering stare.

"Really?" Taylor paused. "I checked the file. Your correspondence listed yourself and Mathew on the letterhead." He paused again. "What do you call that? Or haven't you had to reorder stationery in the past three years since Mathew's death?"

One of the hardest days of her life had been when she removed Mathew's name from all aspects of the business. But she'd kept a stack of the original stationery as a memory of what had been. She had new letterhead. New envelopes. New imprinted bank checks. New licenses. New marketing layouts. New everything. Except for Mathew.

"Yes, the original response letter was on the old letterhead. Yes, I did that to remind you of your friend from college. But I signed that letter with the word Owner beneath my name." She turned to face Taylor. "But I. Did. Not. Put the proposal on the old stationery. If you take a closer look, you will see that has only my name as owner on the letterhead."

He laughed. "You are really something, Ms. Crawford. Really something."

"Thank you. I try to be." Now was definitely not the time to remind him to call her Rylie.

She stared at a piece of lint on the back of the driver's seat. It dawned on her that in the world of high-stakes business, Crawford Enterprises was nothing more than a speck of lint compared to TRED. Question was, how long could the fluff hang on?

"That wasn't a compliment." Taylor propped his elbow on the suitcase wedged between them and continued to stare in her direction. "I'll tell you what you did. You used Mathew's name. And you used his and my friendship from college. You manipulated how I'd look at the proposal without giving yourself a chance to get the contract on your own. Am I right?"

Her stomach churned as she glanced in the rearview mirror, then looked away from the accusing yet sympathetic reflection of the driver's eyes. This wasn't her proudest moment.

"I call it networking." The fluff of lint still clung to the seat.

"I call it a lie." Taylor leaned back.

She couldn't disagree. Not if she were being honest with herself. What had happened to the man in the office that was so upset at the mention of Mathew's death? "Does this mean I don't have a contract?"

Taylor took the time to glance at her briefcase, let his eyes linger longer than a moment. "I didn't say that."

So, what did that exactly mean? She needed to plead her case right now before he made up his mind.

"Okay, I was wrong. I shouldn't have used the letterhead to get your attention. But I have payroll to meet and employees to think about. Families that count on a paycheck and health insurance every day of their lives." She turned to face him. "I did what I had to do, and I'd do it again. I need this contract to save Mathew's company."

"Crawford Enterprises has been around for quite a while. Why do you need TRED now?"

"Other companies have figured out our system and are moving in on our current market share. The only way to keep our place in the field is to move up to the next market level. Understand?" She didn't need to explain about the bookkeeper who'd embezzled a good chunk of the company profits for a couple of years. Embezzlement that had happened because Mathew insisted on being in charge of the company finances, yet never paying enough attention to them.

She didn't wait for Taylor's answer. "Bottom line, Crawford Enterprises needs more clout to move to the next level. With TRED on my company's resume, I can keep the company alive. Uh…I mean…keep the business inching up the ranks."

Taylor frowned as he searched her face with

his gaze, then turned back to the passing world outside the car window. What had he seen in her face? When she looked in the mirror each morning, she usually saw desperation…and loneliness.

She softened her thoughts along with her voice. "Think about it. If the original letterhead hadn't got your attention, would you have requested the Crawford proposal?"

The driver and Taylor shared a brief glance before he bit into the orange, downing it in two bites. She finished her half of the orange segment by segment, then shoved the rind and napkin into the baggie. After setting the package next to her satchel in the floor bed, she settled back in the seat and tried to ignore him.

Taylor pointed at the baggie. "Are you finished with that?"

"Yes. I'll pitch it when I get to a trash bin."

He reached downward just as the limo swerved to avoid a car. The action threw him toward her side of the backseat, and his hand braced against the calf of her leg. She jumped and caught her breath as tiny, soft, titillating tingles shot up her leg.

"Sorry." He looked as shaken as she felt when he held the baggie up for her to see. Quick and to the point, he placed his rinds inside, then jerked the zipper closed again. "Ms. Crawford, you still have your contract."

Her sigh escaped before she could stop the relief. "You won't be disappointed."

"I don't expect to be. Mathew's name may

have gotten you the read. Maybe not. We'll never know." His body eased along with the tone of his words. "You got the contract based on the proposal and today's meeting. Understand me? *You* got the contract. There was no preferential treatment going on in that office today. I don't do business that way."

An inside glow of accomplishment boosted every doubt she'd had about herself as leader of Crawford. "Thank you for saying so."

"Mrs. Parker will have the paperwork in overnight mail this afternoon. You should receive that tomorrow. Just sign off and overnight the contract back to me by the next day."

Rylie tilted her head at his presumptuousness. She was happy for the offer, but she wasn't about to sign off on anything that wasn't in Crawford Enterprise's best interest. "First, I'll look over the contract. If there's anything I have a question on or need changed, I'll contact you. Would you prefer phone, text, or email?"

"Ms. Crawford, I have a standard way of doing business with a standard contract. If it's not to your satisfaction, I suggest we dissolve our association before it begins."

"Mr. Randolph, there's no need to get so upset before I've even requested a modification. Besides, I thought we agreed to call each other by our first names... Taylor." Something about the way his name felt on her tongue, flamed by his corner-of-the-eye look in her direction, only added to her inside's fluttering.

Minutes later, the driver pulled to the curb in

front of the airport and completed the signature receipt with Taylor as Rylie reached in her purse. Leaning over the seat, she handed the cabbie a twenty. "I don't have an extra hundred, but I do appreciate your service."

"Thank you very much." The man glanced in Taylor's direction, then back to her. "I'm glad you got your contract."

"Me, too." Nodding, she walked around the back of the cab. Her future boss waited on the sidewalk.

"You're a soft touch," Taylor said.

"I call it being considerate."

Side-by-side, they headed into the terminal. His long strides seemed deliberate, but she kept up. Two steps to his one. Was he deliberately trying to make her walk fast? Because she sure wouldn't need a workout after this.

"I'll have you know I'm considerate, too," he said, as if to himself.

She stared straight ahead.

Rylie stopped at an overhead departure screen to find the gate she needed. One day in and out for business was the best way to travel. No luggage and no hotel expense, either.

She shook her head. "Whatever you say. By the way, for my information, were you following me when you requested the limo wait?"

"Nope. I was in a hurry. Got to catch a flight to Surryfield, which is the closest town to Nature's Crossing with an airport terminal. Otherwise, I'd have to go by private plane, which would mean more money and flying into one of the little private airports in the county. The Nature's Crossing Town Council Meeting is tonight, and I give them an update every time. Besides which, I've become attached… Wrong word. I've made a lot of friends in that town. People I need in my life…not for business only…for…" He glanced in her direction. "So you see, it was simply a coincidence and nothing else."

What the heck was he talking about?

"My turn." Taylor stepped in front of her. "Did you fill out the paperwork in Human Resources like I told you to?"

Rylie smiled. They both knew she hadn't, didn't plan to, and wouldn't under any circumstances even consider the possibility. "No."

"Is this how you plan to treat all my orders?"

"Orders?" She held her tongue to keep from adding that she would probably never do anything he ordered, exactly the way he ordered. Orders were for ignoring. Or, at least, tweaking.

He huffed. "I didn't mean orders in terms of 'do this or else.' I meant decisions. TRED is my responsibility, and my decisions are final." He raked his fingers through his hair. "Do you plan to carry out my decisions or not?"

"All the time?"

He lowered his overnight suitcase to the floor, then braced his hands on his waist. "Yes. All the time, Ms. Crawford."

Yep. He was magnificent without even trying, but for just a moment there, she'd had him flustered. Her insides quivered with that thought. The woman inside her grappled with the almost forgotten memory of what it was like to fluster a man.

With all her being, she wanted to reach out and plant a big hug around his neck just for the way he'd made her feel alive again. But this was all about business, and CEOs didn't flirt with their emotions. At least she didn't.

He raked his fingers through his hair again and furrowed his brow. "Well?"

"Guess you'll have to wait and see." She shrugged. "Have a good flight, Taylor."

"You, too. By the way, those tennis shoes look really unprofessional with that suit."

"No more so than the orange pulp dribbled on the front of your shirt."

He jerked his head downward and frowned even deeper than before when he saw she was right. His jawline tightened like a man who'd made a fool of himself with no way out of the situation.

"Be sure to run some cold water on that spot." Quirking the side of her mouth, she shook her head, then reached out and touched the stain. Her fingers lingered on the crispness of his shirt, the muscles beneath. Had been a long time since she felt the nearness of a man, and her emotions had reacted.

The warmth of his fingers curling around her own broke the spell as she glanced into his question-filled gaze. She pulled her hand away and stepped back. "Sorry."

He mirrored the movement and nodded. "Me, too."

CHAPTER FIVE

HOURS AND MILES later, Taylor speed-walked through the Surryfield airport, the closest one to his development in Nature's Crossing. Head down, he hoped no one he knew would be in the terminal to see his messy appearance. He had only one precisely folded clean shirt in his bag, and he needed that for this evening's Town Council meeting. Evidently, he needed to start keeping more clothes at the house he'd bought, and remodeled, in Nature's Crossing.

Stepping outside, he spotted his brother Jake parked curbside in one of the black company trucks with gold lettering. As COO of TRED and Vice President of Site Control in Taylor's new nature-oriented developments, Jake had an overview of the workers and work being done on a day-to-day basis across the U.S. But when they'd agreed to start this Missouri development, he'd jumped at the chance to stay onsite for a change.

Jake's rules were to show up on time, do your job, stay clean and sober, plus, don't ever refer to him as a COO or VP. Unless he was in the boardroom or giving his opinion on financial dealings or the good name of the company.

Taylor eased his fingers along a foot-long scratch on the fender, then tossed his bag into the backseat of the extended cab.

"You're right on time," Jake said.

Taylor glanced at his watch as he jumped in the front seat. "What do you mean on time? The flight's almost an hour late."

"Yeah, that's what I mean. I've learned to build an hour into your arrival time."

"I figured I paid you for something. What's with the big scrape along the side?" He insisted his company's appearance stay top-notch, just like its reputation.

"Some guy with lumber hanging out the side of his trailer got too close this morning. I'll get it fixed tomorrow." Jake chuckled to himself. "I thought about covering it with duct tape."

"Those were some good times."

When Taylor's dad had first started out, duct tape was a staple in their advertising. Slap a piece of tape on a flyer and stick it up. Where? Didn't matter as long as it stayed up until someone wanted work done and yanked it down for reference. And, if the sign was gone the next time you passed by, grab some tape and put another one up. Cheapest advertising there'd ever been.

Jake shifted the truck into gear. "Your memory must be fading. All I remember is work after school. Homework finished before bed. And even more work on weekends. Of course, we never had to search for a summer job."

"But thinking back, Dad always made sure we had time for sports. And did you ever notice that when there was some kind of dance or special happening at school, he conveniently didn't need us to help him that day?"

"Yeah." Jake smiled as he merged onto the road leading to Nature's Crossing. "He paid us damn good, too."

Taylor nodded. His dad had also paid them in memories, laughter, and love to last a lifetime. "Hey, what did he say when you told him we were both planning to be onsite at Nature's Crossing?"

"Same thing he's based business on for years." Jake cleared his throat, which meant he was going into his "Dad voice." "Does it keep food on the table? Workers paid? And move the business forward?"

"Yes. Yes. Yes!" Taylor laughed, thinking about how he always used that same set of questions whenever he did business. When discussing TRED in a deal, he also considered what the other person in the contract was getting. After all, business was give and take on both sides. But he never let TRED be taken advantage of at the end of the day. Never. He'd walk away from a deal first.

The early darkness of winter quickly overtook the world around them. Headlights lit the lanes of the highway, but cold weather meant they needed to stay alert for any sign of deer in the tree line by the road.

"By the way, Dad made sure to mention he'd sure like to see some wives or grandkids learning the trade," Jake said.

Taylor felt the twitch at the corner of his eye. "You should get right on that, Jake."

"Not me. Maybe I'll put it under New Business on the next board meeting agenda."

"You mean the brotherly get-together?"

"Yeah, something like that. If we play our cards right, maybe we can convince Michael to take on that project."

Under the new organization of ownership, Taylor, his brothers Jake and Michael, and a few other so-called brothers-in-arms comprised the TRED board. His dad still sat in on the meetings sometimes, but after business preliminaries and catching up on everyone's life, he rarely offered advice.

"Anything new at the site?" Taylor asked.

Jake slowed slightly as they entered a stretch known for deer crossings. "Nothing major. Paperwork's ready for the town meeting tonight. It was the last thing the secretary did. Then she cleaned out her desk and informed me her daughter was in labor. That she was flying to South Dakota to live for a while."

"What does that mean?"

"She quit. And this time it's not my fault." Jake sounded like that was supposed to make everything okay. "Don't worry. I called Mrs. Parker. She's on top of everything."

"Means we'll have to set aside time to interview." Taylor shook his head and sighed. He hated breaking in someone new, no matter what the position. Now there'd be Rylie Crawford *and* a new secretary. "Maybe we don't need anyone in the office."

"Now I know you've lost your mind."

Jake kept the workmen happy, or at least on the job, when the workload got heavy. Not one to back down, he'd wasn't afraid to give Taylor grief over a decision. He also knew when to shut up and pay attention. And he excelled in being the happy-go-lucky face of TRED in their development locations. Taylor was the bottom-line guy. And Michael was the numbers man.

Taylor glanced at the front of his shirt. The fact Rylie had touched the stain hadn't surprised him. Women did things like that without thinking. So why couldn't he get that moment out of his mind? He brushed his hand down the stain, trying to remember what she'd said about not letting the pulp stain set.

"Something wrong?" Jake asked, taking a quick look at the shirt.

Taylor pulled back from his thoughts. "No. I was thinking about my meeting with Crawford Enterprises and…"

"How was he?"

"He was a she, that's how he was."

"Probably someone from their contract department."

"No. Rylie Crawford's the owner all right. Seems Mathew died a few years back. And I didn't even know. I didn't…" Taylor heard the tremble in his voice as he swiped his palm down his face.

Had his and Rylie's sorrow played out at the same time? Had no one let him know? Had he simply pushed it aside and focused on his own problems? Or had he forgotten? Locked it in the safe place of his mind with all the other traumatic events? What else had he missed? Who else had he lost?

Jake glanced in his direction, then slowly nodded as he blinked and turned back to the road. "Sorry to hear about Mathew."

"Me, too. Even if we had lost touch, I always thought we'd get together again. Maybe some school reunion or a conference or…" Taylor shook his head. "Might sound silly, but when I saw his name on the proposal's letterhead, all I could think about was how we could play a round of golf. Talk about college days. Catch up on our lives. You know…old-time acquaintance stuff."

He and Jake had both lost friends in the military…and life…but today, this one had hit him hard. Or was it the way he'd found out that had grabbed his gut and wouldn't let go? Silence filled the truck cab and smothered the emotions.

"So have you decided which company you're offering the contract to?" Jake asked.

"Yes. The best fit for this project is Crawford Enterprises. I liked the proposal. The way they do business. Should be a good fit for TRED and the Nature's Crossing community." Taylor tapped the end of his loose fist against the door side panel. "Rylie may not accept the contract as it's written, though. In fact, I hope she doesn't. I'm not changing one damn thing."

Jake slowed as the car in front of them turned into a driveway on the right. "What makes you say you won't change anything? You're the one always telling us to negotiate the contracts."

"Not this time. I won't change one sentence. Not one word." Taylor closed his fist and thumped it against the side door panel, ending with one final thud. "See how she likes that."

A grin spread across Jake's face. "Sounds like we're having fun now."

"Don't give me any attitude." Taylor spat his words out. He was itching for a fight. A debate. Anything to get the hell of a day over with. Too bad for Jake. He was the only brother handy to feel his wrath. "I say what happens in this company, and I don't need anyone to second guess me. Least of all—"

"You better back off, you big lug. I'll drop your sorry ass by the side of the road." Jake's hands fisted around the steering wheel now, and his voice had lost all humor.

Taylor knew it was time to shut up, but he couldn't. All he could think about was Rylie. Somewhere back there in KC, in the cab, the damn orange, the way he'd accidentally brushed her leg… God help him, the day had turned into more than he could bear.

Never mind the flare-up with Chase. Why wouldn't life just leave him alone?

Jake mumbled something under his breath.

Taylor stared straight ahead. "What did you say?"

"I said it was your lucky day when I was born. Mom and Dad knew what they were doing when they had me and Michael. Someone needs to be around to keep a lid on you."

"Well, you can leave any time you want."

"Damn right." Jake slammed his fist on the truck horn and held for a good five count.

"Damn right," Taylor shouted right back.

The remainder of the drive was tense. If a rabid fox had bolted into the cab of the truck, one of the men would have knocked it back out before it had time to bite. But the so-called fight had been good and just what Taylor needed. Jake would always have his back, just like Taylor would have his. But Jake would also give him one hell of a what-for when he needed one. Made life more bearable to know he cared enough to tell him when he was wrong.

Jake's hands eased from the steering wheel as he pulled to a stop in Taylor's driveway.

Taylor got out, yanked his bag from the backseat, and started for the driver's side of the truck, staring at the ground all the way. Finally, he braced his arms on the driver's side of the roof and shook his head.

Jake powered down the window and leaned his elbow on the rim. "What the hell's the matter with you today?"

"You know I'm just blowing steam."

"Yeah. Me, too. I'll mark it down as another train wreck day for the two of us." Jake grabbed his appointment book and flipped through the pages. "I've been so busy I don't even know what the date is. Here it is. February 27th…"

Taylor bit the inside corner of his mouth. Hard. Stinging salt flooded his eyes, but he regained control along with a few deep breaths.

His brother broke the pen in his fingers before he laid the book back in the seat. "Man, I'm sorry. I wasn't thinking. How you doing?"

"I've been better."

"Anything I can do?"

"No." Taylor stepped back, uncomfortable with the moment. "Hey, I didn't mean all those things I said."

"Never thought you did, or I'd have belted you one." Jake shifted gears on the truck. "You need me at the Town Council this evening?"

"Only if you want to."

"Think I'll pass. Before I head on home, I'll stop by the office. Make sure everything's locked up for the night." Jake looked his brother in the eye. "Sure you don't want me to come in for a beer or two?"

"No. I'm okay. See you tomorrow." Taylor stepped back and turned toward the door before the two of them witnessed the tears neither one of them wanted the other to see. "Good night, Jake. And thanks."

He didn't wait for a reply. Instead, he swung his focus to the two-story Victorian he had bought the same day he closed on the acreage for Nature's Crossing. Tonight, all he wanted was a place to clear his mind. At the door, he fumbled in his pocket for the keys as he vaguely heard the crunch of Jake's truck tires on the gravel as he pulled out of the driveway.

Admitting to himself that he still blocked his emotions surrounding this day, he also knew he'd made a lot of progress since being medevacked off the battlefield four years ago. At first, he'd panicked the 27th of every month. Now the flashbacks seldom came, and he'd learned how to control them.

No, he didn't dread this day anymore. But the sooner the day was past, the better. He glanced at his watch to see how much longer till midnight. Till the day would be over. As the Major always said, "Tomorrow is another day."

"Damn." He'd forgot to return the Major's call from earlier in the office. The only other person Taylor trusted, besides his parents and brothers, was the Major. The Major was also the only other one who'd ever seen Taylor's tears. Or held him up when his mind and body numbed. Or sat with him through beer…and whisky…and talk. The Major might be twenty-five years older, but that just meant he had a good feel for what was waiting ahead in life.

Taylor couldn't believe he and Rylie had shared a moment with the *Airborne* ringtone. Damn it, there he was, thinking about Rylie again. He raked his fingers through his hair, then stared at his hand. That was the third or fourth time today he'd made that move. What was that about?

Once inside the entry hall, Taylor sidetracked to the kitchen and grabbed a soda from the stainless fridge, downing the caffeine on the way upstairs to the master suite. He'd completely remodeled the inside of the house all the way from new electrical and insulation, to jetted tubs, granite counters and top-of-the-line appliances, plus everything in between. Still lots more he planned to do, but he didn't regret the cost. The house was comforting, and the front porch was welcoming.

Every time he stepped into the master bedroom suite, complete with an exercise room, walk-in closet, and top-of-the-line bathroom, he knew it to be worth every dime he'd spent.

He tossed his bag on the luggage rack and proceeded to hang the clothes he needed for the evening's meeting. After setting his shave kit on the bathroom's marble-topped vanity, he flipped on the shower, then shed his shoes and socks.

The Town Council meeting would at least keep his mind off his own problems. Methodical and slow, he removed his shirt and loosened his belt, trying to eat up seconds.

The orange stain caught his attention, and he shoved the shirt under cold running water in the sink. Couldn't hurt to give Rylie's advice a try.

His cell phone sounded with Michael's ringtone. Taylor flipped off the water and waited for the call to go to voicemail. He loved his brother, but Michael was the one who always wanted everyone to talk about their feelings. Tried to get them to meditate. The one who tried to walk the rest of them through their damn stubborn alpha I-can-handle-everything selves. Of course, Michael was just as damn stubborn as he and Jake. More so, in fact.

One thing for sure, though. Taylor wasn't having

this conversation right now. In fact, probably never. Why couldn't everyone just let him hibernate like an old grizzly bear for one day a year? That way, he wouldn't have to remember, not if he didn't want to. Sure, remembering good times was pretty much okay. The hell was remembering the bad. Beginning with his enlistment, fate had shoveled a bucket load of bad his way.

He grabbed the shirt from the sink and hurled it across the room. A spray of water shot back at him a second before the soaked shirt slid down the wall, leaving a trail of water. To hell with the spot. With Rylie. With pretending this day every year didn't rip him to shreds.

Taylor walked into his closet and opened the drawer where he kept military mementos. He pulled out the photo album and flipped through a few pages. Then, there it was—the last picture of his squad all together. The last time they'd all toasted life. The last time… Tears cut a path down his jaw, and he laid the album back in the drawer beneath his military medals.

Two of his men had died that day. He'd saved one before being wounded himself. Medals didn't do a damn bit of good at shutting out the sound of grenades and bullets ripping through the air. Or the screams and moans of his men. The men he'd been responsible for bringing back home alive.

He'd failed that day. Failed a lot of families who'd loved their soldier with all their heart.

One thing for sure, he'd never put himself in the kind of position those spouses had endured.

Of smiling as they opened the door, meeting the eyes of the messenger, whether relative, friend, or uniformed military, and meeting the emptiness of grief.

Falling in love meant the risk of grief. And grief could break a soul. He'd made himself a promise to never marry. Never have children. Never say I love you to a woman. He would not allow love to destroy him. Never.

Time to take a deep breath. He couldn't face this right now. Another deep breath. This whole fucking day had been one disaster after another, and he couldn't take any more. This was too much.

Too. Damn. Much!

Taylor stumbled toward the bathroom, not bothering to remove his pants. Water. He needed water. Stepping in the shower, he flicked the dial to cold. Let the pulsing spray pummel his body. Shrill bullet whines echoed through his mind, mixing with mortar explosions. No matter where he'd been deployed in the Middle East, the sounds of fighting were always the same. Metal-on-metal. Metal disintegrating with a grenade's explosion. Metal and guns. Guns and metal and moans.

Cold water pounded Taylor's face for what seemed like hours. He knew different. Knew the time had been less than a few minutes. He'd shut down the flashback of trauma. Now all he had to do was focus. Focus. He stretched his hands wide and taut till the pain jerked him back.

He was a man in control of everything and

everyone he came in contact with, and he'd be damned if flashbacks and memories conquered him. He stepped from the shower and shed the rest of his clothes.

Time to get back to business. Everything would be okay if he could stay focused on TRED for the rest of the evening. That's why he worked incessantly nowadays. Others called him a workaholic. He called it survival.

He kicked the sopping-wet pants into the shower stall, then absentmindedly grabbed the wet shirt from the corner and tossed it inside the shower as well. So much for Rylie's home remedy for pulp stain. The dry cleaner would get the stain out for him. He paid people to do things like that for him, so he could keep small businesses alive on his developments.

An hour later, he was dressed and ready for the Town Council. For the next few hours, there would be people to see, plans to discuss, and a meeting to navigate—this was what he liked. He jumped in his truck and turned the key, then revved the engine just to hear it roar.

Tonight, he felt like driving through the original part of Nature's Crossing on his way to the town library, where the attached community center provided space for official town meetings. Ms. Lavender, the librarian, made sure there was fresh coffee and tea, while the local bakery, *Eloise's Sunshine Bake Shoppe,* donated leftover pastries. Mr. Peabody always wrangled some of the town folks to help with set up and take down of tables and chairs.

At the four-way stop, in the heart of the old town section, Taylor waved at Mark Garmund and Ashley Lanovan as they locked up their new business, *Serendipity Forever—Gifts, Antiques & Coffee*. Soon to be married, they looked the epitome of happiness as they laughed and waved back to him. Heading on to their SUV, they held hands as if they were young lovers, instead of an early middle-aged couple who'd met less than nine months ago.

Depending on what time he got home, he needed to return the Major's phone call tonight or in the morning. Next thing on his to-do list would be making sure Chase didn't try to retaliate against TRED for being fired this morning.

Last but certainly not least on his list was Crawford Enterprises. More specifically, Rylie Crawford. As soon as she asked for a change on the contract, he'd need to start interviewing again. And there was no doubt in his mind that she would ask for something. A smile started inside him, and before long, he felt it on his lips. No, she'd demand. Of course, from the scuffs on her briefcase, the shine to her cuffs, and what she'd said in the limo, she needed the contract. Her company was in trouble.

She'd come across as all prim and proper, but if that was so, he wondered why her long, slender fingers slid along his when she took the orange from him? Considering the driver evading on-ramp traffic, that could have been an accident. Or maybe his own imagination.

Of course, he had liked the way her shoe

slipped off her heel and balanced on her toes.
How the shoe bounced with her nervous energy
as she spoke. How her foot arched—long, high,
and slender—almost like an invitation. The lump
in his throat tightened. Didn't matter. There'd be
no exceptions. Period. End of discussion.

Besides, he didn't even like blondes.

CHAPTER SIX

RYLIE SNUGGLED INTO the security of her bed at her parents' historic home in Charleston, South Carolina. Half-awake, she fought to hold on to a vanishing dream of hazel-green eyes, orange pulp, and a hand caressing the calf of her leg with slow, easy movements like liquid velvet.

"Ummmmm." The dream escaped, and she burrowed deeper under the covers.

Her flight had arrived late the previous night, so she'd took a taxi instead of calling Gwen to pick her up. House-sitting while their parents were in Europe had brought the sisters close once again. Still, waking someone in the middle of the night when they were already mad hadn't seemed the best idea.

A couple months ago, when their mom had called with the house-sitting idea, Rylie had just finished a project and had been trying to decide on where to stay for a short vacation. And since Gwen had recently quit a job she'd started only a few months back, she also needed a place to stay while her finances were "in flux" once again.

Hence the story behind the sisters sharing the house and trying like crazy to stay out of each other's lives had all fallen into place. And hence the reason Rylie didn't want to pull herself out of bed to face Gwen before she figured out how to apologize.

Rylie heard her bedroom door open with a soft squeak, then lightweight footsteps stomped to the side of the bed. Gradually, she cracked open her eyelids, hoping she'd dreamed the door opening. No such luck.

There stood Gwen peering back, clad in her usual oversized white T-shirt for sleeping and her dark brown hair pointing to the four corners of the world. She'd braced her hands on her non-existent hips and raised her eyebrows on a face entirely too perky for this early in the morning. If it was still morning.

Gwen cleared her throat. "So, you're here after all."

"Go away. I'm tired," Rylie said.

"You're tired? Well, so am I, but do you see me lying around in bed all day?"

Attempting to muffle her sister's tirade, Rylie pulled the covers over her ears. Usually, she was the one up at the break of dawn, but yesterday had been draining. For once, she'd like to sleep in. Was that too much to ask?

"No answer? Well, let me tell you what I've been up to this morning." Gwen tapped her foot in time with the words. "I'm the one answering the door for your FedEx delivery."

Son-of-a-gun, Taylor had said the contract

would be here today, but Rylie prayed that was only a figure of speech. She should have known better where Mr. Serious was concerned. She eased her head from under the covers. "Where is it?"

"On the kitchen table right next to a chair you can sit in if you ever get out of bed." Gwen popped her lightly on the behind. "Rise and shine, sister of mine."

"You're crazy. What time did you get up?"

"Early." Her sister yanked the corner of the covers for emphasis. "Real early."

In all likelihood, early to her sister probably meant ten minutes ago. Still, Rylie hauled herself to a sitting position on the side of the bed, then closed her eyes as she stretched for the ceiling.

"By the way, some guy named Jake from T-Randolph Environmental Development called on your business line." Gwen plopped cross-legged on the foot of the bed.

"Who's Jake?" Rylie moaned.

"I don't know. He rattled off some kind of title that sounded like it might have been vice president of something, but I was still half-asleep, so I only got half of what he said." Gwen shrugged. "Said he's with TRED in Nature's Crossing."

"What did he want?"

"Oh, you're gonna love this." Lips pursed and head bobbing, her sister spoke in a deep, sharp voice. "Tell Ms. Crawford not to worry about renting a car when she flies into the area. We'll have a black company truck made up for her to use. Let us know what to paint on the side."

Rylie plastered her fingers over her ears. "Please don't do voices this early in the day. What time is it anyhow?"

"It's 10:28, to be exact, and that's the way he talked. Honest-soda-crackers, he did. So first, I informed him that you did not drive trucks."

"Good girl." Rylie emphasized her words with a sharp nod of her head.

"Then I told him that if in your wildest dreams you did drive a truck, it would be something like red or royal blue. Might even have splashes of color down the side." Gwen painted the air with her hands.

"What did he say to that?"

"Said you'd have to take that up with the boss. And, when I asked who the boss was, he said… Mr. Taylor Randolph."

Mister? Really?

Rylie arched an eyebrow and got to her feet, smoothing her purple nightshirt that stopped at her upper thighs. "Let's get some coffee started."

"Already did. Want a bagel?"

"Sure."

Gwen bounded down the stairs while Rylie brought up the rear after pulling on a pair of yoga pants to go with her nightshirt. With each downward step, her fingers skimmed the edges on a few of the many picture frames hung on the wall. Each held faces, places, and moments from the past. Rylie had noticed she didn't so much choose the picture each day as her emotions reached for the strength of a memory. Felt nice to be home for a while.

Sunshine poured through the kitchen windows as Rylie poured herself a cup of morning wake-up. Then, eyeing the FedEx envelope, she took a seat at the table. Here it was. The contract.

"You gonna open that?" Gwen sat the toasted bagels, butter, and cream cheese in the middle of the table and took a seat.

"I'm thinking about it."

"Is Taylor Randolph as good-looking in person as he is on television?"

"Ummmm, I didn't notice." Rylie's heart drummed with her sister's question and her own lie. She'd noticed. He was handsome…and then some.

Gwen grabbed the envelope, pulled the zip open, and laid the stack of papers on the return FedEx envelope. "See? It's just a cover letter and the contract. What's the big deal?"

Rylie pushed the documents away. "He said there'd be no changes."

"Maybe you won't need any changes. It's a contract. Look at the thing."

"You should have heard him. He's all business and bravado. You know how I hate that in a person. Someone being inflexible. I can't work with someone who's not open to change."

Gwen gave a fake laugh. "Right. 'Cause you're sooooooo flexible."

True though it might be, the jab pricked a nerve. Rylie stuck her tongue out at her sister. They might be grown women, at least in years—thirty-five and thirty-two, but when they got together, they quickly reverted to annoying each other as if they were still teens.

She walked to the window and gazed into the backyard garden. "At least I care about people. Care about what each day brings. I don't want to be around anyone ever again who only thinks about business. Life's too short to…"

Her hand trembled along with her chin as she bit her lips together to still the storm. It had been a while since she'd had an emotional binge, and she sure didn't need one now.

For years, Mathew had put business ahead of everything else, including her. Others might not have noticed, but she did. Before their wedding, she'd been first. But with the start of the business and the company's growth and the travel to keep customers happy, everyday life had slipped away from them. She'd never worried about there being another woman. Mathew wouldn't have taken time to notice.

Still, she loved him through every slight she ever felt. He did what he thought was right for them and their future. Too bad their future would never be lived.

Damn it all, she'd become just like him now. Business, business, and more business.

Gwen took the mug from Rylie's trembling hand and set it on the counter before wrapping her arms around her. "Aren't the azaleas beautiful this year?" Gwen whispered.

"Almost as beautiful as they were last year."

Rylie realized this was how the two of them had always consoled each other from childhood on. Give a hug. Change the subject. Time to move on. What would she do without her sister? Rylie brushed her cheeks just in case a tear had strayed from the corners of her eyes.

"Did you notice nothing ever seems as good as the last time? I believe it's just our mind that plays tricks on us." Gwen smiled as she spoke, but Rylie knew behind that smile were a thousand drops of sadness hiding in crazy hair and accents. "Whatcha think?"

Rylie mussed her sister's hair. "I think you're one smart woman to be such a ditz. Wasn't this mane bright orange or red before I left for Kansas City?"

"Yeah, but I thought I might need to look more grown-up if I expect to land a good job. Can't live off my family forever, you know."

The sisters reminisced about hair colors and cuts from the past. They laughed at the memory of the time they convinced their mom to put pink streaks in her own hair. How their dad had surprised the three of them when he walked in the door two days early from a tour of overseas duty. The look on his face had been priceless as he fingered her mother's hair. Then he'd burst out laughing and given each of them a giant bear hug.

More years ago than she could remember, their dad had insisted they purchase this house in Charleston. The family had always flitted from base-to-base with his Army career, but suddenly he'd insisted on a place that could be their family's base. At first, they only stayed a day here, a week there, but before long, they had a childhood home, so to say.

Dad had been right. Everyone needed a base. Someday she'd make one for herself. Maybe. For now, Crawford Enterprises was her life.

Gwen headed to the staircase. "You okay now?"

"I'm fine. Thanks for asking."

"Anytime. I'll be back down as soon as I shower."

Rylie refilled her mug and read through the contract. Twice. She even had Gwen read it when she came back downstairs. They agreed the wording was straightforward and precise. All the timeframes, percentages, and bonuses were correct. Notation of Crawford Enterprises' presence in the town had been spelled out with T-Randolph Environmental Development to pick up the tab for the office. The expectation for both sides was explicit and written in clear, understandable English.

Nothing needed changing. No need to waste money on an attorney's okay.

Sure, there'd been the clause about her living in Nature's Crossing, but even that wasn't overbearing in its wording. She just had to live inside the city limits, otherwise, the contract would be null and void. And that she needed to be onsite in ten days.

Okay. She could do that.

Taylor's accidental touch in the limo had been the most she'd allowed herself to feel in the past few years. His heat had felt good. Stirred her core, making her want to reach out and pull him close, but she could resist. Might mean some sleepless nights or ones with Taylor-filled dreams, but she'd survive.

After all, he was a Type-A businessman—the exact opposite of what she would ever allow into her life again. Even if the nearness of him made her wonder what being in his arms would feel like, she'd rein in her needs and work alongside him for the good of Crawford Enterprises.

She grabbed a pen, signed, and dated both contracts. "That's that. Now maybe I'll have a few days to rest before heading to Nature's Crossing. Want to take a ride on one of the tourist carriages this afternoon? Maybe have a bowl of She Crab Soup at Fleet's Landing?"

"Sounds like fun. All my job hunting is depressing." Gwen's generic ringtone blasted through the air. "Wait a minute. Let me get this call."

Rylie headed upstairs and at the second-floor landing, she paused to fluff the silk arrangement of flowers on the side table, then leaned over the banister waiting for her sister. Sounded like she was into a long conversation with a friend.

Listening to her sister's concern about needing to find a job, Rylie realized the two of them had been in the same boat. At least part of her own worries had lightened. In fact, she felt so confident in the company's future, she'd treat Gwen to lunch and shopping. Time for a sister's day of fun. In fact, everything was in its place for the time being. Mom and Dad would be back tomorrow. And she had her own new contract. Life was good.

She wondered what Nature's Crossing would be like. More so, she wondered what working with Taylor Randolph would be like. If she was lucky, he'd miss the hustle of Kansas City and move back in a couple of weeks. She had learned through the years that the fewer people who knew about her business dealings, the better.

CHAPTER SEVEN

AFTER A GOOD night's sleep, Taylor wanted nothing more than to sit on the Victorian's front porch and have his coffee. One of the reasons for being in Nature's Crossing was to take time to re-energize. He hadn't done that in over a year. He was smart enough to know when he was running on fumes, which was for damn sure what he'd done the past few months.

He glanced at the yellow legal pad on the kitchen counter. Almost every line on the page was full, which meant he had one busy day ahead of him.

First, he needed to make the final decision on the Major's request during last night's phone call. The Major was a full-bird Colonel, retired, but to Taylor, he'd always be the Major. Just like Taylor would always be the Captain.

After he'd got off the phone last night, Taylor'd run ten miles on his treadmill, then spent an hour lifting weights. Heavy weights. Heavy enough to lighten the load of a decision already made. Then, yesterday, due to security and time zones of the Major's travel arrangements, Taylor hadn't been able to reach him with an answer.

Instead, he'd spent time remembering when Captain Taylor Randolph was the one who'd lived on the adrenaline rush special assignments brought him. He'd gobbled them up like pizza on a Friday night until one dusty, dirty hill. Wrong place. Wrong time.

That mission threatened to destroy him. Sometimes still did.

Last night, the Major had said he planned to publish a book on life in the military. Planned for it to be more of an anthology where service members he'd served with wrote about a moment in time that changed their world— good, bad, humorous, whatever they wanted. Planned for the book to touch on various ranks. Various locations. Various battles. He asked him to be one of the lead authors in the first book. Taylor told the Major he'd need to think about it, but he already knew he'd meet the challenge, the obligation, head-on. Not because he liked reliving the past. But because the Major asked.

It was the least Taylor could do for the man who'd led the group that rescued him and the others in his squad years ago. The man who'd brought the ones who survived off the mountain along with the ones who didn't. The man who'd made sure the soldiers had all received the best medical assistance possible.

Taylor carried his coffee to the front porch. Felt good to relax in the open air. Barely a wind blowing. Still, the leaves on the trees stirred enough to flicker the sunlight peeking through the branches. A car passed on the road in front, birds twittered their early morning song, and when he sat, his Cracker Barrel rocker crunched on the grit from the porch.

His cell phone rang, and when he checked the caller ID, it was Rylie Crawford. Now was not a good time, so he let it ring, figuring she could leave a message this time. Instead, the phone stopped ringing before his automatic voicemail kicked in. Just as well. He didn't need anything else messing with his mind at the moment.

He went inside to grab a pen and paper. First thing needed would be an outline. A list of topics—physical, mental, emotional—then specifics. Lasting effects? Yeah, he'd share those, too.

He could do this. Hell, he'd lived through it. Putting it on paper was the easy part.

Returning to the front porch, he eased into the rocking chair and listened to the crunching sound of the rocker's movement. The light still flickered through the branches, but the breeze felt cooler. He stared at the paper for a long time before he listed the topics he wanted to cover.

After a while, his hands began to tremble. Words on the paper blurred. Then, like a bull charging a red cape, the door to his mind's past unlocked, and the visions charged forth.

The pen and paper dropped from his hands. Cold sweat broke on his face. Shivers ransacked his body. Stomach clenched. Heart pounded and pounded, fast and faster, hard and harder until, finally, Taylor slammed the front screen door open and charged to the kitchen. He opened the upper corner cabinet and peered up to the top shelf at the unopened bottle of Jack Daniels.

The Major had given Taylor the first bottle after the nightmares began once he was discharged from hospital recovery. He'd gone through that whisky like a man dying of thirst who'd stumbled on an oasis. A week later, the second bottle arrived only half full, the third week a quarter bottle. The Major had personally handed him the fourth bottle. There'd been two shots inside, one for each of them.

After they'd toasted each other and drank it down, the Major had given him some advice. Something along the line of how the true mark of a man was to be threatened with destruction, face it down, and come through stronger. Now move on. Life's too short to let a few fucking days of hell ruin the rest.

That day, the Major had handed him the same unopened bottle sitting on the top shelf. Told him not to break the seal. Just keep it close. Someplace easy for you to flip off. And he'd told him the words Taylor'd never forget, words that had helped him in not only controlling flashbacks, but also in business.

Every single time the fucking world punches you in the gut, go tell this piece of liquid gold to bring it on. You're not afraid of anything. 'Cause you've already walked through hell and come out the other side!

Taylor focused on the unopened Jack, staring into the hell called his past. The hell called a mountain. The hell called just another mission.

He slammed the cabinet door closed. "Bring it on, world! Bring it on!

No one would blame him if he opened the bottle. Took a drink to numb the memory. But if he did, then he'd know the past had defeated him. Some people might say he should toss the bottle before he crossed a line and broke the seal some night, but he knew different. The unopened Jack gave him hope, just like the Major gave him hope years ago.

Defiance bit his mind, and a touch of calm entered his soul. He turned his attention to the clock over the sink, and his breathing slowly returned to normal, his pulse evened.

He reopened the cabinet door and smiled in defiance a second before he flipped off the symbol on the shelf. The Major also told him there would come a day he no longer needed the symbol. The day he'd pick up the bottle and chuck it in the trash. Go on with his life, safe and secure in his own self. This wasn't that day. Instead, he closed the cabinet door just as if nothing out of the ordinary had happened.

Taylor might be successful. Might be confident. Might be way past needing the symbol on the shelf. Still, he kept the bottle around as a connection to the Major. As a remembrance of all the men Taylor had served alongside. And every so often to open the cabinet door and tell destiny he still had control.

Cadence sounded on his cell phone, and Taylor answered. "Yeah?"

"You okay?" the Major asked, concern in his

voice.

"Depends. What's okay?"

"Figured you might need a call about now. Everything coming back?"

"Yeah." He poured himself another tall mug of coffee. "I'll do what you asked. Sounds like a form of therapy. Who else is on board?"

"As soon as I have the group together, I'll email you their contact info," the Major said. "Some names you'll recognize. Some you won't."

Within seconds of ending his call with the Major, his phone rang with its generic tone. He glanced at the display—Rylie Crawford again. He needed to program her number with a specific ringtone. Maybe something like Elle King's "American Sweetheart" or Bebe Rexha's "Meant to Be." After all, Rylie was blonde, and so were they.

With a flick of his finger, he transferred her call to voicemail. He'd check for the message when his voicemail beeped. After a few minutes, he realized there'd been no beep. No voicemail. She'd have to learn to be more professional with her phone calls or he—

The phone rang again. Rylie. Once again, he transferred it to voicemail. Waited. Before long, his message beep sounded, and he clicked to hear the voice mail.

"Hi, this is Rylie Crawford. Sorry about not leaving a message before. Just as I was calling you, my mom and dad walked in. They've been out of the country on vacation for a while. Well, not really. It was more of a vacation for my mother and military business for him. So, I really wanted to talk to him. Make sure he didn't have to head out again."

He paused the message. She sure rambled a lot. He'd point out to her how much she went on and on with her emails and now her voicemails.

Of course, she's got her dad in the military, and I've got my Major. Kind of the same situation. "I guess I'll let her have that one."

He pushed the button on the voicemail again, and Rylie's voice continued.

"Sometimes, there's not a lot of time for him to make a call. Anyhow, he's okay, and I knew you'd understand once I explained."

Understand? Why should he understand that something, someone else, had taken precedence over business? Of course, he let the Major's requests be priority.

The message went on, "Want to hear something funny? Oh, never mind, I'll tell you later. Anyhow, the reason I called was to thank you once again for the contract. Have a great day. Bye."

He blew out a sigh and shook his head. Just when he tried to be upset with her, she made everything cheerful. Hopefully, that wouldn't be an ongoing thing. He liked his life, and his business, just the way they were. Well-organized. And serious.

No need to think of a ringtone for Rylie. This would all be over soon.

CHAPTER EIGHT

THE MOMENT RYLIE turned on her cell phone the next day, she checked her voicemail. Mrs. Parker had left a message assuring Rylie the contract arrived, and everything was finalized. Further questions should be directed to Taylor, who was already on location in Nature's Crossing. He had asked Mrs. Parker to remind Rylie she was to be onsite within ten days. Hopefully sooner.

Rylie had no intention of arriving in Nature's Crossing one day sooner than stated. For the next few days, she reveled in the springtime show of azaleas, ate her fill of fresh seafood, and lazed on the porch. Her walks by the water invigorated her, and the drives in her red convertible freed her mind and hair. The break between jobs was wonderful. Just what she needed before a new project.

Time spent with her parents and Gwen had given her a boost also. The four of them spent a couple of days out on the water, plus trips to Sullivan Island and Folly Beach. Rylie loved everything from the cool breeze to the squishy sand beneath her toes at the water's edge, but she was ready for work. Time to make the payroll.

Nature's Crossing was on her horizon, and as much as she hated to, Rylie dialed the onsite office of TRED on day six. The phone rang a dozen times before someone answered.

"Yeah," a rough, out-of-breath voice shouted.

"Taylor?" Rylie asked.

"Yeah. Who's this?"

"Rylie."

"Who?"

"Rylie Crawford. Crawford Enterprises." She looked across the room at her sister and pointed to the phone, giving a he's-crazy finger twirl.

Taylor's voice calmed a bit. "I thought you were another supplier calling to tell me my order isn't here. Never mind the fact it's our fault because it never got ordered. Hold a minute."

Through a muffled receiver, she heard him yelling again. "I don't know where it is, Jake. Look in the files for yourself. I can't find a damn thing in there. And answer that blasted phone."

Rylie flinched at the sudden silence on the line right before the dial tone kicked in. She hung up and looked at her watch.

Gwen strolled over with three glasses of sweet tea, then sat down next to their mom already sitting on a stool at the counter. "Did he hang up on you?"

"I'm not sure. He may have ripped the cord right out of the wall." Rylie sipped the cool liquid for the next five minutes, then redialed Nature's Crossing.

"TRED," Taylor answered.

"I'll assume we were accidentally disconnected."

"Sorry about that."

Sorry? The man actually said the word sorry? "What's going on?"

"It's utter chaos here. The secretary quit. Moved out of town. We can't figure out what she ordered. Who knows where the forms are. When can you get here?"

The image of Taylor flailing his arms about with orange pulp on his shirt flitted through Rylie's mind and made her smile. The image was quickly replaced with the broad-shouldered back and cocky stance of him against the skyline. Her insides tingled with that vision.

"I'll be there in four days like the contract calls for. But you better find somebody else to help you. I'm not your office manager."

Quiet on the other end made her think Taylor probably counted to ten before he answered. "Don't you think I've tried to find someone? This isn't just a front desk job, you know. I need someone with experience in construction and plats and ordering. There aren't a whole lot of people with that background around here. Get the picture?"

"Maybe I can help." Rylie glanced at her sister. "I know someone who's currently looking for a position in the Midwest and has great credentials. She comes from a family with connections to development. What she doesn't know, she'll pick up right away."

Gwen tilted her head and rounded her eyes

before waving her hands no.

Taylor exhaled loudly. "That might work. See when she can be here, and tell her the job pays twenty-nine thousand."

"No wonder you lost your employee. This woman's not just someone to answer your phones and order supplies. She's got an IT degree, has managed offices, and exhibits the kind of personality that puts people at ease."

Her sister propped her elbows on the table and dropped her head into her hands. Their mom walked into the kitchen and watched Gwen shake her head from side to side.

"What pay do you think she'd want?" Taylor grumped.

"You'd be lucky to get her for sixty."

Gwen straightened in her chair and leaned back. Raised her eyebrows and smiled.

His voice reverberated through the phone. "What? I'm not paying a penny more than forty-five."

"I could try to talk her down to fifty-six. Of course, I don't even know if she's still available. She's usually in high demand." Rylie turned away from her ditzy sister and focused on the bird at the feeder outside the window.

"What's her name?"

"Gwen...Gwen Prescott."

"Hold a second while I Google her and pull up her LinkedIn profile."

Rylie knew there'd be no problem there. Everyone in their family kept their web info up to date.

"Looks like she's got the right experience for the job. Great references," Taylor said. "Fifty-four. Salaried. Final offer."

A phone rang in the background on his end. "Why don't I see if she'll take fifty-five?"

Silence. A lot of silence. She could imagine the clench of Taylor's jaw from their first meeting. She might have pushed too far.

Rylie yielded. "On second thought, I think you're right. Fifty-four thousand with a salary review in six months."

There was the slam of a door on his end, and then two men shouted in the background. They both yelled for Taylor at the same time.

She closed her eyes and crossed her fingers. "Of course, as a permanent employee of TRED, she'd expect travel expenses, health benefits, 401K—"

"Are you sure you'll vouch for this lady?"

"Absolutely. I'd trust her with my life. And my business." Rylie knew everything she'd said in this conversation was absolutely true. And she meant everything she'd said about trusting her sister.

"Fine. I'll have Mrs. Parker call you for the particulars to finalize the paperwork. Just make sure this Gwen…Prescott is here day after tomorrow." Taylor sighed as another phone rang in the background. "I've got to go."

Her sister squealed the moment Rylie hung up the phone. Then they high-fived and swung around like they were teenagers again. Exhausted, they sat back down at the table.

Mom smiled and patted her hands together. "Isn't this nice? My two daughters will be working together."

Rylie's head crashed to the table. "What have I done?"

Gwen hurried to her sister and massaged her shoulders. "Don't worry. It'll be fun."

"This is a job. Not a party."

"I know. But there's always time for fun." Her sister's smile turned downward. "Just one thing, though, I didn't get this job all on my own."

"Yes, you did. He took time to Google you and even checked LinkedIn before he agreed to hire you. Besides, he knows you as Gwen Prescott. And he knows me as Rylie Crawford." She felt herself grin a second before she heard herself laugh. "You got the job on your own merits because Taylor Randolph doesn't know you're my sister."

Rylie nibbled on her handful of cookies as she walked across the hallway back to the living room. As she neared the doorway, she heard her parents in one of their mini-tug-of-wars. She'd always loved their back-and-forth banter.

"You should tell her about the Captain," her mother said.

"I will." Her dad picked up the paper by his chair.

"You know this is all your fault."

"How so? I was halfway around the world when this started." Dad rustled his paper and gave it a pop. "And just so you know, I'm not responsible for people being in the same place at the same time, wanting the same thing."

Her mother cleared her throat in an attention getting, listen-to-me type of way. "Tell her about the Captain."

"What Captain?" Rylie asked.

Both of her parents jerked their head in her direction, their expressions a cross between surprise and secretive.

"How long have you been standing there?" Mom asked.

"Just now." She slid onto the sofa and offered her one of the cookies. "Now what's this about a Captain? You know how I like to stay up on everything."

"Oh, nothing. Just news about an acquaintance. If anything good comes of it, you'll be the first to know," Dad said.

"Well, that was clever." Her mother set her glass on the table with a thud, staring at her husband. A thud she'd learned in rebuttal to his so-called clever jokes through the years. "Very, very clever."

"Thought you'd like that." Dad winked in salute.

Rylie had hoped that was how her marriage would turn out, long and full of spirit. "If somebody doesn't tell me something soon, I'm going to take a walk."

Her dad inched his hands back in place on the newspaper again and gave it a snap, then quickly folded it back together. Thoughtfully, he glanced to her mother, then outside, before finally settling on Rylie. "I just wanted to tell you how proud I am of the way you've handled yourself these past few years. I know it hasn't been easy to pull yourself out of bed every day and face the world since Mathew's death."

Praise from her Dad was always appreciated because he didn't give recognition easily, but there seemed to be more to this conversation. She was touched by his sincerity.

"You're not the only one in this world who's suffered a loss," he continued. "Lots of people don't come to grips with life, even when they think they have. Now, I say this because I love you. Maybe it's time you thought about your future instead of just Crawford Enterprises."

He reached over to pat her mother's arm. "After all, you're just like your mother. A beautiful woman with a lot of love to offer the world and…" He straightened in his chair, his cheeks and forehead crimson red for a moment.

"All I'm trying to say is, don't let life pass you by and end up alone with nothing but memories. That's not the Rylie we raised."

"Thanks, Dad." She gave him a hug, then returned to the sofa.

Her mother headed toward the kitchen, stopping long enough to tussle his hair and kiss his forehead. "That was real nice."

He pulled her mother's hand down and kissed her palm. "I love you, too. Now why don't you two skedaddle out of here so I can catch up on the news."

Rylie flipped the television on as she left the room. "Look. Look. That's him. Taylor Randolph."

The screen filled with his presence, alongside

others, on a panel about building within environmental and climate change standards. Polished and assured, Taylor sat in the seat as if he ruled the world. Fielded questions, laughed, frowned, smiled.

She flicked the sound up to listen to the interview. Turned it back to normal when he finished. "Can you believe how serious he is? How controlled he comes across? Can you imagine me and him working together?"

Her mother smiled weakly.

"I mean, we are so opposite."

"Really?"

Rylie inhaled deep, exhaled long, thoughtfully. "Of course. Can't you see the difference?"

Dad reached for the remote. "If you ask me, he looks like a man who needs a life."

"Are you kidding? He's one of the most successful men in the development industry today. Consults with dignitaries all over the world. Plans development only in the best interest of the environment." Why was she defending her new boss?

"I still say he needs a life." Dad crossed his arms. "How did you hear about an opening with this company anyway?"

"You." Rylie looked pleased with herself. "The day you and Mom left for Europe, you called from the airport. Said you forgot to tell me there was something about a job on your desk. Something I might be interested in pursuing. Don't you remember?"

Dad frowned. "Of course, I remember the

phone call. But I left you an ad about a new development by a local builder on the outskirts of Charleston. Not with this TRED Corporation or Taylor Randolph."

"Well, that's what I found after I picked up the stack of paper that had evidently fallen off your desk and scattered across the floor." She smiled. "In the end, everything worked out for the best."

"What do you mean?"

"I got the contract."

He sighed. "Guess time will tell."

Where were all these deep observations coming from? Her dad usually kept pretty superficial in his observations of people. Heck, he hadn't even met Taylor. She had. The man was anything but lost.

Rylie pursed her lips. Dad was wrong this time. "How can you say that? He's got everything in life he could possibly want. In fact, if there's anybody in this world who has his life in order, it's him. He's the type who's got a five-year, ten-year, and twenty-year plan for his company."

Dad picked up the paper, opened it in front of him, and snapped it once again. "I wasn't talking about business."

CHAPTER NINE

TAYLOR SLAMMED HIS palms on his desk and pressed himself upward. His office at the end of the construction trailer left something to be desired. Mainly peace and quiet. The sooner the clubhouse for Nature's Crossing was complete, the sooner he could function in a soundproof environment.

Voices from within the trailer grew in volume and intensity as he headed to settle the ruckus in the front office. He'd sent Jake to pick up the new office manager at the Surryfield Airport over two hours ago. His phone app showed the plane had arrived on time, so they should be back by now.

Barely one step out of his office, he jerked his eyes to the sound of the front door being yanked open with authority. In stomped a no-nonsense-looking woman with chopped hair scattered to the winds. Gold hoops dangled from her ears, almost touching her shoulders. Tight jeans, a form-fitting top emblazoned Go Army, and three-inch—at least—heeled boots said she was who she was. Get over it.

She glanced around and spied the vacant desk.

Her work-out-daily body pushed between two tree-sized men and one spindly guy holding his own in the shouting match that had been taking place for the past five minutes.

"My name is Gwen Prescott, and I'm the new office manager for TRED here in Nature's Crossing. I've just arrived, so I'm not sure who has an appointment and who doesn't."

The room was small. Cluttered. Crammed with bodies and noise. But from the look on the woman's face, that was about to end. The men all opened their mouths at once. Each claiming to be the first one there.

Her double crash of the metal trash can against the side of the file cabinet echoed through the close confines, and one of the men dropped his folder. Another visibly jerked. And the third stared at her as if she didn't impress him one bit.

Taylor stepped back into his office doorway and watched as Jake glanced into the trailer, then quickly retreated back outside.

Turning her gaze to the three men in the main area, Gwen pointed her finger at each of the three loudmouths. "Gentlemen, and I use the term loosely, this is not a verbal boxing ring. This is a place of business and will be treated as such. Understand?"

Two of the men cowered like boys caught with their hands in the cookie jar. The other huffed and stared at the clock on the wall. Evidently, he was supposed to be someplace else…soon. Quick, loud, and rude, the men started their loud complaints once again.

A second later, the trash can-file cabinet clash sounded again. The men quieted.

Gwen sat the trash can down, smiled, and pointed to the clock-watching man. "Do you have an appointment?"

"No."

On to the next. "Do you have an appointment?"

"No, but—"

Her hand shot up to silence the explanation, then on to the final man. "Do you have an appointment?"

Subdued, he responded. "No."

She handed each of them a clean sheet of paper and pen. "In three short bullet points, list why you need an appointment with Mr. Randolph today. Then, if you'll be kind enough to wait outside, I'll see what I can do about time for each of you."

The men obediently did as asked and left the building as Jake ventured in through the back door with a look of amazement.

"Chicken," Gwen said.

"Yep," Jake replied.

Taylor's door inched open. "Whatever I'm paying you is not enough."

Gwen smiled. "We'll talk about that later. Right now, let's get a little organization around here. Where's the appointment book?"

The two men looked at her with blank expressions. "We have no idea."

"Do you have a personal calendar, Mr. Randolph?" Gwen asked.

"Taylor. Call me Taylor. I'll get it for you."

Jake brushed past his brother in the narrow

hallway leading to the executive office. "We need to talk."

"What's up?" Taylor followed, closing the door behind him as he entered his office.

"There's a problem with the new office manager."

From everything that had happened so far, she seemed like a gift from heaven. "I can't believe there's any problem that could outweigh the quiet in that front office right now."

Jake opened his mouth to speak, then cocked his head to the side and blew out a sigh.

If his brother was at a loss for words, then this wasn't going to be good. And if Jake had already upset the woman…well. Damn, Taylor knew he should have picked her up from the airport himself. "What did you do?"

"It's not what I did. It's what you did."

"Me?" Taylor's exasperated tone stilled the air. "What did I do?"

Jake huffed. "You hired her."

"Yeah. Her former employers raved about her work." He braced his hands on his hips. "What's the problem?"

"Did they happen to talk to anyone from Crawford Enterprises?"

"How the hell should I know. Now, what's the damn problem?"

"Oh, this is good. This is really good." Laughing, Jake plopped into the side chair. Taylor'd had enough. "Well, I hope you're enjoying the entertainment at my expense."

"You don't know. You really don't know." His

brother roared with laughter again. "You've gone and hired Rylie's sister."

Sister? Heat rushed to Taylor's brain, to the part he used for negotiations. Rylie'd hoodwinked him again. Well, he hired Gwen Prescott. He could fire Gwen Prescott.

Taylor slammed open his office door, then charged to the front office. "Sister?"

Methodically, Gwen cleared a spot on the piled-high non-visible desktop and then dusted off the seat of the swivel chair. She sat down, opening and closing one desk drawer after the other.

Taylor leaned on her desk, arms braced wide apart. "You're related to Ms. Crawford?"

"Yes, sir. Rylie's my sister," Gwen said as she stood again.

"Did she put you up to this?"

"No, sir. She knew you needed help. Knew I was looking for a new job. Knew I have fantastic experience that would be just right for this project. And for TRED." She used her fingers to count the topics. "Rylie simply puzzled everything together, and here we are. A win for you. A win for me." She smiled. "Everyone has what they need."

"Do you always work for her?"

"No. This is the first time we'll have ever been on the same job. Is there a problem?"

Taylor straightened. Glowered.

Gwen shrugged. Nervously, rotated a pen over and over and over in her fingers. She met his stare with one of her own, but not in a confrontational way. Yet her expression never changed to being intimidated, either.

He liked employees who didn't cower to him. "Let's get one thing clear right now. You work for me. Not Rylie. Me. Is that understood?" Taylor said.

"Clear as…" She glanced at Jake.

"Well?" Taylor asked.

"Yes, sir. You pay my salary, and I work for you."

Taylor scrubbed his hand down his face. "Maybe. Maybe not. I need to think about this."

Gwen stepped around the edge of the desk, blocking his path back to his office.

"I'm a good office manager. Confidentiality is not a problem. I promise not to tell her anything you don't want me to. Bottom line…you and I will get along fine." Her hands embellished the air. "Mr. Randolph, I really want this job, and it's not just the money. I need to prove to Rylie that I can be successful without any help from her."

"That is between you and her."

Gwen's shoulders slumped. "At least give me a chance."

He took in her honesty, her plea to be given a chance. Many a time, he'd done the same. Proved himself and rose another rung on the ladder.

Glancing at his brother, Taylor weighed his options. "I'm probably gonna live to regret this."

Jake smirked. "Probably. But what the hell?"

Taylor felt the tension in his shoulders loosen as he extended his hand in Gwen's direction. "Taylor. My onsite employees call me Taylor."

Ten minutes later, Taylor tossed a folder on Gwen's desk. "File my copy of the Crawford contract and give your si— Ms. Cra— Rylie her copy of the initialed page."

He and Jake moved to the property plat tacked to the wall, moving colored pins first one place, then another. One of these days, the whole development would fall into place. Always did, but not before a lot of strategic planning was done, which meant a lot of colored pins moving over a lot of terrain. Sure, he had the same system on his computer, but he still liked the old-fashioned way his dad had taught him.

Besides, one of Taylor's skills in the development world was knowing when the perfect fit had been achieved. Not everyone had the mindset, but Taylor had that gift. And Nature's Crossing was close to coming together. Just in time for Rylie to make the land sales to the builders.

Jake got a call from one of the workers and walked outside, letting the door slam behind him, but Taylor stayed at the property plat, more to watch his new office manager than the pens on the wall. She seemed at ease and right at home behind the desk, answering the phones and making appointments as she sorted and straightened folders and paperwork scattered on top of her desk.

Satisfied she knew what she was doing, he headed to his office, then glanced back. Two sisters in one office. What had he got himself—and Jake—into?

Between the roadwork and no phone service,

Rylie's drive from Charleston to Nature's Crossing had been frustrating. If Gwen hadn't had to begin work with TRED two days ago, they could have ridden out together. Having her for company along the way would have made for a faster trip in her mind.

Besides which, she figured her sister was probably ready to pull her hair out after two days in the office with Taylor.

"How's Mr. Serious?" Rylie asked when her cell phone finally had bars again and she reached her sister.

"Who?" Gwen answered.

"Mr. Serious. Taylor."

"He's fine once you get to know him. That and the fact I put the fear of God in all the suppliers the first day I got here."

"How'd he take to you being my sister?" Rylie asked.

"Okay." Gwen's tone even sounded like things were fine on her end. Her sister's voice lowered to a whisper. "He's not happy that you aren't here already. Where are you, anyhow? "

"I'll be there before the day's out. Probably about four if I don't hit more road construction. Besides, the contract doesn't say what time, just the date." Maybe she would drive up at a quarter to midnight. No, she was more professional than that.

Gwen bombarded her with the ins and outs of the office and suppliers. Told her of the town folk she'd met. The peacefulness of the community. Mentioned she got to drive one of the company vehicles as her own. Ended with the fact she'd decided to live in Henton, the county seat about five miles away.

"You'd like Henton. The condo I leased has two bedrooms." Gwen paused. "Would be great if we could share the place."

Rylie didn't want anything to go wrong regarding the agreement with TRED. Her company needed this influx of money. "Thanks for the offer, but the contract specifically says I need to live in the city limits of Nature's Crossing. Taylor and I agreed on it, and I plan to uphold my side. Did he have you find me a place?"

"Yes. I have everything lined up for you."

CHAPTER TEN

"WHEN'S RYLIE GETTING in?" Taylor charged down the hall to the front window of the construction trailer.

His voice rose a little every time he mentioned Rylie's name. For the life of him, he couldn't figure out why. Hell, he couldn't figure out why he kept thinking of her long neck and blonde hair, either. No, he wasn't a fool. He knew perfectly well why.

Besides, this was the contract start date. If she didn't arrive before the day was out, then he wouldn't have to deal with Crawford Enterprises or her.

Gwen stared at the paperwork on her desk. "Soon. I just talked to her. She hit road construction but should be clear the rest of the way."

Covered with dirt, Jake walked in during the middle of their conversation. "She here yet?"

"No, and by the time she is, it'll be time to close up shop for the day," Taylor said.

Gwen's phone rang, and she answered with her usual professional response. Suddenly, her face jerked into a round-eyed-wrinkled-brow expression. "Oh my gosh, Chadwick! When did this happen?…Was anyone hurt?…Good. So when *will* this be available?"

Taylor and Jake moved, as one, closer to her desk.

She held up her palm to quiet them. "Yes, yes, I understand, but…what else have you got here in Nature's Crossing?" Gwen switched between nodding and shaking her head. "No…No… No, that won't do, either. It *has* to be in Nature's Crossing. What have you—"

She flinched and jerked the phone away from her ear. Stared at it for a moment. Listened, from a short distance, once again. Then laid her phone down. "He hung up on me."

"Who?"

"Chadwick Andrews. The man I leased Rylie's Nature's Crossing house from."

"You mean that unscrupulous real estate broker over in Henton?"

"Yes," Gwen's shoulders slouched. "And before you ask why I dealt with him…he's the only one who had anything for lease in Nature's Crossing."

Jake dusted off the dirt from the worksite he'd been on earlier, then perched on the corner of Gwen's desk. "Okay. What did he want?"

Gwen's complexion paled. Taylor hoped she wasn't getting sick because ever since she arrived, the office had run smooth as a triple-sanded piece of handrail. She was just what he'd needed in the office all along, and so far, she was on top of everything. Organized like him.

"Long story short. He's been having repairs done on the property. And they found an unstable portion of the foundation, so they've been working on it." Gwen looked like she was almost in shock. "About an hour ago, as they were finishing up, the back corner wall collapsed."

Taylor straightened. "Anyone hurt?"

"No. Once they got all the utilities turned off, Chadwick called to let us know. And the worst part is that he thinks it may not be worth the money to repair." She glanced up toward him. "He'll probably just tear the house down."

Taylor started pacing. "From your side of the conversation we could hear, I assume there is nothing else to lease in Nature's Crossing."

"Exactly."

All three of them focused on what that meant. How they could make things work to find a place for Rylie to live. As quick as one of them had an idea, another rebutted with a reason why it wouldn't work.

"Okay, here's what we can do for the moment." Jake walked toward his brother, shaking his finger in thought. "Taylor, that house you bought, renovated, and currently live in is big enough for the two of you."

"The two of who?" Taylor shouted.

"You and Rylie."

"Not funny."

"Hear me out." Jake took a deep breath. "Evidently, Rylie living in Nature's Crossing is important to the contract, so—"

"Why?" Taylor asked.

"Why what?"

Taylor crossed his arms over his chest. "Why is it important that she live in Nature's Crossing?"

"Don't ask me." Jake shook his head as he jabbed his finger at himself. "You're the one who put the clause in the contract. You must have had a good reason."

For the life of him, Taylor couldn't remember exactly what that reason had been. In fact, this whole conversation had him doubting his own decision. But there was no way he would be the one to request a change in the agreement. "Sure…sure, I had a reason."

Jake waited. Stared at him for a full minute. Then half laughed before rolling his eyes. "Okay, I get the picture. Well, until you can figure out what else to do. Share your house with her."

"Nope. This is her problem." Taylor had the solution in his hand. Rylie was gone. Crawford Enterprises was out. So why didn't he feel better about the outcome? He shrugged Jake away.

"Whose problem?" Gwen questioned. "I work for TRED, so I took care of the arrangements. Now, through no fault of mine, the place is unavailable, and Rylie's almost here." She softly banged the end of her fist on her desk. "Bottom line is, it falls back on TRED. If you can't come up with a place for her to stay here in Nature's Crossing, you'll have been the cause of the broken contract."

Jake turned in Gwen's direction and nodded. "Well played," he said.

Taylor flipped Gwen's words through his brain

over and over and over. They didn't make sense. Yet they did. This had been a long day, and his mind was tired. What was he missing? How could this be his problem? TRED's problem?

"What are you saying?" Taylor asked.

Jake jumped in. "Like I said, your place is big. You could live on the upper floor and Rylie on the bottom. Plenty of space."

"There's only one kitchen."

"Share the damn kitchen!" Gwen screeched.

Both men jumped at the shrillness that vibrated through the air. Had she completely lost her mind? No, she was probably just tired like him. Jake reached out and gave her hand a pat.

"What do you think?" Jake asked, looking at Taylor.

"Sounds good to me," Gwen said.

Jake leaned against the wall. "Then again, you could give Rylie the entire house."

Taylor shot his brother an eye-roll. "And just where would I go? I'm sure as hell not moving into that condo with you."

His mind told him to agree to the arrangement. Not to worry. Besides, Rylie'd never agree to live in the same house as him. He'd win all the way around. He'd come across as flexible. Understanding. She'd refuse the arrangement. Ultimately, she'd be the one who requested a change in the contract.

He smiled. "One week. I'll give her one week to find another place."

Satisfied with his plan, he went to his office and closed the door. Something still seemed off about that whole conversation. Besides which, if he broke the contract with Rylie, would Gwen quit and leave, too? That might be more than TRED—or himself—could stand at the moment. In the short time she'd been there, she had already mastered the contractors, half the town folk, and all the workers, never mind the peace and quiet of the office.

The pulsating sound of "Girls Just Want to Have Fun" wiggled through the open window of the construction trailer. Louder every second, the air seemed to reverberate with energy.

Taylor burst back into the front office. "What the hell is that?"

"She's here." Gwen smiled and raced to the window. "Rylie's finally here."

CHAPTER ELEVEN

RYLIE FREED HER hair from the scrunchie and shook her head as her hair tumbled free around her face. She might have upset people with her blasting of the radio, but she figured blasting "Girls Just Want to Have Fun" would make her sister happy. Might even give herself a boost.

Every Friday afternoon during high school, Rylie used to pull into her parents' driveway with the song blaring from her convertible. Gwen would run outside in some kooky outfit or new hairstyle, and the two of them would dance around the yard. Might be a new convertible, but the song brought back the memories—Fridays, weekends, fun times. Sisters.

The construction trailer door burst open as Taylor charged onto the porch with an expression on his face that said he was breathing fire on the inside. Close behind him, a tall man with linebacker shoulders and a running back waist immerged. Dark hair framed the amused expression on his face.

Taylor tore down the stairs and into the small

parking lot, then planted himself on the gravel. He looked like a man who'd reached his limit of aggravation for one day as his index finger pointed at her to emphasize his shouting.

The shouting increased her defiance. Finger-pointing tripled her stubbornness.

Of course, she couldn't hear him over the music blaring from the way-way-too-loud car stereo. Her own ears were about to explode, but so was he. No way she'd turn it down…yet.

She never looked away from him until Gwen ran down the steps to meet her, arms waving overhead and dancing just as crazy as they used to. Oh, what the heck. Rylie turned the ignition to Accessories and jumped out of the car. The two sisters danced around each other until the song ended. Beaming, Rylie reached in, turned the stereo off, and retrieved her keys from the ignition.

The quiet was deafening.

"He's really not happy with you," Gwen whispered in Rylie's ear.

"So, I see. Maybe you better get back into the office before your boss fires you."

Rylie hung her sunglasses in the vee of her top, grabbed her briefcase from the backseat, and walked toward Taylor. With his hands propped on his hips and one heck of a cocky stance, he came across as a contender for sexiest man of the year in her mind. The crazy thought that if she'd been walking away from him, putting an extra swing in her backside, shot an even crazier sensation to her core.

She extended her hand. "It's nice to see you again, Mr. Randolph. Oh, we agreed to call each other by our first names, didn't we? Taylor... right?"

Before he could comment, a car pulled into the lot and parked next to her convertible. A loud a-ooooga sounded from the horn a second before a dapper gray-haired elderly gentleman stepped out of a restored 1955 Chevy. Suspenders and white Reeboks showed his spunk. Support of a cherry wood cane showed his age.

A smile spread across the at least eighty-something man's wrinkled face as he eyed her car. "Well, will you look at that shiny red convertible? She's a beauty. If I was younger, I'd get one for myself."

Rylie reached out her hand, she liked the gentleman already. "Hello, I'm Rylie Crawford."

"I'm Mr. Peabody. I've been anxious to meet you ever since your sister got to town. She raves about you to everyone. Says you're one heck of a salesperson." His age-spotted hand clasped hers in a genuine handshake and covered with the other. "Yep, Gwen's a real sweetie."

"That she is."

Rylie had done her homework on Nature's Crossing and knew from the defining suspenders, he was one of the town elders involved in the resurrection of the area. From what she'd read, after a stint in the military, a banking career, and being married to the same woman for over fifty years until her death, he now stayed involved in his beloved hometown. His appearance and attitude were everything she'd expected. Her snap decision was that Mr. Peabody was one person in town she could always trust.

Rylie dangled her key chain in front of him. "You're welcome to take her for a spin." "Don't mind if I do." He slid into the seat and smiled. "Won't be gone long. Just around the block."

"Take all the time you want. By the way, I look forward to our meeting we have scheduled day after tomorrow. Gwen says you're the right person to show me around Nature's Crossing." Rylie caught a slight sideways glance from Taylor standing next to her.

"Ten o'clock. I'll be here. By the way, just call me Peabody." He turned the ignition and smiled with the engine's purr. As if transported to another time and place, he caressed the dashboard, then grinned with a slow nod.

"Have a nice drive," Rylie said.

Peabody shifted his gaze to Taylor. "You've done good. She'll fit in fine around here."

Taylor's hands slid off his hips as he quickly nodded and shook his head as the red convertible tooled down the street with Mr. Peabody behind the wheel. "You're not in town five minutes, and you get to call him Peabody…just Peabody."

"What are you muttering about?" Sore from the hours on the road, Rylie bypassed him and climbed the steps to the construction trailer slowly.

"Nothing."

What she'd seen of the small town so far seemed to touch a happy spot within her she'd almost forgot existed. Like weekends she used to spend at her grandparents every so often. Too early for azaleas to bloom farther north yet, but she'd make sure some were planted wherever she ended up living. Rylie turned to look at Taylor as he stomped to the foot of the stairs and crossed his arms over his chest.

First shouting and finger-pointing. Then hands on hips. Now crossed arms. He was certainly not a master at making someone feel welcome.

"About time you got here. I've been waiting all day to meet with you," Taylor grumped.

"We can still meet unless you have to be someplace."

"I expect professionalism, and that includes meetings in a timely manner."

Enough was enough. Rylie stepped down two stairs, which put the two of them on a more even stance. She leaned toward him. "You and I both know that Gwen and the man wearing the muscle-hugging black shirt are inside listening to everything we say."

"Jake. His name's Jake. And for the record, he's my brother."

So much for her rationalization that Jake might be old because he'd said Mister Taylor Randolph. "Okay, Gwen and Jake."

Taylor glanced at the window and nodded.

"Okie-dokie. I'll say this in a soft voice so it's just between me and you." She leaned closer, toward the scent she was fast learning by heart. "Stop being such a grump. Your crossed arms and glares don't scare me one bit."

He leaned toward her in return. "You might want to watch what you say. Understand?"

"Oh, I understand you want to make a point about being in charge and being all business. But lighten up. You're acting like a child." Yes, her company needed this contract, but, personally, she had her own set of lines that wouldn't be crossed.

His jaw clenched a second before his hands found his hips again. His expression became defensive as he cocked his head. Tension in the air quadrupled. She probably shouldn't have used the word child because he certainly wasn't a boy.

Her insides tingled with chemistry's recognition, the heat heading lower and lower. She should have paid more attention to the casual attraction she'd felt back in his office in New York. Now here she was, trapped in a small town with him, trapped in close working conditions, trapped... Heaven help her, because Taylor Randolph was a man. All man. One that left no doubt about his abilities. Anywhere. Any time. Any place.

With a forced smile at the corners of her mouth, she extended her hand. "Let's start over. Hi, Taylor. It's nice to see you again."

With a deep sigh, he took her offer. "Nice to see you, too...Rylie."

The two proceeded inside, where Gwen kept her eyes on the papers covering her desk, and Jake fiddled with files in the cabinet.

"Gwen, take a company check and go pick up some bedding for the daybed in the alcove off the living room. Get some towels and anything else your sister might need for the next couple of days." Taylor blew his cheeks out with a sigh.

"What about food?" Gwen asked.

Taylor briefly glanced at Rylie, then sighed again. "Yeah. Get whatever she likes."

"Is this about where I'm going to live?" Rylie smiled.

Her sister cleared her throat and glanced at her sister. "Yes, I'll explain later."

Rylie wanted nothing more than to crawl into bed and sleep for eight hours. Her hands and arms ached from gripping the steering wheel all day, and her backside ached from sitting. Plus, her mind already ached from keeping up with her new boss.

"Nothing to explain. I'm just glad it's all arranged. Where is it?" she asked.

"Not far." Gwen fidgeted.

Rylie guessed there was more to the story. "Where?"

"Tell her." Taylor's manner changed as he headed toward his office.

The shift of his shoulders, the gait of his walk, that infuriating corner-of-the-eye glance he gave her along with a little gotcha grin all shouted "beware." Whatever the problem was, he seemed to think he was in control and enjoying the moment.

"It's the first floor of a beautiful Victorian right in the heart of Nature's Crossing," Gwen's voice quivered a bit. "You just have to share the kitchen."

"Share a kitchen?" Rylie tried to process the

arrangement. The premise sounded silly. Even sounded tacky. She softly sighed. Sounded like something that might be done in a small town. Besides, sharing a kitchen couldn't be all that bad.

"Tell her the rest," Taylor called from his office, a touch of humor in his voice.

Jake closed the cabinet drawer and headed outside. "Night, everybody. See you tomorrow."

"Chicken," Gwen whispered.

"Damn right." The door closed behind him.

"What else, Gwen?" Rylie asked.

"It's a house Taylor owns here in town."

That shouldn't be a problem. Lots of people owned investment properties. "So?"

"So…" Gwen grabbed her purse and headed out the front door. "You'll be on the first floor. He'll be on the second floor. And you'll both share the kitchen. Good night."

The door slammed shut behind her sister.

Took a moment for the words to sink in, but when they did, Rylie was speechless. Livid, she stomped into Taylor's office. "These are the living arrangements you had Gwen set up for me?"

"Not exactly." He sighed, then proceeded to explain the whole situation that had just happened. "So, this is the best we can do on short notice."

Her own bottom line was that she should be happy to at least have a place to live. She couldn't afford to lose the contract by being headstrong. Her employees and her company needed this contract.

She ended her steps in Taylor's office and took a

seat in the chair across the desk from his, another high-backed black leather executive chair just like in New York.

After opening her briefcase, she pulled out her date planner and cleared her throat. "If you've got time, I'd like to show you the companies I've already made contact with here in Nature's Crossing and the surrounding towns. I figure to start locally with construction companies and work my way to other parts of the state if need be."

He followed her lead and returned to his desk. For the next hour, Taylor and Rylie discussed the community, the development, and their respective calendars for appointment times and deadlines. They agreed on a number of marketing scenarios, tabling the ones that would require more research.

Finally, he stood and turned off the desk light. "I'm impressed. You seem to understand what this place is all about."

"Thanks. I take pride in my work. You won't find me or Crawford Enterprises lacking."

"Never thought I would."

She repacked her briefcase. "By the way, I like the name and slogan you picked for the development. Peaceful Lake Acres…*A place for people, wildlife, and nature to coexist.* Very nice."

Smiling at the thought, Rylie walked out on the porch and stood by the rail, staring down the street. "Wait till I get my hands on her."

Brushing up beside her, he braced himself against the railing. "Sorry if I come across a little grumpy sometimes. It's just…"

When had he gotten so close? She stepped away from him and to the side. Living in the same house might be difficult, but she could handle the situation for a few days until she found another place to live.

Rylie glanced over to where Peabody had parked her car when he returned. Keys dangled in the ignition. That said a lot for the safety in Nature's Crossing. She noticed he hadn't completed the sentence, but that didn't matter. He'd actually said he was sorry. "Don't worry. We'll have everything worked out by the end of this contract. But, for now, could we head to this house of yours? I'm kind of tired after the drive."

Taylor tossed his briefcase in his truck, then turned back around. "You're right. It's been a long day. I'll lock up, and you can follow me over to the house."

Once back inside the construction office, he watched Rylie through the window. She got into her car and reclined the driver's seat back a notch. Then, as she stared up at the sky, she slow and easy reached overhead and stretched before fluttering her fingers through her loosened hair.

He shifted his stance and looked away. This whole evening had played a trick with his emotions, and he needed to focus on business. He grabbed another stack of papers to work on later tonight and a set of office keys for her before heading back out.

"Isn't the sky beautiful tonight?" she said when he stopped by the car to give her the keys.

Dark blackness full of bright white stars filled his view when he looked up. This was better than being in the city with all its bright lights obscuring any sign of starlight for the most part.

"Yeah. Don't get this kind of weather very often this time of year. Supposed to be a cold wave coming in. Maybe rain." Taylor said. "Better put your top up, or you'll be bailing water from the backseat tomorrow."

"I will. Thanks for telling me." She raised the seat back and started her engine. "Taylor?"

"Yeah?"

"Thanks for letting me stay at your house."

He nodded in return. Who was he kidding? This arrangement was one giant problem waiting to explode. He climbed into his truck and turned the ignition, revving the engine to get himself back on track. Tomorrow, he'd insist she drive one of his company trucks.

Jake had said she didn't want one. But Taylor would take time to explain why.

After all, driving the country roads could be treacherous. They were narrow in spots, with dips in the road. Hill crests that could catapult a car through the air. Sometimes not even a proper shoulder if you had to pull off. Plus, gravel roads were the worst. Get too far to the side, and you slide right in the ditch. She'd understand…might take a while, but she'd come around.

After the day his unit had been attacked years ago, he'd made it a point to never ride in anything open air. No roll-up-sided Jeeps. No dune buggies. No convertibles.

Heading down the road, he looked in his side rearview mirror and saw her hair blowing in the wind, a smile on her face. On second thought, the truck might be the least of his problems. She'd called him a grump. He wasn't. But that was the only defense he seemed to have against whatever pull she had over him.

A few minutes later, she drove up the driveway and parked next to his truck. For a moment, the soft sounds of Frank Sinatra's "Strangers in the Night" floated through the air as she raised the top. When she caught him watching, she quickly turned away, but not before he saw exhaustion etched on her face.

He grabbed his keys and started to the door. "Need help with your bags?"

"I'm too tired to unpack tonight. I'll just take this small one in for now."

The back door stuck as he pushed it open, reminding him he'd never updated the door or locks. He'd send someone over tomorrow to get them in order. Truth was, he hadn't been concerned with the locks when he'd been the only one there, but now that Rylie would be sleeping downstairs, he needed the windows and doors to lock tight. This was a safe little community, but he'd feel better following his instincts on the locks.

He stepped aside for her to enter, and a light floral scent tickled his nose as she walked past, pulling her suitcase. The wheels hung on the threshold and jerked the case from her hands. Before she could reach back, he picked up the case and sat it inside. The warmth of her touch hugged the handle, then clung to his hand.

"Thanks," she said.

"You're welcome."

Standing in the middle of the kitchen, Rylie looked more like a lost waif than the CEO of her own company. She wasn't weak. After all, she'd just driven halfway across the country alone. Something inside him wanted to pull her into his arms and tell her they'd find her a place. A really nice place all her own. He suddenly wanted to let her know that everything would be okay.

Meaning—he'd try to stop making her life miserable.

Taylor quickly surveyed the counters and opened the French doors on the refrigerator. "Looks like Gwen's been here already. Are you hungry?"

She shook her head. "Maybe later. If you point me in the direction of my bedroom and bath, I'll be fine."

Leading the way, he gave her a brief tour of the downstairs living room, dining room, bath, and the alcove with the daybed now turned back with pink and green sheets along with a comforter. A smile crossed Rylie's face as her fingers skimmed a pink throw tossed across one of his front porch rockers that had been conveniently relocated to the room. Her sister had done a good job setting up the space.

"If you need anything else, just let Gwen know,"

Taylor said.

"That's very nice of you, but I won't be here long." Rylie eased into the chair, eyes closing as the rocker whispered on the floor.

Right. What was he thinking? He'd given her a week, that's all—nine days tops. He walked back toward the kitchen, stopping long enough to pick up a couple of vinyls and a book from the shelf in the living room. At the doorway, he glanced over his shoulder. She'd already curled up on the daybed with the afghan from the chair.

He turned around to face the now spent bundle of energy. She appeared tired and vulnerable at the moment, but he wouldn't deceive himself into believing her compliance would last. Eight hours from now, she'd be back on her feet with that full-steam-ahead approach, along with her stand-up attitude he'd been privy to a few times. The one that didn't quaver from confrontation.

She crunched the pillow under her head and wiggled into place. Her eyes fluttered open for a moment and stared into his own, then closed. "Ummmmm… Good night, Taylor."

"Good night, Rylie." He flicked the living room lights off before he stepped into the kitchen.

Heaven help him.

Two weeks. No more!

CHAPTER TWELVE

"TOMORROW I'LL HAVE been here three weeks. Can you believe it?" Rylie's voice drifted to Taylor from the corner table in Eloise's Sunshine Bake Shoppe.

Didn't surprise him to see Peabody seated at her table. The elderly gentleman and most of the town had taken her under their wing. Always saying what a fine job she seemed to be doing. Taylor still didn't understand what it was about her that made people smile. Made them want to be around her.

He had to admit, there were even times he found himself wanting to be around her at the house during the evenings. But he'd made sure to keep a good distance between them at the Victorian. Every night, he got his food and went upstairs. She got hers and disappeared into the dining room. You could barely even tell there was more than one person living in the house. Except for a lingering floral scent on the first floor… Rylie's scent.

And that was another thing, why was she still in his house?

Of course, he'd lost his damn mind and told her she could stay until something nice came open in Nature's Crossing. Sure, he'd checked the last time anything came up for rent in the community. Answer—never. At least nothing acceptable for her to move into.

The Sunshine Bake Shoppe was nestled in the middle of a long row of white block buildings in the old part of Nature's Crossing. Morning time, the bakery was the place most people viewed as the meet-up. Lunchtime get-togethers were usually at Gus and Lorna's barbeque cafe a few doors down. Or a quick pop-in to grab a deli sandwich over at Red's Corner Market at the four-way stop near the edge of town.

Taylor glanced over his shoulder at Rylie, and their looks met for a brief moment. Her hand quivered as she set her cup down, or it could have been his vision that shivered.

The woman was becoming a fixture not only in town and the development, but also in his mind. And when she wasn't, people were talking about what a nice lady she was. Yeah, he liked the idea of her job skills. But, as far as the nice lady part? He didn't know. Didn't want to know.

"Good morning, Taylor," she called out.

"Good morning, Rylie," he grumped.

"Mornin'." Peabody dipped his oversized muffin in his coffee, his look bouncing between the couple. "Join us?"

Taylor shook his head. "Thanks, but I've got a full schedule plus one for today. Just stopped in for my usual."

"Maybe another time." Peabody returned to his conversation. "Now, convertible girl, three weeks can't be right. Seems like you've been here forever."

Rylie nibbled the icing from her chocolate donut. "Nope, but I know what you mean. Feels like home around here."

"That's because you fit in so good with everyone." Sheila, the part-time waitress, refreshed coffee one table at a time.

Taylor noticed Rylie's gaze turned back to him. Why was he still looking at her? She smiled. That sweet, friendly, sexy one that she used all the time. Of course, he doubted anyone else noticed the sexy part. That seemed to be his own personal angst.

"Did you need me to do something for you?" Rylie asked.

"No." Good lord, had he been staring at her all this time? Evidently. To top it off, everyone in the bakery seemed to have noticed, too.

"You're next, Taylor," Eloise said from behind the bakery counter as her always-in-place white-gray hair framed her advanced years. So far, she was the nicest person he knew in town, and not just because she was Peabody's sister. Alert and spry, age had not defeated her.

"Oh…uh…I'll have my usual." Taylor grimaced, he didn't have a usual. He never knew what he wanted when he came in the shop. Most times it was coffee. Black caffeinated coffee. So why had he said he had a usual? To impress Rylie? To fit in? Heat rushed to his face.

Eloise glanced at Rylie's table, then the elderly lady smiled and winked at him. "Let's see, that's a large black coffee to go. And a…" Her hand hovered in the display case, her eyes shifting up toward him.

At the bear claw, he gave a slight nod. Thank goodness Eloise felt his predicament. He was going to send her flowers. A whole lot of flowers. She might be as good at getting him out of predicaments as Mrs. Parker was at the office in KC.

"Bear claw. And, if memory serves me, you want two." Eloise acted as though they did this daily.

Peabody moseyed to the counter. "I was talking to Rylie and just couldn't tear myself away. Such a nice lady."

"Right. A nice lady." Taylor took his coffee and the bag of pastries from Eloise. "Thank you."

"Anytime." The elderly lady smiled, then moved on to the next customer.

"How's that house arrangement working for you?" Peabody asked.

Taylor's grip on the pastry bag tightened. "What do you mean, how's it working? Rylie's on her floor, and I'm on mine. Nothing else."

Peabody chuckled, causing half the store to look in their direction. "Well now, thanks for the update, but I meant the plumbing. You know the pipes in that old place have seen better days. Thought they might be acting up."

Again, warmth from embarrassment flooded Taylor's body. All he wanted was to escape the bakery, get in his F-150, lock the door, and drive away from any idea of him and Rylie. Instead, he cleared his throat. "The plumbing's fine. I had that and the electrical updated when the house was remodeled."

"Good, good." Peabody glanced in Rylie's direction. "That there is one cutie-pie. Don't you agree?"

Talking on her cell phone, she seemed oblivious to the going-on between the two men.

Taylor heaved a sigh. "I never paid much attention, so I wouldn't know."

Chuckling, Peabody patted him on the shoulder. "Good thing you don't lie for a living. You'd starve the first week."

After that, Taylor made a hasty retreat. He didn't even return Rylie's wave when he went out the door. They'd succeeded in only scheduled meetings for the most part since she arrived in Nature's Crossing. That way, days were easy. Evenings were a different story. Wasn't his fault there were no places for rent in Nature's Crossing. Thank goodness he flew back to KC for meetings at least twice a week.

He'd discovered the house arrangement contained more entrapments than a field of land mines. Seemed like they were both in the kitchen at the same time every night. Both reaching for the refrigerator. A cabinet door. Fork…spoon. For the most part, though, they stayed on opposite sides of the kitchen island. Both of them quiet.

Still, the air around them sparked with an energy he didn't want to evaluate and didn't plan to act on because whether the air sparked or not, he was the boss. She, his employee. Plain and simple and painful. Peabody was right, though. She was one cutie-pie, to use the man's words. His own words would have run along the lines of beautiful and classy and stimulating. And she didn't even realize her attraction.

Maybe he could spend most of the week in KC and only two days in Nature's Crossing. No, he needed to be here. Not just for the project, but because he liked being out of the rat race of the city. Besides, the fresh air and community's friendliness had him hooked.

He also hoped to figure out just how badly Rylie needed this contract. There'd been rumors about Crawford Enterprise's loss in market share, and he'd done a little checking on his own. Other companies had picked up her business idea, great that it was, and surpassed her with the larger influx of capital. There'd also been something about an accountant's embezzlement creating a slow downward slide for the company.

He figured she was smart enough to see the outcome. Savvy enough to know the end was waiting in the wings. Still, she held on. Why?

When he subtly questioned Gwen about Rylie's business, she had offered up nothing. He hadn't pushed. Gwen worked for him, and he figured she would be true to her word about TRED, yet, at the same time, the two women were sisters. If he'd been in her position, he'd have safeguarded his family the same way.

Taylor pulled into Red's Corner Market to fill up with gas. The day he first arrived in town, he'd stopped in and made fast friends with the owners, Patrick and Janie Horton.

Transplants from the East Coast, they blended in with the rest of the town residents, except for Janie's tiny Southern accent. Petite and perky, she fit nicely into her husband's side when they walked arm-in-arm. Her strawberry-blonde hair was only a few shades lighter than the red cap Patrick wore most days. He walked with a limp, but his back was straight and his shoulders broad, and together they made a nice couple. One Taylor envied.

Patrick had agreed to run a tab for Taylor's company, so most times the drivers could just look toward the front window and see one of the owners wave them on after filling. Today, Taylor felt like a little hometown banter and strolled inside.

Busy with early morning workers who stopped in for everything from cupcakes to potato chips, honey in little bear-like containers to steaks in the freezer, three-cycle oil to bug repellant, Patrick waved then went on ringing the register.

From what Taylor knew, the owners had completely remodeled the building when they moved to town, but from the looks of it, no one could tell it had been updated. The checkerboard tile flooring and tin signs hung close to the ceiling keeping the old small-town feel of the renovated building. Yet the coolers were top of the line, lighting bright and efficient, and even the checkout register was computerized but hidden beneath an antique cash register shell.

Red's was also known to have a small bait shop area for travelers on the way to the big lake. It supplied most things the fishermen might need, including worms, crickets, minnows, ice, and beer.

Spotting Mark Garmund farther back in the store, Taylor gravitated to the fishing area. He knew Mark and Patrick were friends, which explained why Mark spent so much time at the market whenever he was in town. Of course, Taylor still hadn't figured out Mark's line of work because all he did when he came to town was mosey around.

The few times Taylor and Mark had talked in depth, he'd said he used to work for a marketing firm but never gave the name of the company. He wondered if marketing was just another word for a secretive government job. Word had it, he worked for the National Park Service now, but if he did, he seemed to have a lot of free time.

"You like to fish?" Mark asked.

"I've landed some big ones in the Atlantic. Once things settle down at Nature's Crossing, I thought I'd try the Missouri lakes for some bass." Taylor fingered the artificial worms and buzz bait. "What do you recommend?"

From behind the counter, Patrick's laughter filled the air as the last customer closed the door behind them. "Don't ask Mark. He's not a fisherman."

"I think I take offense at that. I like fish just as well as the next person. Just don't like to catch them," Mark said.

"Then what are you doing in the sporting goods section?" Taylor asked.

The two men gave each other space and respect when they met, and, so far, Taylor liked the man. Now if he could just figure out who and what the man was.

Mark held up a tiny handheld net as water droplets plunked back into the big, aerated tank and grinned. "What I always do. Chase minnows around."

The front entrance bell jingled, and Mark dropped the net as he swung his right arm down to his side, inching behind his back. He seemed to eyeball the customer from the corner of his eye, and then just as fast, he eased, picked up the small net floating in the tank and returned to the minnow game.

Strange behavior for Nature's Crossing, for anywhere, unless… Taylor thought for a moment of how the reactions had been vaguely familiar. Even reminded him of himself sometimes. Being in the military had taught him to always watch the door, the window, the area in front of you. Even now, he kept his back to the wall whenever possible.

"How you doing, Clayton?" Patrick asked the customer who had walked in.

"Good. Yourself?"

"Never better. What have you been up to?"

"Not much. Keepin' busy."

Taylor grinned at the small-town banter.

Mark walked to the front to stand by the man called Clayton. "Caught any bass lately?"

"A few." Clayton's hands eased up in front of him and inched apart. "Didn't think you liked to fish."

"It's not that I don't like to fish. The fish just never seem to like my bait." Mark nodded toward the sporting goods area. "Taylor said he'd be interested in catching some bass, though."

Taylor grabbed some bait and headed to the counter. He held out his hand. "Hello. I'm Taylor Randolph. I don't think we've met."

"I'm Clayton Mason. And any other time, I'd love to talk fish with you. But right now, I've got to get home and get one kid to baseball practice and the other to get a haircut." He grasped Taylor's hand in a firm handshake before walking to the back of the store. "Patrick, I need to grab something for dinner. Those boys of mine are kicking my budget this month. Hungry all the time."

The owner followed along to the deli. "Probably having a growth spurt what with spring in the air."

Patrick and Clayton returned to the cash register and settled the bill, said their goodbyes.

"See ya, Mark." Clayton opened the front door and nodded. "Nice to meet you, Taylor. We'll talk about worms and stink bait another day."

"Say hello to your boys for me. Tell your oldest he did a heck of a job at last week's soccer game," Mark said.

"Sure thing. Tim loves his sports. Hoping it gets him a scholarship one of these days." Clayton stepped outside.

Taylor held the door open as the man rushed out, heading for home, heading to his boys. Loaded down with three bags of groceries, two jugs of milk, and a list of things to do, Clayton still had a smile on his face.

"Funny, I haven't seen him around town before," Taylor said.

"None of us get to see much of him." Mark waved through the storefront window as the man drove away. "He's either busy with work or his boys or a million other things. I don't know how he does it some days."

"He's got a little construction business in town. Maybe you heard of it, Clayton & Sons Construction. He's a hard-working man." Patrick poured himself a cup of coffee.

"Doing everything yourself is still hard when you're alone."

"Oh, for some reason he struck me as being married," Taylor said.

Mark cleared his throat. "He was. Probably still feels like he is."

"Cancer took his wife Jenna a couple years back. Left him with a lot of medical bills. Now, he's just trying to raise his boys since she passed on. Doing a good job."

"And his sons are all mighty fine, too."

"If he needs work, send him my way," Taylor said.

"He put a bid in when your ads went out but didn't get the contract. From what I've heard, he's pretty well booked up for the summer at this point. Besides his usual remodeling jobs, his company's known for building the best decks and pergolas and gazebos in a fifty-mile radius. Keeps him busy this time of year." Patrick disappeared through the curtained doorway to the back room.

Clayton & Sons Construction sounded like the kind of company Taylor liked to hire. Too bad TRED had missed its chance. Chase had been in charge of hiring local contractors. Maybe that hadn't been such a good idea after all. Taylor figured he should take a look back through all the bids. See who else had been rejected.

Nonchalant, Mark leaned against the counter. "Lloyd and Dot Gregory are in town for a few days to finish up a few things they didn't get done before they moved to Florida. So Ashley and I are holding a small barbeque out at the house this weekend. Nothing big, just a few friends. Ashley said to invite you if I happened to see you around town."

"Sounds good. When?" Taylor asked.

"Saturday about three."

"I'll be there."

Broom in hand, Patrick came through the backroom curtain and headed straight out the front door. Taylor and Mark talked a while longer as they harassed Patrick through the storefront window. Patrick finally slapped his red hat against his pants leg and stomped back inside.

"You two are gonna be banned from my store one of these days."

Mark slapped his friend on the back. "Don't scare me one bit. Janie will let us back inside."

Much as Taylor liked the guys, he had work to

do, so he started for the door, too. "Hey, I gotta get going. See you Saturday."

Mark raised his cup of coffee in acknowledgment. "Sounds good."

"Sure thing." Taylor left the store, heading to his truck.

"I almost forgot," Mark shouted across the parking lot as Patrick walked back inside of Red's. "Ashley said you should bring Rylie."

Taylor scowled to himself, then shifted to face his new best friend. "I'd rather not."

Mark laughed. "She said you'd say as much."

"Besides, I doubt Rylie'd come if I asked."

"Tell her Ashley said she wouldn't take no for an answer." Mark grinned.

"All right, I'll tell Rylie about the picnic, but I guarantee nothing." Taylor walked to the driver's side of his truck, then braced his forearms against the hood as he stared back at Mark. "Got any more requests?"

"Not today. But like I said…" Mark tapped two fingers against his forehead in a casual salute. "…we'll talk about a fishing getaway Saturday. Maybe head up to Canada. Rent a houseboat. Just you, me, Clayton, and few other guys I know who need to take a break and enjoy life in the open air."

CHAPTER THIRTEEN

RYLIE PAUSED FROM tackling the next item on her to-do list and focused on Gwen and a new arrival's conversation. She couldn't place the voice, but he was arrogant, rude, and demeaning. Didn't sound like a supplier or contractor. In fact, she'd never heard him in the construction trailer before.

"Sir, you're not allowed on this side of the desk," Gwen said. "Sir—"

"I'm Chase Andrews, and I can go wherever the hell I please. Where's Taylor?"

Rylie tensed. She'd done some research and knew that was the creep Taylor had fired back in KC. The same man who had shoved her against the wall as he evaded security and flipped Taylor off that day.

"Mr. Randolph is out at the moment. Would you like me to call him?" Gwen asked.

Chase's laugh sounded sinister. "Not likely, honey."

"Sir, you can't come behind the desk." Gwen raised her voice.

"Now, honey, we're just gonna get to know

each other a little better."

Rylie shoved open her office door and stepped into her doorway. Utter anger raced through her body as she saw that the man had her sister trapped behind the desk by blocking the way out. "Mr. Andrews, is there something I can do for you?"

Chase stopped and turned toward her, then his tongue twitched between his lips like a snake warming on a sunny rock. "Well, look who's here."

His slow saunter around the front edge of Gwen's desk sent chills down Rylie's back. She stood her ground and kept her eyes firmly focused on his as he invaded her personal space.

Bracing his hands against the doorjamb, Chase leaned in her direction. "I heard you got the job. You must be good. Real good."

Rylie noticed her sister on the phone and hoped she'd been able to reach Taylor or Jake. Chase leaned even farther until his nearness, plus what smelled like beer and whisky on his breath, sickened her stomach.

"Please, step back, Mr. Andrews." Rylie felt her hand compact into a tight fist. She and Gwen both knew how to defend themselves. Their dad had made sure they attended self-defense classes on base. And even some individual hand-to-hand combat training.

"Or what?"

She focused on the next moves she'd make if he didn't back off. Knee, jerk, run. She might not be able to take him down alone, but between her and Gwen, they'd make a damn good dent on his manhood.

Chase licked his lips again as he brushed the back of his hand across her arm. "Why don't you show me just how good you are, hon—"

The front door burst open a moment before Taylor charged inside and grabbed Chase by the shoulder, slamming him face-first against the wall. "What the hell do you think you're doing?"

Taylor's adrenaline pumped, and veins bulged in his neck as he wrenched the man's arm up behind him. Calm and powerful at the same time, his manner said he was in charge. His other forearm anchored across Chase's shoulders and power-pressed him against the wall.

If Rylie hadn't been so frightened by Chase, the look on Taylor's face would've been priceless. As it was, she closed her eyes and swallowed the lump in her throat, while an involuntary tremble raked her skin. Gwen stood at the end of her desk, trashcan in hand.

"Man, I was just jokin' around with the girls." Chase gave a feeble laugh.

"You've been drinking again. You haven't learned a thing since I fired you." Taylor eased his hold. Volleyed his look between Rylie and Gwen. "You two okay?"

Rylie and Gwen nodded.

"Don't ever bother either one of these women again." Taylor growled his words deep in his throat. "Or anyone else in TRED for that matter. Understand?"

Chase nodded. "You've got my word."

Rylie figured that wasn't worth the breath wasted on the statement.

"What are you doing here anyhow?" Taylor asked.

"I just stopped by to…to…" Cowered for a moment, Chase smoothed his clothes as if searching for time to regroup himself. Suddenly, his expression switched to amiable with a trace of remorsefulness. Or it could be he'd found his next lie and was ready to give it a test drive. "To apologize for the way, I misspoke back in Kansas City. I sure hope you don't tell my uncle about our little misunderstanding."

"Misunderstanding? Not hardly. You were insubordinate and hungover, which I had come to expect from you occasionally. But threatening to blackmail me and my company is a whole different matter. That's why I fired you." Taylor's hand clenched, then released. "End of story."

Chase held up his hands, patting them outward to calm the situation. "Okay, okay. I got a little out of line that day. What say we sweep everything under the rug and move forward? I've learned my lesson, and if you'll just give me another chance, I'll—"

"Get out, Chase."

"Your loss." The jerk stood in the doorway as if goading Taylor. "Thought you might want to know, Uncle Chadwick may be selling his real estate business over in Henton. If I talk to him man-to-man, he might let me run the place for him instead."

"Why would I care?"

Chase popped a toothpick in the corner of his mouth, then twirled it with his tongue. "Oh, you know. You in development. Me in sales. I'm sure we could work something out to make it a lucrative deal for both of us. Nothing wrong with making a few bucks on the side."

Taylor's jaw clenched. "Did he ask you to talk to me?"

"Hell no!" Chase's face reddened. "That old coot's nothing but a conniving moneybag still stuck in the way business used to be run. I figure you and me could show him how the big boys play in the corporate world. You know…a dollar here, ten there."

The crunch of tires on rocks in the front parking lot caught Rylie's attention, and she glanced out the front window. Jake was out of his truck in a flash and headed to the front door. Wheat McIntosh, the local State Trooper, had stopped his car at the farther end of the block as if waiting to see if he was needed.

"You still seem to be following the same line of conversation you were before." Taylor's brown furrowed as he rolled his fingers in and out on a set rhythm.

Chase backed out the door. "Listen, I swear on my mother's grave I'm not involved with that. Why, if I tried to muscle in on that type of deal in Kansas City or New York, I'd be fish food before the day was over." With a quiver to his tone, Chase grinned. "Besides, you know me. I'm just a local boy trying to make a name in the big city."

"Then stay away from the Peaceful Acres Lake

development. Away from TRED. And away from these ladies." Taylor held the front door open as he stepped outside. "Because the next time I catch you anywhere near my dealings uninvited—" he pointed in the direction of the State Patrol car, "—I'll have you picked up. And I'll personally call your Uncle Chadwick. Understood?"

Rylie inched up to peer out the front door as the two men stepped onto the porch. She reached out and laid her hand in the middle of Taylor's back, slightly tugging on his shirt. He was furious at the moment. Even his voice seemed like someone else's, but she and Gwen were okay, so he didn't need to push any further. The twitch of his muscle beneath her fingers told her he felt her warning, but he stayed shielding the doorway with his body.

"Sure, man. Sure." Chase staggered down the steps, holding up his hands for everyone to see. "I'll stay away from TRED. You've got my word on that. In fact, I've got a job offer up in New York that sounds better than anything you could offer anyhow."

Minutes later, back inside the construction trailer, secure within his office with the door closed, Taylor paced between the walled-in confines. Angered with his downright lack of foresight in the matter of Chase, he was angrier with himself. How could he have let the man hang around as an employee for so long?

The man who had saved his life in Afghanistan

only asked him to give his stepbrother a chance. Not let him take advantage of the situation. In fact, it was hard to believe they had been related.

Instead, Taylor realized he'd let himself get swept into… What? A promise? No, that was the wrong word. Responsibility? That was a better word, but still wrong. Obligation? Duty? Debt? Better words, but still he'd been wrong.

Sweat beaded on his brow as the flash of lights blinded his vision. Taylor swallowed hard, struggling to keep himself in the moment. He knew the words. Knew others who'd had the same reaction. Knew he'd denied the possibility for years. To the Major. To the VA counselor. To himself.

Maybe if he said the words out loud, everything would be better. He'd be cured. Hell, nobody was ever cured. You just learned to live with the…

"Guilt. Survivor guilt."

A tiny relief took hold in his mind. He'd finally said the words along with the acceptance that he did feel guilty at being the one to survive. The bullet had been headed straight for him when Chase's stepbrother stepped in front of him. There was also guilt for so many things that had saved him in business through the years. The times he'd been given a contract when others needed it more. All the things he'd been given by destiny's choice.

He'd been a fool to let Chase take advantage of the situation, but no more. That horse had left the barn. He just hoped he hadn't waited so long that he'd put others in danger.

Back in New York, the rumor mill at the office had brought Chase's low regard of women to his attention. The situation had been handled with employee counseling, which the man had attended. At the KC office, the problem had been the drinking and insubordination.

But rumors around Nature's Crossing about Chase's gambling habit had been there from the beginning. Word around Nature's Crossing was that the man had riled more than one person with his attitude, but few were willing to go against the nephew of one of the richest and most powerful men in the state, Chadwick Andrews. Still, Chase had spent more than one night in the county jail.

He might be mostly mouth and attitude, but what was to say he wouldn't cross that line one day. What would have happened to Rylie and Gwen today if no one had walked into the office? Taylor hated to ask for favors, but this had to be done. He scrolled through his phone's contact list and pushed the dial button.

"This is Mark."

"Taylor Randolph here. I've got a favor to ask."

"Go for it."

"Do you know of a security firm that could hook up a couple of places quick?"

"Trouble?"

"Chase Andrews. Found him bothering Rylie and Gwen when I got to the office." Taylor paused a moment to allow Mark to take in what he'd just said. "I had fired him over a month ago. Today, I've banned him from the Peaceful Lake Acres development, but I'd rather not make this a legal matter. Besides, the office is already on a security system. But I'd feel better if the women had some protection at home, too."

"That man's never gonna learn, is he?" Mark's caustic laugh broke the air. "Yeah, I'm acquainted with a few people who can get one place hooked up tonight. The other tomorrow morning. Just tell me where?"

Even before he asked, Taylor knew Mark only had to make a phone call, and things would happen. "Do Gwen's first. I'll be at the house to watch out for Rylie tonight."

The men exchanged particulars, then ended their call.

Taylor returned to his chair and opened the left-hand bottom drawer of his desk. As his mouth went arid dry, he pulled out a black folder tucked at the bottom of the stack. Survivor guilt came in many packages for many things. This one was personal. He stared at the last photo of him and his unit. Stared at the men who'd lost their lives less than a week later. Stared at the ones who, like him, had survived.

Some of the men had come to work for TRED and followed developments from site to site. Others kept in touch by text or email or the occasional phone call.

Fate had raised its ugly head at him that day on the battlefield. The Major had told him it was a matter of wrong place, wrong time. Taylor figured it had to do with his destiny. Destiny that could have been changed in only a second, a step, a breath. He wouldn't stop searching for the tiny thing that could have changed everything that day. The second he'd lost had to be hiding in the past, and someday he'd find the hiding space. Maybe that would bring him peace.

CHAPTER FOURTEEN

SITTING AT HER desk, Rylie fought to push the past minutes out of her mind. Thinking about what might have happened if Taylor hadn't got there in time would do nothing but increase her calming panic. And that was the last thing she needed right now.

Hoping to reorient herself, she let her gaze focus on the progress of two robins building their nest in the tree outside her window. They'd started yesterday, and even now, they still looked eager to start their own family. The robins were making this community their home, why couldn't she?

Spring had grabbed a toehold on the area later than South Carolina, but that didn't matter. The new grass smell and tweets of the birds in the trees surrounding the Victorian lured her outside each morning, cup of coffee in hand. She'd even dreamed of making the house her home.

"What's got your attention?" Taylor asked from the doorway.

She turned to face him. "Robins building a nest."

The intensity of his green eyes softened as they

skittered from her hair to her lips to her eyes. Her pulse fluttered as he pulled his gaze up to the ceiling as if their energy hadn't just sparked. The ignoring was all right with her because she sure didn't need any more complications right now. Besides which, her body had already let her know he could be a complication. Maybe even a catastrophe.

His eyes drifted back to hers, and then he tucked his hands in his pockets instead of on his hips. And, damn, if she didn't like that look, too. Breathe. Just breathe, she told herself.

He walked over and braced his hands on her desk, leaning next to her as he stared out the window. His essence permeated her senses, and she remembered the scent of his cologne in the taxi. Her mind shouted no, but her hormones had their own idea. Ridiculous! All she wanted out of this contract was a great reference and the bonus. Her company needed money. She needed to focus.

"Where?" he asked.

Her arm brushed his as she pointed to the construction birds, but he didn't seem to notice.

"Let me know when the eggs hatch," he said.

"You think there'll be baby birds?"

"They didn't build the nest for no reason."

The two turned to face each other at the same time. He was close. Way too close. Close enough to get them in trouble.

He must have felt the same because he eased back. Slow and easy. Finally, he walked to the other side of the room. "You okay from before?"

"Yes. Thanks for getting here in time. I don't know what Chase is capable of, but he's a little frightening.

"Let me know if he bothers you again. By the way, I sent Gwen in search of a plat on file over in Henton. Afterward, I gave her the rest of the day off."

Rylie realized there were only the two of them in the trailer. With him in her office, she should try to make chit-chat. Maybe they could at least be friends. "Peabody gave me another grand tour around town this morning. I met Sheila's children at the thrift shop that adjoins the bakery. Do you know them? They're such sweeties."

Rylie heard herself rambling but couldn't seem to stop. If she hushed, the silence would carry too much weight. Or worse, Taylor would leave her office, and for some reason, she liked him right where he was at the moment. "Did you know there's an annual strawberry festival being planned here in Nature's Crossing?"

"I heard something about it at the Town Council meeting. What date did they decide on?"

"Sometime in the latter part of June. We'll have to go. Maybe sponsor an information booth for Peaceful Lake Acres." She should hush. Maybe say she had work to do. Push him out of her office. But try as she might, she couldn't. "Peabody told me about his wife. Do you know that after she died, he sold her cafe for fifty-six dollars? One dollar for each year they'd been married. I could tell how much he loved her and…and…how hard…" She cleared her throat.

Seeming uncomfortable, Taylor left the room.

Pity? Was that why he'd backed away. How dare he think she couldn't get through her pain? Memories didn't immobilize her anymore like they did right after Mathew died. Now, she was thankful for the moments to remember, and had learned to stare down the pain and move on.

What gave Taylor the right to presume he understood her sorrow? He couldn't know how she felt. Life-changing anguish could only be understood if you lived through the event. She had. He hadn't. Who was he to feel sorry for her?

She charged across her office to follow Taylor. "I wasn't finished."

On a dime, he turned back to face her, and even though his eyes had saddened, his hands still found his waist. He used that stance a lot. One of these days, she really, really, really needed to point that out to him. Not today…but someday.

"Anyhow, the strawberry thing isn't really a dinner," Rylie said, "but more like a town picnic and—"

"I knew there was something I'm supposed to tell you." Taylor's arms fell to his sides. "We're invited to Ashley and Mark's for a barbeque. Evidently, the previous owners of their home are going to be in town, so Ashley's organizing a barbeque on Saturday."

"We? As in me and you?" Her mind stumbled over the idea. We?

"Yes. Mark said Ashley would like to get to know you better. We'll head over there about four if you can be ready by then."

She couldn't do *we* with him. Especially when his mere presence flustered her like hell, and the way he was staring at her heated her insides.

"What?" she asked.

His stance shifted. "I said, do you have meetings that afternoon or can we—"

"We...aren't heading anyplace. I knew everyone in town would get the wrong idea from us living in the same house. This is only the beginning."

"They didn't mean anything by inviting both of us. You're new around here and work for me. That's all. Nothing else."

Taylor strode toward his office, then turned back at his door. "This is not some kind of date, if that's what you think."

"Darn right!" Why was she so angry? This man made her edgy without even trying.

"Damn right, it's not! I told Mark you wouldn't come if I asked."

They faced each other in a field of unknown territory, shouting at each other for no valid reason. Especially since she was fairly trembling with the need to touch him, to fold her hand in his and clasp their fingers. Instead, she brushed her fingers through her hair. Once. Twice. Three times. Then crunched for volume.

"Ouch! Ouch! Ouch!" She flailed to free her bracelet from being caught in her hair.

"Hold still a second." He steadied her with his hands, then tenderly touched her fingers. "Stop pulling." He leaned closer, his breath sliding against her ear as he gently worked on the clasp. "Let me see what I can do."

A few seconds later, her bracelet was free, and her hand fell to his shoulder. "Thank you. Otherwise, I might have had to cut my hair to get it loose."

He slid his fingers through her hair and brushed it back from her cheek, letting the side of his hand caress down the side of her neck. "Hey, I'm sorry about calling you bossy." He stroked her hair back once again. "It's just that you…you…"

She rested her hand against his chest. Fingered the shirt. "Did you get the orange pulp out of the other shirt?"

"No, but I did try. Then I sent it to the dry cleaners." He closed his hand around hers and squeezed, and for a moment, they simply looked into each other's eyes. "Rylie, we're not twenty-somethings playing a game. Life has thrown us some curves along the way. And the thirties have been tough. So, if I'm too abrupt at times, you keep right on reminding me there's two sides to everything."

Her inner voice nudged to give an inch as she pulled her hand from beneath his. "Me, too. We've had a stressful afternoon. The barbeque on Saturday sounds great."

"Be ready by four, okay?"

"Fine." She returned to the door of her office. "Why don't I put the top down on my car and drive us over?"

He headed to his office. "We'll take my truck."

"If you're worried about my driving, I can assure you you'll get there in one piece."

His shoulders jerked as he glanced back at her

with that I-will-not-budge attitude. "We'll take my truck."

"Why? My car would be a great way to start a picnic." She thrilled at the thought.

In the short time she'd been in Nature's Crossing and shared the house, she'd learned his walls-up demeanor and knew how to avoid a confrontation. Plus, they'd already had more than one conversation about her driving a truck. Each time, she let him think she would just to get him to stop forcing the issue. Then, the next morning she'd get in her convertible, turn the radio on and drive away.

In her mind, the matter had been settled, but once again, here was the truck issue. Only now, he didn't just want the truck for her workdays, but also her time off. Too bad.

This time she dug in for the come-what-may battle. "My car—"

"We'll take. My. Truck!"

"Then I'll. Drive. My. Self!"

"Good. That way everyone will know for sure we're not a we." He shoved the door to his office closed behind him.

"Darn it," she whispered, walking back to her office. "Double dang darn it."

His door opened a second before she heard him heading in her direction. "By the way, I'm having a security system installed at Gwen's place this evening."

She quieted with the seriousness of his tone. "Okay. I was a little worried that she's there by herself. So, thank you kindly."

"The one at our ho— where we live, will be put in tomorrow morning." His stare locked with hers. "I want you to use it all the time."

Rylie nodded. She wasn't good at remembering to set alarms, but she'd try. "What code?"

"What?"

"What do you want set as the passcode?"

He shook his head. "I don't care. You decide. And one more thing…"

Tired of all the recital of dos and don'ts, Rylie opened her mouth to say so, then paused. The security system was a good idea, but what else could he possibly be going to rule on?

"I'm sorry, could you repeat that? I wasn't paying attention," Rylie quirked the corners of her lips into her sweetest smile.

His irritation at not being paid attention to showed in the set of his mouth as the look from his eyes questioned why she wouldn't pay attention to what he said. She liked that look, that tell. Now be nice, she told herself, no matter what he says, be nice.

"I said, I'll be sleeping on the sofa in front of your bedroom door tonight."

Lord, help her that was all she needed. "Why?"

"In case Chase decides to make an appearance. Don't try to change my mind. Like it or not, that's where I'll be tonight."

At least he hadn't said he'd sit in a chair by her bed all night. Where the heck had he gotten such a protector attitude? She could understand his concern for her and her sister's safety, so she'd give him this one.

"Makes sense," Rylie said. "Thank you."

Made sense to her, but she sure wouldn't get much rest because she'd be awake all night listening to him breathe. Listening to his movements. Listening to that quiet, relaxed sound men made when they were in a deep sleep.

"Alright then. It's settled." He started to close the door again.

Rylie's spinning mind spun to a stop. "Robins."

"What?" His half-glance over his shoulder obscured his face.

"The passcode for the security system. Robins. Okay?" She wanted his approval on this. Needed his approval.

He nodded. "Sounds good."

Great. For once, they'd agreed on something personal and spoken to each other like a rational man and woman not bent on confronting each other. Maybe they'd turned a corner.

"Will you please ride to the picnic in my truck?" he asked.

So much for the corner. "No. How about the convertible?"

He shook his head and started back to his office, then stopped and glanced over his shoulder. "If I asked you on a date, would you say yes?"

Stunned by the question's directness, she lifted her face to gaze into his eyes. The idea hadn't crossed her mind, and she'd tried to push all thoughts of them as a *we* as far away as possible. But from the expression on his face, he was serious. Standing there, waiting for an answer, he waited. And she couldn't reason an appropriate response.

Yes. No. Maybe…maybe later…maybe never… Maybe…just maybe. What was the answer? What was *her* answer?

She'd hope he'd never ask that question. Not that he didn't appeal to her. Not that she wouldn't love to be lost in arms. Not that there weren't times the nearness of him overwhelmed her all the way to her core. But if he asked, that would mean she had to make a decision.

"I don't know. I truly don't know."

"Fair enough." He walked into his office and turned back to face her once again. "Have you ever gone out with anyone since Mathew's death?"

Slowly, she shook her head. "No."

He nodded, then shut his office door. Not loud. Not soft. Just closed.

CHAPTER FIFTEEN

RYLIE MARVELED AT how good life in Nature's Crossing had turned out. The past few days had felt like she'd lived there all her life. In fact, except for the Chase incident, everything had gone better than she could have hoped. True to his word, Taylor had slept outside her door that night. She'd been drawn into the rhythm of his breathing, letting herself relax as she slipped into her own dreams. Even getting used to the security system at the Victorian had been easier than she'd expected.

Her appointments with construction companies had gone well, and two tracts of land were already signed, sealed, and sold. But just when she thought she and Taylor were more on a friendship line of thinking, he took his couple days' trip to KC, then picked back up on his business and business only manner when he returned.

Didn't matter, she had her own company worries to think about. Besides her work here at Nature's Crossing, she had to stay on top of the day-to-day business of Crawford Enterprises.

She loved Peaceful Lake Acres, a development

of eight communities, where each small village within the complex would be built by a different contractor, which in turn would offer different prices, styles, and buyer appeal. The houses all had to complement the setting of woods and trails, nature and green space, family values, and enjoyment. When she'd signed the contract with TRED, she hadn't realized how much she'd enjoy being part of a housing development friendly to the environment. She had also discovered how deep Taylor's integrity ran with his company and with others. If she ever needed a business confidante, he'd be right at the top of her list.

The development's clubhouse, which would soon house the TRED offices, was almost finished, and weather permitting, the pool and deck were to break ground in a couple of weeks. Of course, in construction, everything depended on the whim of the weather, and today had been a watershed filled with bucketloads of rain. Thank goodness the day was almost over.

Rylie pulled into the construction trailer parking lot and parked as close as possible to the entrance, then sprinted through the current downpour. She'd barely stepped inside when the door behind her flung open once again, and Taylor crashed inside, bumping into her with enough force to knock her off her feet. Reactively, he bent as his arm encircled her waist and grabbed her against him before she hit the floor.

Feeling the heat of a blush on her cheeks, she knew spoons in a drawer wouldn't have nestled any better than the two of them at the moment.

Evidently, he'd felt the familiarity, too, because after a few seconds, he planted her feet on the floor and stepped aside.

Easing past her, his chest brushed her arm. "Excuse me."

She had no reply.

All she could think of was how her hair seemed plastered to the sides of her head. Water droplets trickled down her cheeks and the back of her neck. She swiped her palm across her face and discovered her mascara had started to run. Before long, if not already, she'd look like someone had given her two black eyes.

When he turned to face her, she noticed his shirt had wicked to his arms and shoulders. Never mind the suction of cloth to skin over his muscled abs as the material disappeared into his jeans.

Taylor cleared his throat, and she realized he'd seen her staring at him. Well, that was awkward. No, that was embarrassing as heck.

Flustered beyond her senses, she said the first thing that bounced into her mind as she raised her gaze to meet his. "I was just wondering. Why do you stand with your hands on your hips all the time?"

His hands stayed put, but he angled his head and grinned. "You sure that's what you were wondering?"

"Yes, of course. What else would I be thinking?" She remained motionless for fear she'd lose her concentrated stare into his eyes and let her own eyes stray downward.

"Okay. If that's the way you want it." He quirked the side of his mouth and nodded. "Maybe my hands are on my waist because I don't have any other place to put them."

The trailer door flung open again, and in charged Gwen and Jake. Like a train collision, Gwen slammed into her sister, and Rylie stumbled forward into Taylor. Once again, he grabbed her to him. This time, face-to-face and close.

She didn't remember moving them, but she realized her arms were clasped around his shoulders, and her toes didn't touch the ground. At least she kept her presence of mind not to wrap her legs around Taylor. But her imagination was running crazy.

For a moment, the only thing she longed for was to lay her head against his chest and let his rain-soaked clothing melt with her own. His lips were within easy reach, his scent pulling her even closer. How much longer could she deny the attraction? Deny herself? Him?

Her fingers brushed against his neck, and he trembled. Pressing his hand against her back, he didn't look away. One kiss. What would it matter if they shared one kiss? Just one and then never again. Their lips inched closer. Had she leaned in? Had he? Just one.

No, she couldn't allow herself to want him. What would Mathew say?

From a hazy distance, Gwen giggled.

"Ahem," Jake said.

Rylie blinked and jerked back as her arms slid from his shoulders and hung at her side. She pointed her toes, reaching for the solid surface of the floor. "You can put me down now."

Slow, easy, and so close she heard his heartbeat, he lowered her to her feet before his hands released her and fell to his own sides. He didn't turn away. Neither did she. After a moment, he stroked her rain-drenched hair from her cheek, then slid his hand around to the back of her head as if to guide her to his lips. Her mouth parted with the upward stretch of her neck, willing and waiting and...

No, no, no. She couldn't betray Mathew. He might be gone, but she couldn't betray his love, his trust, his kiss. Lowering her chin, she closed her lips.

Jake cleared his throat again. "Thought you'd want to know they're calling for floods in the area, Taylor. Might be a good time to see if the far end of the creek overflows."

She and Taylor's moment broke like a fragile limb in a strong wind, and each turned away.

"Good idea. I'll grab my poncho, and we'll drive out there." Taylor walked into his office.

Rylie glanced at her sister, then back to the floor. Whatever had just happened left her confused, and all she knew was that her insides were churning with peaks and valleys, too intense to ignore.

By the time Taylor came back out, Rylie had moved to the side of the front office, giving him plenty of room to pass, but he stopped beside her. Confused and unsure, she didn't look up.

"You have any more appointments today?" he

asked quietly with a touch of husky softness to his tone that made it sound like the most intimate of questions.

"Not till tomorrow afternoon." Rylie crossed her arms with a slight shiver. The cold rain soaked through her clothes, and she shivered from the cold mixed with…something else. Need? Want?

He lobbed the poncho over his head. "Good. Don't go out driving around just to look at the community in this kind of weather. I don't want anybody caught in a flash flood. Okay?"

Rylie thought she nodded.

Evidently not because he reached out and tipped her chin up, and before she could stop herself, she gazed into his eyes, realizing his expression made her feel as if she'd be protected forever. Even when she didn't know she needed to be.

Her insides struggled with the realization that this man—Taylor with the Type A personality, the uber-successful CEO, the man known for his steeled emotions—cared about her.

That couldn't be. She wouldn't allow another workaholic man in her life. Mathew had known nothing but work, work, work. She wouldn't go through that again.

"Okay?" Taylor asked as his thumb caressed across her cheek.

"Okay."

Then he turned and followed Jake out the front door. Once the door closed and the two men's voices faded into the rain, she turned to face her sister and stood there quietly. Words weren't needed for the sisters to understand each other. They were connected by a past of happy and sad…there was nothing to be said, only felt.

Gwen pulled a couple of towels from the restroom and handed one to Rylie. "You look like a drenched Yorkie."

"Feel like one, too." Shivering, Rylie rubbed her rain-soaked hair with the soft terrycloth but couldn't move from the spot.

"Here, let me wipe your face." Gwen took the end of the towel and patted beneath her sister's eyes.

"I should never have come here," Rylie choked out in a whisper.

"Why not?"

"Taylor…being around Taylor. It's too much. I can't do this."

"What do you mean?"

Rylie looked back at the floor and bit her lip. "He makes me feel things. Things I felt with… with…Mathew."

Gwen touched her shoulder. "Mathew would want you to enjoy your life. Maybe it's time to move on. "

"I don't want to move on." Rylie heard the words she'd spoken, but they seemed jumbled with her expanding sniffles of pain. Hiccup-sobs, like the time she fell from a tree and broke her arm, shook her insides. Partly pain…partly fear.

"Sure you do. Otherwise, you wouldn't be so upset. You're just not quite ready yet." Gwen whispered. "Remember years ago, when you told me it was okay to be confused…to be afraid? The same's true for you, too."

Tears rolled down Rylie's cheeks and her hands trembled as she wiped them away on her wet sleeves. It had been a long time since she broke down, but suddenly, the wall she'd built around her grief crumbled and she reached out for Gwen, who folded her into her arms and didn't let her fall. Her sister had stood tall through her own loss years ago and survived, now amid shuddering sobs Rylie needed her sister's strength more than ever.

Gwen rocked the two of them gently. "Shhhh, it'll all work out. You're strong. Strong enough to walk through this."

There they were—the words the girls had heeded from their mother all their life. Even when their mother's muffled tears had echoed through their parent's bedroom door once their dad left on extended duty, the woman had never shown anything but strength to the world. Gwen and Rylie had learned their mother's strength well, yet life still didn't come easy sometimes.

"Closing the door on what Mathew and I had is hard. Harder than anything I've ever done in my life." Rylie shivered with the cold uncertainty tugging at her heart and mind. "I'm not sure I can do that. Not now. Not ever."

CHAPTER SIXTEEN

TAYLOR DROVE THROUGH the rain in silence. Jake sat in the passenger seat as they covered every roadway in Nature's Crossing, sometimes twice. Each man scanned the roads and hillsides for unplanned water runoff or worse. High powered spotlights lay in the jump seat, ready for in-depth surveillance from the truck or on-foot if necessary.

A blocked culvert caught Taylor's eye and he pulled to a stop. People in Nature's Crossing had told him the past few days of downpours had been highly unusual, but that didn't matter in his development world. He had to build to withstand the elements without harming the environment, that was part of what his company stood for.

Good work. Good planning. Good infrastructure. This culvert wasn't good.

He and Jake grabbed the lights and trekked up the hillside, following the run to its origin. Jake made notes in a handheld recorder as they stomped back down the hillside, leaving flag stakes in the muddy ground at key problem points. Once back in the cab of the truck, he drew diagrams in his zippered notebook before they drove on to the next area of trouble. The minutes stretched into over an hour. Finally they reached the creek.

"If that sucker's gonna flood, it'll be here," Taylor shouted, jumping from the truck.

Jake followed him up the hillside as they both stayed well back from the edge of the water just in case there'd been an undercut from the rushing water. Rain pelted them as fast as the high creek water surged downstream.

Eyes vigilant, bodies on alert, instincts sharp to danger, reminded Taylor of guard duty years ago in the military. He glanced at Jake. Did he feel the same from his days in the Marines?

Taylor wiped his face with his palm, little that it helped. "Looks like the creek's running good. Be sure to get those extra trees planted and some ground cover up the sides. That should help with erosion."

"I'll get Bennett on it first thing Monday," Jake shouted above the roar of the gushing water.

"Make sure we don't alter the flow downstream either. We sure as hell don't want our project to damage anybody else's property." Taylor was as mindful of spending money on a project as any other CEO, but when it came to keeping other people's property unaffected by TRED development, he'd spend whatever it took.

The two men headed down the hill, digging the heels of their boots into the mud to stay upright. They stopped at a rock outcropping.

"Damn rain. Crews won't be able to work for

a day or two," Taylor knew that meant they'd be behind schedule. Jake should be on top of these issues, not handing them over to Bennett. The man already had enough to do as foreman on the site. In fact, Taylor didn't understand why the man's name kept popping up in the daily night reports lately. "Maybe we could dig out the creek bed a few feet all the way across our property. Might help eliminate flooding downstream. Be sure to check with the Department of Natural Resources first."

"When I talk to Bennett, I'll tell him to get hold of our contacts in the local Conservation office, too." Jake stared off in the distance as if the rain were the least of his worries. "You'll like working with Bennett. He's a good man. Takes the environment as seriously as TRED does."

Taylor wiped his face again and eyed his brother. Something wasn't right. "Spit it out. What are you trying to tell me?"

Jake pushed back the hood on his rain poncho, letting the rain pound against his face. "Let's go back to the office and talk."

The two of them trudged the rest of the way to the truck, tossed their rain ponchos in the back and climbed inside. Drenched and quiet, each of them seemed lost in their own thoughts.

Taylor started the truck, then turn it off and flipped on the overhead light. Leaned back against the door. "Let's talk here. What's going on?"

"I've been waiting to tell you till more was in place. But, I guess now's as good a time as any." Jake turned and braced his back against the passenger door, making sure the two of them were face to face. "A lot of the logistics are still in the planning stages, but the guys in Washington have asked a group of developers to look into possible improvements in South America. See what could be done in respect to living conditions in some areas."

"How long have you known this might be in the works?"

"They contacted dad about six months ago. Someone had remembered he did some work in Peru and Brazil, years and years ago. Wanted his advice. Wanted him to be involved." Jake paused. "When he told them his health wasn't what it used to be, they asked for a recommendation. He called to see if I'd be interested. I said yes. He told them and they agreed. The rest is history."

The idea sounded promising. And there was no doubt that Jake was a leader in the construction field for seeing the possibilities of a piece of land, long before others laid everything out on the computer. Still, worry hit Taylor in the gut. Yes, this was business. Nothing to do with fighting or the past. But, Jake's last tour of duty in the Middle East had been hard. Sure, he'd managed to pull his life back in place after a few months being home. But, what if... Taylor couldn't help but worry sometimes. He was forever reminded of how much he loved his family, loved his brothers.

"When do you leave?" Taylor asked.

"About a week. I've made arrangements to hold some preliminary meetings down at Fort Campbell." Jake swiped his palm down his face to no avail. Water still trickled from his hair onto his forehead. "Then we'll head on to Washington, D.C."

The two of them glanced away from each other. Listened to the rain. The thunder. The lightning. Each lost in their own thoughts.

"You sure you want to do this?" Taylor asked. "I mean—"

"Yeah, I know what you mean. And I'm good." Jake grinned. "Sure, I was caught by surprise when the idea was first brought up. Had to let myself face some things." Jake turned toward him. "But you know what? The more the idea took shape, the more confident I became. And when they suggested I be in charge of the entire committee… Well, that was a grow-up moment. My mind kicked into overdrive on so many levels. And every single one was business, business, business."

"One thing for sure, they've picked the right man and the right company to keep things above board and on track." Taylor held out his hand. "Man, I'm so proud of you. So damn proud. Anything you need. Anything. Ever. You. Just. Call. Day or night, I'm always here for you, brother. Always."

Jake cleared his throat as he returned the clasp. "Thanks. That means one hell of a lot to me. And just so you know, we've already got some big money behind this project."

"Now that I like to hear. Maybe something will get done this time." Smiling, Taylor turned the key in the ignition and flipped off the interior light. Time to move on. "We'll need to get you a going-away party lined up. The guys will—"

"I'd rather you didn't. Except for you and Bennett, no one needs to know for now. There's already a get-together next weekend, so let's just make sure it's a happy one." Jake's tone sounded like any other time he planned a party. "You call a meeting for the Monday morning after that. I'll tell everyone. Then, take off that afternoon."

"Okay, if that's what you want."

For the rest of the ride, the two of them discussed TRED's possible involvement, with some pro bono work, as the plans developed. Discussed how to handle working with some of their business competitors. Most important, they brainstormed on staying healthy, staying alive and staying out of the cartel's way. South America might not be half-way around the world, but there were still a lot of dangerous scenarios to consider.

By the time they pulled into the construction parking lot, the lights were off in the trailer. Seemed like weeks instead of hours since Taylor had walked out the door with Rylie on his mind and his shirt. The touch of her fingers still lingered on his neck, but not as warm and soft as before.

Jake grabbed his notebook and recorder. "I'll talk to Bennett tomorrow and schedule a meeting between the three of us some evening this week."

"Sounds good. Make sure to increase his salary and benefits." Taylor eased back in the seat, accepting the inevitable. For him, life would go on. Always did. Fate and destiny were tough taskmasters to him, but he'd learned how to survive. His shields were in place, and he'd keep them there. "Won't be the same around here without you to give me what-for when I'm wrong."

"I don't think you have to worry about that. Rylie will probably pick right up where I leave off."

"What do you mean?"

"She's got your number, buddy." Jake jokingly punched him in the shoulder. "And she's for damn sure not gonna take any guff from you."

"Well, I've got her number, too." Taylor didn't plan to take any from her, either. In fact, he would make sure their interactions were strictly business from now on. That was his forte, no one better. She was one of his contractors, nothing else. Aw, hell. He'd already overstepped that rule a few hours ago when he'd come close to kissing her till she begged for more.

"Yeah, I noticed that earlier. Did me and Gwen interrupt something?" Jake asked.

Taylor didn't want to pursue that thought. At least not right now.

Jake slid out the passenger side into the dark, slamming the door behind him, then grabbed his rain poncho from the truck bed before walking to the driver's side of the truck. With a big grin on his face, Jake knocked on the window, and Taylor powered it down.

"Here's the situation as I see it," Jake said.

"Which one?"

"You and Rylie."

Taylor's blood surged. For a moment, he remembered him and Jake in high school, razzing each other about girls. Tossing around their bravado and saying how they'd never get caught by a woman. He'd sure miss his brother's ribbing while he was gone. With him around, Taylor could remember where he'd come from not just the man he'd become.

"So what's your take?" Taylor asked.

Jake hauled back and laughed. "My money's on Rylie. Hell, I figure by the time I return, you'll be married with one in the oven."

"Not hardly," Taylor shouted as his brother trotted to his own truck and drove away.

Then as if on cue, lightning crackled through the air, and a flash in the near distance indicated a tree somewhere in the development had been hit. The deluge of rain notched up and poured like a broken faucet, while his windshield wipers fought to keep up.

Taylor didn't feel like heading inside to his office to work. Didn't want to go get anything to eat, either. But considering what had happened between him and Rylie earlier, he sure as hell didn't want to run into her again tonight.

All he wanted was to go home, climb the stairs unseen, and have a good long workout in his gym. He flipped the defrost on, and Rylie's lingering fragrance on his shirt mingled with the air. That same smell was invading the recesses of his house, too.

He shook his head and shifted the truck into

gear. Maybe he should spend the night sleeping out in the cold rain. Might bring him to his senses.

CHAPTER SEVENTEEN

TAYLOR TOSSED THE rain poncho he'd worn from the truck to the house back outside on the porch. Walking into the kitchen, he caught sight of Rylie perched on the kitchen counter, wearing a gown short enough to make a grown man cry. Instantly, everything from his belt down went on high alert.

As she turned to face him, he caught sight of her clutching the bottle of Jack Daniels from the top shelf. "I thought I saw this up here and decided a drink might be good about now."

"Put it back."

"I'll buy you another one."

"Put it back, Rylie. It's got nothing to do with you buying anything."

She turned and set the bottle back on the shelf. "You don't have to be such a bear, you know. It's just a bottle of whiskey."

"Put it back, and then get down before you fall and break a leg or arm..." Taylor couldn't take his eyes off her legs or the way the silky material outlined her breasts and butt in perfect detail. Every delicate little detail. "Or something."

Pushing the bottle back to where it had been, she stood on her tiptoes and stretched upward, causing her gown to rise and slide up her thighs. Way up. His body reacted even more. For once, she had done what he asked, and her response might just kill him in return. Damn his body. He needed the heat and hard like he needed another problem. Where was his rain poncho now that he needed something to hold in front of him?

"You got bottoms for that top?" he asked as he stepped behind the kitchen island.

Her hand grabbed the edge of the silk and tugged downward. "Yes, but I didn't expect you home. Usually, you stay at the office much later. Besides, I have undies on. And, for your information, this top covers more than my swimsuit."

He couldn't argue with that logic since he'd never seen her in a swimsuit, but his imagination filled in the blanks. "Well, I'm home tonight. Put the bottoms on."

Each had called this place home. What was up with that? He needed to make sure she understood this arrangement was only temporary. Had she found another place to live? Tomorrow. It could wait until tomorrow.

She crouched on the cabinet's granite countertop, eyeing the floor. "Didn't seem this far up when I jumped on the counter. Could you help me down?"

Rain-soaked and dripping onto the ceramic floor, he considered the circumstances. Yes would surely get him in trouble. Maybe even get him what his body told him he wanted because all he had to do was pick her up in his arms and see if she leaned in for his kiss like she had back in the office earlier that night.

"Well, can you help me?" she asked.

He blew out a simple cheek-puffing sigh as he scanned his eyes from the red on her toenails to the glow of her blonde hair and every spot in between. Lord have mercy. If this was one of life's little tests, he was about to fail no matter what he answered.

"No!" He escaped up the stairs and headed to his exercise room.

From downstairs, her voice followed him up, but he couldn't make out the words, only the tone. She was mad. He chuckled and grinned to himself. Real mad. And, probably sassy…and hot…and…

Flicking on the shower to full cold, he stepped inside. Too hell with getting undressed. First, he needed to cool off.

Over an hour later, fresh from his workout and shower, Taylor headed to the kitchen, which he hoped would be empty by now. It was, except for that damned floral scent of Rylie's.

A shaft of light shown under the pocket door to the dining room, and considering how quiet the whole place seemed to be, he pushed the door open to turn off the light. To his surprise, not only was the table covered in stacks of papers, Rylie was seated at the far end of the table, holding her head in her hands.

"Sorry. I figured you'd gone to bed," he said.

"No, I'm still working on Crawford Enterprise

business." She tilted her head just enough to look at the screen on her laptop, quickly scribbled on the yellow legal pad beside the computer, pushed a few buttons on the calculator, then popped her pen in a nervous fidget against her cheek.

"Something wrong?"

"No…uh, yes. No. I mean no." She met his gaze. "What I meant to say was there's nothing wrong with Nature's Crossing or my contract with TRED."

To him, she looked like a child who'd just said what she thought the teacher wanted to hear. Considering the way his evening had gone so far, he wasn't about to pursue the fact that obviously, something was very wrong in her business world.

"Okay. I'm about to make dinner. You hungry?" Taylor asked.

She was up now and making notes on Post-Its, slamming them on the stacks of paper and folders as she walked around the table. He noticed she still didn't have the pajama bottoms on, but he decided this wasn't the time to bring that to her attention. Biting her lip, she threw the notepad in the middle of the table along with her pen. "Damn it."

"What's the matter?"

She jumped at the sound of his voice. Evidently, she'd forgotten he was there because her hand slid to the hem of her sleep shirt and tugged downward.

"Embezzlement," she said.

The businessman inside him snapped to attention. "Have you found someone siphoning money from Crawford Enterprises?"

"Not now, but…." She squinted at the laptop again. "Long story short, the accountant Mathew insisted we use had been diverting profits into her own bank account for years. When I took over all aspects of the company, I had an audit done by a credible outside firm. That's when the discrepancies showed up."

"Want me to take a look at any of this?"

"No. Thank you kindly." Rylie jerked her head up and glared at him with anger in her eyes.

A tiny twitch at the corner of her right eye said he'd done something she considered an insult to her ability. Amazing how much he'd picked up on her tells during the past days. He always figured that one reason he did so well in the cutthroat world of development had been his ability to read other people.

Another plus had been when he learned how to admit when he was wrong. But all he'd done was ask if he could be of help. She always seemed to think she could do everything by herself. Maybe he'd stepped on her ego even though he hadn't meant to. Wouldn't hurt to make a peace offering this time.

"You're right. Your business is yours. Mine is mine." He walked back to the kitchen, easing the pocket door to the dining room closed behind him. Dinner…he'd come down to make a really late dinner for himself. Something easy. Staring into the refrigerator, he gradually began to fill the island counter with fresh vegetables.

The pocket door inched open, and Rylie stood

in the doorway with matching long silky pants beneath the top.

"I think I need…uh, could you…" She paused and cleared her throat. "If you've got time, I'd like to take you up on your offer to look over my company's paperwork." Her pained expression deepened.

He nodded and put the knife down from chopping green peppers, then waited for her to continue at her own pace. "Show me whatever you want. I'll keep everything confidential. But you need to understand upfront that I'll give you my best opinion. Straight, tough, and to the point. Deal?"

"That's what I'm looking for. Honesty on all fronts."

She walked back into the dining room, and he followed. Those long silky bottoms might cover her body, but they sure didn't hide the curves. And the way they teased across her bottom with every step she took was a walking timebomb for him. Still, he followed her into the dining room, ready to do battle with himself and her paperwork.

His mind absorbed the rundown Rylie gave him regarding each stack on the table. And even though it annoyed the hell out of him, he let her explain things her own way. He liked things short and concise. She liked short and concise with all the background, some of which didn't interest him. Plus, at times, he wasn't quite sure where she was headed with her explanations, but he listened, and eventually, a few specifics came through loud and clear.

The biggest thing he gathered from her tone and words, expression and voice quivers, was that Rylie still clung to Mathew through the company. She hadn't faced his death entirely. Because Mathew lived on in Crawford Enterprises, she appeared perfectly fine to the world at large. From what she'd just laid out on the table for review, life might not give her that connection much longer.

Taylor knew it hurt like hell to release the past, but he'd taken steps to at least compartmentalize his demons. Could Rylie do the same? Maybe… maybe not.

Finally finished, she offered Taylor the chair in front of her laptop. One glance at the screen told him she trusted him enough to share her company's innermost secrets because the spreadsheets pulled up were specific and confidential. Right now, he wasn't so sure he wanted to be part of her possible collapse, but he had offered.

She pulled a side chair next to him. "So, here's the problem. Problems, I should say. The day before I got here, my CPA told me that even with all the cuts and reinvestments we've done, Crawford is still staying in the red each month. And he gave me a spreadsheet—" she moved it to the front of the screen, "—detailing a few scenarios for me dipping further into my personal finances to keep the company afloat for another year. Some long-range projections. And finally, some other options I might want to consider."

"May I ask what those options are?"

She balked. Looked away. "I want *your* opinion

before I tell you the CPA's recommendation."

Taylor wasn't one to give false hope. Yet, his gut clenched at the thought of the tables being reversed. If TRED were the one on the chopping block, he'd want the cold hard facts plus the bottom line. Somehow, he doubted that was what Rylie wanted.

"You want me to look this over and check the info in the stacks? The contracts?" He pointed to the laptop and table.

"Anything you want. I need someone to bounce this off since Mat—since my accountant isn't here. And, frankly, I don't want to share this with anyone in my company yet."

His eyes scanned her figures. "Is this why you climbed up to get the whiskey?"

"Yeah. Guess I looked pretty stupid."

He wasn't about to tell her just how sexy she'd looked on her tiptoes reaching for the top shelf. At least not right now. "When you came in the kitchen just now, I was about to make something simple to eat. Open a bottle of wine. Would you like a glass?"

"I can open it. I'll even make us something to eat while you look this over."

"Sounds good." His eyes strayed from the computer screen for only a moment as the silky swish of her pajamas caught his ear. Everything would be a whole lot easier on him if she wore flannel. Maybe.

Didn't take him long to see that if her numbers on the spreadsheet were right, Crawford Enterprises was in deep trouble. She was right, though. The quieter she kept the possible problem, the better for her company's reputation. And possible sale price.

He checked and rechecked different facts, always coming to the same conclusion. Even he'd begun to hope he was wrong, that he'd missed something, anything. He headed into the paperwork from a different direction, but nothing changed in the final outcome.

Rylie was a good businesswoman, and her figures all made sense. Less money coming in meant she could cover hard expenses and pay her employees their current salaries for about six months. Then, do a gradual cut back on staff.

His conclusion…Crawford Enterprises would die a slow death unless she restructured and downsized drastically and ASAP. Even then, the long haul didn't look promising.

After a bit, the smell of green peppers, mushrooms, and cheese wafted from the kitchen, and when he glanced at the clock on the hutch, he couldn't believe almost an hour had passed.

"Food's ready," Rylie called from the doorway.

He grabbed each developer's contract and walked into the kitchen.

Standing at the island, he shoveled the hot food into his mouth from the plate she'd set in front of him, then, one by one, he flipped through the pages of each contract another time. They were good, well-written to cover Crawford Enterprises, but as all business people knew, there were extenuating circumstances even in a nailed-tight contract. He kept each one open to the same section on default.

Suddenly, his taste buds shifted to cool, and when he glanced down, Rylie had placed a bowl of cantaloupe and grapes in front of him.

He laid the paperwork aside. "Sorry. Once I get into financial dealings, I sometimes zone everything else out."

"That's okay." She picked up a piece of his cantaloupe and nibbled the edge.

"Thanks for the food. It was good."

"Really? What exactly did you have to eat?" she asked as she smiled.

"I have no idea." He laughed, offering a grape to her lips which she took eagerly. "But it was good."

She cleared away the dishes as he spread the contracts, moving his thoughts from his mind to the legal pad he'd brought from the dining room. Then he laid the pen down. He was done.

"You need some stools for the counter," Rylie said.

"Why?"

"To sit on, silly."

He'd never noticed. Mainly because he'd never had time to sit when he came in from a day's work. Most times he'd simply been running in to change clothes on the way to another meeting.

She leaned forward on the island, and he could feel she was ready for his summation. He knew she'd try to shield her feelings as he presented his conclusion, but he wouldn't help by sugarcoating the bottom line. True and fast was the best way.

"From what I can tell, your figures are right,"

He started with what she already knew. "When that accountant siphoned off your money, he gradually stalled any momentum for growth in the future."

A slight pallor encompassed her face as her expression dulled.

"Our only difference is in the timeframe for paying your employees. You figure a year. I figure six months." He knew he was right, but at the same time he already knew what she would say.

Rylie straightened. "You're right. Six months out of the company's funds, but then I can pull from my personal accounts. That should get me another six months."

Finally, there it was. Out in the open. Raw on the table. She planned to throw good money after bad if it saved Crawford Enterprises. If it saved a part of Mathew. If she didn't have to let go of what might have been.

"Have you considered approaching outside investors for more money?" Taylor asked.

"No. I don't want anyone else involved in our company."

"Our?"

"Mathew and mine's company." She lowered her eyes toward the floor. Bit her lip as it quivered. "My. I mean *my* company."

There was the answer to everything. In that moment, he knew that no matter what he said about being fiscally responsible to her and her business, she wouldn't take his advice. Because no matter what, she didn't want to face the impending doom of Crawford Enterprises. All she needed to hold on to her reluctance was for him, or anyone, to give her an ounce of hope for the company's survival. From "our company" to "my company" to no company at all, would be a hard chunk to swallow.

She opened the outside kitchen door, and the sound of a slow rain filled the silent void as the aromas of the past meal converged with the smell of wet dirt. Clearly, whatever business friendship they'd shared an hour ago was quickly dissipating, and two minutes from now, he knew she'd hate him with a passion reserved for her enemies.

He could shut up now and let her hold on to her dream to the bitter end, but that wasn't his way. He wouldn't do that to Mathew's memory. And he wouldn't do that to the woman Mathew had loved enough to marry.

"You're too smart to risk everything on a dying company." Taylor held his voice to a businessman's tone. "Yet that's exactly what you're about to do. Why? Have you asked yourself why?"

Rylie turned and shot him a look. One that said he'd stepped over a line. Too bad. He had nothing to lose by having his say. Hopefully, though, maybe something in his words would save her from her financial self-destruction. To him, that was worth her wrath.

"You need to think about yourself. Not just Crawford Enterprises," Taylor urged.

She stormed to the counter and shuffled the paperwork into her arms, angry to the point of trembling. This was what he'd feared would happen when she asked him to look over the paperwork. She'd wanted the truth if the truth helped her company. It hadn't. And she didn't want to hear the outcome now.

His demeanor softened. "Rylie——"

"No." Scrunching her arms tight against her sides as if fighting her collapse with all she had inside her. "You don't know what you're talking about. I can't lose this company. Mathew would want me to put everything into it. Everything. You're wrong."

"No. You're wrong." Taylor braced his hands against the island's granite countertop to keep from pulling her close. This was not the time to offer comfort. "From the times Mathew and I talked after college, I know he loved you. Looking over your figures, knowing what I've just reviewed, I also know he'd want you to be safe and secure. He'd want you to be the businesswoman you were when the two of you started your company. He'd want you to have money to live a good life."

"Leave me alone." She stumbled around the end of the island.

He turned and blocked her way, but she shoulder-shoved at him to move while tears drenched her cheeks and she shivered with emotions.

"Rylie…Rylie!"

Angry and defiant, her gaze shifted to his. He could tell she was down to her last ounce of strength. But there was one more thing he needed to do. Of course, that would mean he'd lose any chance they might have for a future together. Still, he had to say the words. Somehow, he needed to free her from the past and in this case, there'd be no bottle of whiskey for her demons, only his words.

"Get out of my way, Taylor," she muttered.

"Not until you listen to me."

"No. I shouldn't have trusted you. Now leave me alone."

"Losing Crawford Enterprises is not losing Mathew." His insides clawed at his throat. "Damn it, Rylie. You kissed him goodbye that morning. The plane crashed. He didn't survive. It's time you accept that."

Her feelings gurgled in silent sobs jerking her chest. "I can't...I can't let him go."

"You have to." Taylor fought the urge to take her in his arms. "Now, I'm not saying Mathew and I were close friends, but we knew each other. Knew who we planned to be in life. Knew what that long-term vision included. And one thing I know for sure. Mathew would not want you to give up everything *you* are just to save a failing company. All you'll end up doing is withering away to a shell of yourself. Don't make that his legacy to you."

She stared at the floor as if in limbo. Shaking her head as her eyes darted from one wall to another.

"I know how hard this is for you to accept, but Mathew's not on some extended business trip." Softening his voice, Taylor touched her hand as she clutched tight to the papers she'd picked up. "He'll never walk through the door again. Never kiss you. Never touch you. Never..."

She shook her head until her body vibrated

with denial.

"Rylie, hold onto your memories and the love you had for him. But Mathew's gone." Taylor's voice cracked. "No matter how much you try, there's nothing in this world that will ever bring him back. Believe me when I say, nothing will ever give you that one extra second that might have changed everything."

Only the drip of water from an overflowing gutter outside broke their silence as she slowly calmed herself.

"What do you know about love? Or death? You don't know anything," she said in a quiet, sadness filled tone of voice. "You've never even been married. What gives you the right to think you know how it feels to lose someone close to you? To lose someone in an instant. You know nothing…nothing."

CHAPTER EIGHTEEN

TAYLOR WATCHED AS Rylie bolted out of the room and stumbled to her bedroom. The agony of her sobs as she closed the French doors behind her ripped at his heart. Raking his fingers through his hair, he knew he'd pushed too far. Said too much.

Business or personal, he couldn't help her if she wouldn't accept his offer, but at least he'd talked about the elephant in the room. Just like the Major had talked to him years ago.

Sure, Rylie wasn't a soldier, but inside she was strong like one. Trouble was, she hadn't let herself fall yet. Hadn't let herself heal before she charged the next battlefront. To heal, first she had to fall to the bottom of the pit by realizing Mathew was gone and the company was nothing but a business. And businesses needed to make money.

Even a soldier in battle had to rest and renew at some point. Rylie hadn't. She'd just kept the brave face and fought the bottom day after day after day for the past few years. Life had a funny way of deciding when a person reached their breaking point. Once there, though, the strong rose again…stronger and better.

Taylor glanced down to where she'd left the legal pad with his notes scribbled on the pages, then picked it up. He'd look at the numbers one more time, but deep inside, he knew there'd be no change in the bottom line. The clock over the counter showed two a.m., so he headed upstairs. This had been one hell of a long day, and he needed some sleep.

The stairs creaked with his weight as he trudged up each step. What did he know about death? More than he wanted. That specter stood ready to raise its ugly head at a moment's notice.

This was why he'd never let himself fall for a woman completely. Never let himself say the words I love you. Love would lead to marriage. To children. To memories and life and happiness. Then, suddenly, without notice, fate might snatch everything away. Like a knife to the chest, he'd be racked with pain again. Just like he'd been after the attack on his unit. Pain so intense he might not be able to break the hold this time.

He doubted a bottle of whiskey would heal that pain again, and he couldn't risk what lay beyond his next breaking point.

His feelings for Rylie were more than attraction. Just what, he didn't know, but one thing for sure, if it became too heavy a load, he'd do something he'd never done in his life—turn and run. Love would not claim him on this path.

Hell, if there weren't so many people who depended on him for their job, their family's income, he'd call himself back into the military.

Go to the front line where the enemy was real and tangible. Where he could fight them and still be standing at the end of the day. Not like the opponents that ran through him at the moment, tearing at his heart and soul, teasing him with life's dreams.

Taylor noticed Rylie's scent all the way to the top of the stairs. She permeated the house more and more every day. Truth be told, he even felt something nice every time he turned in the driveway and saw the lights on. The fact she'd be inside. That maybe he'd bump into her. Share a smile.

This had to stop.

There'd be no more climbing around on the countertops, either. She could have been hurt. She needed to move out, and the faster the better. He'd talk to her about moving tomorrow—today.

Standing in his bedroom, he dropped his clothes to the floor and tumbled into the big, empty king-sized bed. Wiped out from the day's events, he scrunched the pillow beneath his head, praying for sleep to take him in for the night. None came. Instead, silky pajamas flitted through his mind. Bottoms or tops, those pajamas needed to stay on. He'd talk to her about them, too.

Wait, no need to do that, she'd be out of the house in a couple of days. Good. Get rid of that infuriating smell, too. He punched the pillow tighter under his head. Waited for sleep. Even in his bedroom on the second floor, he could still hear her sobs from downstairs. Finally, he turned on his back and stared at the ceiling, shoving all the other pillows off the bed.

Damn it to hell, when had his life gotten so complicated?

Rylie was a female persona of himself. Yet, she was soft and beautiful. Passionate, too. Was she the person she'd dreamed of being as a little girl? Probably not entirely. She was a scarred soul, damaged and hurt. Feelings he knew well. Nobody dreamed of being that person.

He couldn't let her go, she needed him. Even if she didn't know it yet, she needed him. Not for the long term, of course, but just for the time being. Might even be a slight possibility that he needed her, too. For the short term. He chuckled to himself. Slight? That was an understatement.

What would happen if he told her how a man had taken the bullet for him? Would she listen? Understand his pain? Comfort him? Tell him he should live the rest of his life trying to repay the outcome of life and death? Pity him? Pity! He didn't want that from anybody.

His mind slowed its pulse, and his eyelids drooped as he settled under the covers. *Be yourself.* He'd carried his facade, his armor, for so long he wasn't sure who Taylor Randolph really was anymore. His breathing slowed. *Try. At least try.* That he could do.

What was it the Major had told him? Things are never just two ways. There's usually a third choice. The gray area. Rylie wasn't an alternative, a gray area. She was a woman. Worse yet, a woman he'd made cry even if it had been for the right reasons.

Adrenaline pumped as he strained to listen for

sounds from below. Now there were only sniffles, then the French doors squeaked open. Moments later, he heard Rylie's steps in the kitchen. A cabinet door. The refrigerator opening. More sobs in the living room. She was in a pain so deep, he felt the pulses beating inside himself.

A yawn tugged at his mouth.

No way would he go down there again tonight unless she asked. But his soul ached for her to climb the steps to him.

CHAPTER NINETEEN

SHUT OFF FROM the world behind the French doors to her bedroom, Rylie huddled on her bed, pressing the phone against her ear as she clutched one of Mathew's shirts to her cheek. The shirt she kept in the bag by the nightstand. The one she'd never washed. The one that soothed her loneliness when the ache was too real.

During the past hour, she'd composed herself, evaluated what Taylor said, and didn't like the outcome staring her in the face. He might be right. She needed someone to tell her otherwise. Someone to say Taylor was wrong about her and Crawford Enterprises. Someone to understand she had to hold on to the past.

Her call was answered on the other end. "Dad?"

"What's wrong?" Her dad's voice sounded sleepy.

She glanced at the clock, then realized how panicked seeing her phone number at this time of night had to be for him and her mother. "I'm sorry, I should have noticed the time before I called. But I...I..."

"Doesn't matter what time it is. What's wrong?" His voice came through alert and awake this time. "What did he do?"

"Who?"

"The Cap— Taylor. Taylor Randolph. What did he do to upset you?"

Her mind shook with wonder at why her dad would jump to that conclusion. Chin quivering, she bit her lip as she focused on the clock numbers, stifling a sob with a whimper. "He didn't do anything. Not really. He's just…just very honest in his opinions." A moan escaped her lips. "Dad, am I…"

"Are you what? Just tell me what he said." Her dad's voice was calm with a touch of soothing. And like any other time she'd called with a problem, he was waiting for her to continue.

This was the way he always got in an emergency. His battlefield take-charge mode blended with knowing how to help the other person. Through the years, she'd learned to expect nothing less from him when she needed help.

Tonight, though, she wanted him to take her side. To blast the blatantly wrong idea. Say it was alright to stay with her dreams, her memories. All she had to do was tell him what had happened, and he'd agree with her. Then, why was it so hard to tell him? To need his counsel? Because her dad was honest. Just like Taylor, her dad wouldn't sugarcoat his response once she asked the question.

Suddenly, she felt lost. Afraid that the answer to her question would be the best for her, but not the one she wanted to hear. She didn't need another dose of reality tonight, so she wouldn't ask. She just wouldn't ask if Taylor was right.

"I shouldn't have called. We'll talk later."

Dad cleared his throat. A sign he was serious. "Rylie Crawford, don't lock the bedroom door like you're seven years old. Talk to me. To us. Your mother's on the other phone."

"Hi, honey. What's wrong?" The sound of her mother's voice broke the dam, and Rylie sobbed and sobbed.

After punching the phone to speaker mode, she curled up on her bed, pulling her knees to her chest. Clutched them to her.

Her mother's own sniffles echoed through the phone. "Honey, I'm right here. I've got my arms around you. Can you feel my arms? My love?"

Rylie felt like she was seven years old with a skinned knee, but she wasn't. She was a full-grown woman. A widow. A woman in so much pain she couldn't hide any longer. "Mathew's gone, Mother. He's really gone."

"Yes, honey. I know."

"I don't want him to be gone. I don't. I don't. I don't." She railed against her pillow with punch after punch. "Change it, Dad. Make it not real. Because…because it was too real tonight."

Her dad's silence spoke volumes. Had he stood waiting for this day all these years?

Rylie slid to her knees on the floor beside the bed like she had at the gravesite years ago. Her parents and Gwen had stood beside her and let her grieve, then comforted her with their tenderness and love.

"He's gone forever and…he's never… Never coming back." Her hands clenched the covers on the bed as she spread her arms in front of her. Leaning her cheek against the pink coverlet, she muffled her sobs. "He's…never…coming…back. I can't do this, Mother. I can't do this."

"Yes, you can, Rylie." Her mother's voice sounded strong. "Listen to me. You're a strong woman. Strong enough to take whatever life gives you and walk right through it."

"I don't want Mathew to be gone." Rylie heard her own whimpers, the ones of a little girl, the ones of an empty woman, the ones of realization. "I don't want him to be gone…"

"No, but he is gone. And nothing will ever bring him back." Her dad's voice shook her with its finality. How many times had he faced death in battle? Made a phone call to a relative of one who didn't make it home? Written a letter to go along with the soldier's personal belongings to his or her family? How did he do that? How?

He'd once told her and her mother that each step was acceptance and healing to allow the family to move forward. Had that been what he'd been doing, waiting for her to move forward in more than just her outward persona and business?

And if she let herself move forward inside, let her memories be memories and nothing more, let herself feel her needs and wants once again— would that be betrayal to Mathew? Would she forget him?

Rylie's sobs returned full force. There was

no stopping them, and she didn't want to. She needed to let the pain out because holding it in was harder than letting it go and she realized her mind had known that all along. Only now her heart and soul knew the same thing.

She cried. She cried. She cried.

"Let's rock, honey." Her mother's soft voice returned, seeping through the torment. "Feel my arms around you and just rock. Like we used to when you were little. Just cry and rock. You and me. No one else in the world, but you and me."

Rylie swayed back and forth with the rhythm of her mother's voice. Back to her childhood. Back to when a skinned knee was her biggest problem. Back and forth, back and forth, till gradually the sobs eased to sniffles, and then to tiny jerks of sadness. Sadness and defeat.

Reality pummeled through her emotions. Of course, she'd never forget Mathew or the life they had together, but it was time. Time to move forward and live the life she'd swept under Crawford Enterprises business survival for the past few years. "Thanks, Mother. I love you."

"I love you, too."

"Are you better now?" Dad's voice completed the circle of love between her and her parents. They always knew what and when to give whatever she needed. "Now, what did Taylor say that brought this on?"

"I told him about some problems my company's having. He agreed the outcome didn't look good." Rylie leaned back against the bed and wiped her face with the sleeve of her pajamas. "I've had to let people go. And even now, making payroll for the skeleton staff around the country is… Well, suffice it to say Crawford Enterprises is running in the red every month. The embezzler did a job on the investments money, and I can't catch up no matter what I try."

Her dad was quiet for a while. "I figured as much when you not only took the contract with TRED but agreed to work it yourself. That wasn't like you."

She managed a tiny snuffling laugh. "Think you know me pretty well, don't you?"

"For the most part."

Silence. Awkward, patient silence. She knew her parents would stay on the phone as long as she needed them. And she figured her dad wouldn't let her get away without telling him what she hadn't said yet.

"Plain and simple, Taylor said Mathew would never walk through the door again no matter how long I fought to keep the company afloat." Her chin trembled, and she breathed deep, blew the breath out long and slow. "He wasn't being mean. Just honest. Almost like he understood on a personal level what I was doing."

Rylie sighed and wiped her eyes. "Do you think he's right? Am I holding onto Crawford Enterprises to hold onto Mathew?"

Her mother's continued silence held her answer.

"That's for you to decide," Dad said. "What do you think?"

Rylie grabbed a handful of pictures from her bag by the nightstand. Photos of her and Mathew and good time and happy memories. She clutched the shirt tighter. "I think I've answered my own question in the past few minutes. Taylor's right. I've been a fool to keep holding on. Had you already figured this out?"

Now, her dad's silence spoke.

"I've been a fool," Rylie said. "All this time I've been a fool."

"No, honey. You've been a woman coming to grips with life. You've done the best you could," her mother said. "We knew this day would come when you were ready. It's here now. What you do with the future is up to you."

Dad cleared his throat. "Why don't you go upstairs and get Taylor to come sit with you for a while. Talk if you need to."

Rylie opened the French doors and glanced upstairs. Should she? Should she ask for his comfort? No. If she made the climb, if she knocked on his door tonight, she might not be able to resist falling into his arms.

No, tonight was about letting go of Mathew and moving forward for her. She needed tonight to say goodbye. The memories would stay with her, but she'd loosen her hold on the past, and she'd never forget, but she'd look to the future taking it one day at a time.

Tomorrow would be soon enough for Taylor. Maybe she wouldn't even need him.

Taylor's body jerked awake with one thought—what the hell was that? Red numbers on the clock showed three a.m., but he'd heard a noise. The crash had been loud enough to wake him. Loud enough to have not been a dream.

Chase? Could the man have broken in the house?

He'd set the security alarm before coming upstairs, but the system was still new. Maybe he'd missed a letter in the passcode. He jumped up, yanked his jeans on, and grabbed his steel flashlight from beneath the bed.

Rylie. He needed to get to Rylie before the intruder got to her. His stealth mode slammed in place as he moved fast, but quiet through the upstairs hallway, then down the stairs into the kitchen. She must be frightened. Terrified. That's all she needed tonight.

If there were someone desperate enough to break in when they knew people were at home, they were probably drugged or past caring. Either way wasn't a good scenario. What if there was more than one?

A glow showed through the doorway to the living room as he inched toward the opening and peered around the doorframe. Nothing. No movement. No sound. He slid around the corner and hugged the wall.

Then he saw the broken wine goblet on the hardwood floor next to the end table. That had been the crash he'd heard. Of course, since his very first military deployment years ago, he'd always slept light, so it would make sense the glass sounded like a crash.

Taylor stepped farther into the room and

eased around the recliner. His insides jerked an involuntary push of misery into his gut as he saw Rylie, asleep and huddled in the recliner that was three times bigger than her.

Photos of her and Mathew littered her lap, and she clutched a blanket and quilt against her as if fighting the cold. Tissues dotted the floor around the chair while others were wadded up and appeared thrown across the room.

He stroked the strands of still-damp tear-trapped hair from her cheeks, smoothing the straight blonde silkiness. Still, she slept. Her nose was red, her cheeks were red, and her body still jerked with tiny snuffles. He'd never seen anything so beautiful in his life.

Sliding his arms beneath her, he rolled her against his chest as he stood, and the covers slid from her hold. She snuggled against him, mumbling as her hand grasped the front of his shirt. He wondered who she thought she clung to. Mathew? Probably.

"Let's get you into bed, baby. Before you make yourself sick."

Her body relaxed and melted even further into him. "Thank you…Taylor."

He twinged with the realization she knew he was the one who held her. Something about that made him feel good, and lonely at the same time. For a moment, he rested his cheek against the top of her head and the softness gathered him in. What if he gave his heart to her? Would she accept it? Accept him? No, she hated him.

Hell, she could barely stand to be in the same

house with him, and someday she'd be strong enough to leave, leave him in a flash. He wasn't a fool. Besides, how could she possibly want someone like him? An inconsiderate workaholic who filled his days with work to keep his secrets from the past locked away.

She snuggled closer. "Ummmmm…"

If he intended to pursue this strong-willed woman who'd folded into his arms like they'd been together forever, there was one thing he had to face. In the end, he'd be the one hurt if it didn't work out. If she couldn't be satisfied with what he could give, she'd walk away. His question to himself was simple Was a few moments happiness worth a lifetime of agony later?

This felt like the times he'd took a chance on a failing company when he knew it could turn-around and be worth millions. Always some what-ifs, some oh-hells, and some why'd-I-do-that moments, but with time and perseverance the risks had made a profit. He'd done that many times.

Of course, there'd been that one time when he lost his investment plus a million. Brazenly, he had taken the loss public, and his reputation had held. People actually thought he'd taken on the company for a tax write-off and even though he'd let them think their thoughts—he'd known he lost.

He damn well knew how to play the business world with a poker face. And he knew how to keep his private life private. Only one problem with that theory—he couldn't keep his private life private from himself.

Rylie's breath warmed his chest along with her cheek. The pajamas she'd had on earlier left little between them now that she burrowed against him, and the rise and fall of her breathing was one long torment.

"Cold," she whisper-mumbled. "I'm cold."

He nestled her closer, and his emotions betrayed him along with his body. Cold. She was cold. For him, she was the warmest thing he'd felt in years. Warmer than the sun on a hot July day. Rylie wasn't just another woman. She was different. Different enough for him to feel her attraction. He'd need to be diligent, or he might find himself drowning in her.

Nope, if he pursued her, she'd need to realize it was purely a physical attraction, a hollow need. Nothing more. He had no more to give. If he got too close to her and let his guard down or set his emotions free, he'd have to find the strength to push her away. That was the only way to protect her from the cruel fate destiny always seemed to shove at him. The only way to protect himself, too.

He maneuvered his way to her room and placed her in the middle of the bed. Her fingers didn't let go until he gently unclasped them. As he walked into the living room, he picked up the blanket and quilt that had fallen next to her chair. Sliding from between the covers, something white fell to the floor.

Taylor bent to pick it up, then straightened empty handed. A man's shirt, streaked with dried and fresh streaks of mascara and tears, lay crumpled on the floor. When he saw the initials inside the collar—M.C.—a heavy sigh escaped his lips. Mathew Crawford. She'd been clutching Mathew's shirt and dropped it when Taylor picked her up.

He left the shirt where it lay, then walked back in her room with the covers he'd picked up, spreading them across her. She looked so damn beautiful he couldn't stop the backs of his fingers from brushing her cheek. Her face reactively turned toward his touch, her lips unconsciously skimmed his fingers.

Hot liquid surged through his veins. He jerked and stood away from the flame.

"Taylor, you were right?" she muttered through her drowsiness. "About the company…and Mathew."

"Get some rest, Rylie. Sleep for a while."

Her eyes never opened. "Work…meetings…"

"Gwen will reschedule them."

Rylie snuggled deeper into the covers and he watched her drift toward sleep before he turned to leave.

"Taylor?"

"Yes."

"I shouldn't have pushed you away. I'm sorry…" Her voice withered.

"Don't worry about it. We'll talk later."

"Hmmmmm, later."

He closed the French doors to her sanctuary, picked up the broken pieces of the wine glass beside the chair and walked to the kitchen, trying to tamp down his body's reaction. Finally, he walked out on to the front porch as a drizzle of rain still fell and a cold chill filled the night air. Spring was close, but winter still had a slight edge.

Rocking in the same chair he'd rocked in so many times before, it wasn't his past that poked at him. This time, it was Mathew who taunted him from the crumpled material of the shirt in the living room. Daring him to pick it up. Taylor's jaw clenched tighter and tighter as he rocked faster and faster.

"Damn it to hell!" Taylor raced inside, grabbed the shirt from the floor and flung it at the grandfather clock in the corner. After a few deep breaths, he picked it up, buttoned the front of the shirt and cuffs, then folded it into a fresh-as-new look. He hoped like hell that Mathew had realized how blessed he'd been to have a woman like Rylie love him.

"I'm not afraid of your memory, you know?" Taylor said to the air as he laid the shirt on the chair. "If you don't want me to have her, that's one thing. But you've still got to let her go."

What the hell? Now he was talking to shirts? Since sleep seemed out of the question at this point, he might as well go into the office.

He stepped to the front door for one more dose of rainy drizzle, but a strong swirl of morning wind percolated the air outside, rustling unraked leaves from last fall amid the scents of spring, then swished across the porch, rocking the chair with an easy creak, and finally bursting inside through the open doorway.

The shirt slid to the floor, landing still folded as if waiting to be put away.

The wind stopped just as suddenly as it has begun.

He'd take that as an okay from Mathew. Taylor quirked the side of his mouth and nodded as he scooped up the shirt and placed it on the seat of the chair again. Message received loud and clear.

"Trust me…I won't let you down, buddy," Taylor said.

After a glance at the French doors to Rylie' room, he raced upstairs, showered, and dressed, then locked up the house and climbed in his truck. What the hell, it was only five in the morning. He still had time to drive to the largest lake in the Peaceful Lake development and enjoy the sunrise.

For such a bad end to yesterday and strange start to today, he felt good. Better than he had in a long, long time. Maybe there'd never be another touch between him and Rylie. Then again, maybe there would. Whatever she wanted. He'd let her lead the way. In the end, he'd take what fate and destiny brought him, for as long as possible. When she left? He'd take that, too. At least he'd feel like he belonged for a while.

Don't worry, Rylie. I've got your back for as long as you need me.

His cell phone rang with "Airborne Cadence." Seemed kind of early for the Major, but then again, the man was a time-zone ahead.

"What's going on?" Taylor answered.

"Nothing," the Major said. "I was just up early

and thought I'd see how you're doing."

"Well, the last twelve hours have sucked big time. But overall, I'm good." Taylor smiled with his thoughts. "Better than I've been in years."

CHAPTER TWENTY

THE PAST FEW days around the office had been awkward for Rylie, never mind in the house every night, but Saturday had finally arrived. Something had changed between her and Taylor, but she wasn't sure exactly what and didn't even want to let her imagination consider the array of possibilities. After their flare-up over her company and Mathew, she'd apologized for her reaction. After all, she'd asked for Taylor's honest opinion.

He had acted as if she had nothing to apologize for and went right on with his Type A demeanor. Except for one thing. He seemed gentler, not in a condescending way, just gentler. She couldn't explain her feeling or exactly how he was different, but he was…or maybe it was the fact she felt different. Maybe he was more than Type A. Maybe he was also considerate.

She hadn't asked how Mathew's shirt ended up nice and neat on the chair, but since she hadn't been the one to put it there, that left no one but Taylor.

Her new outlook on life had allowed her to

wash the shirt, fold it into loving respect, and stow the memory away in the bottom of her suitcase. The lightness she felt after her night of goodbyes had given her new hope, along with a plan to sell Crawford Enterprises. She'd already notified anyone she thought might be interested in buying her company. If she didn't get an offer in a couple weeks, she'd put word out to a larger group of possible buyers. New, smaller business possibilities kept popping into her mind lately, ones she could enjoy starting from scratch just for herself.

"You about ready to go?" Taylor asked, walking into the kitchen.

Rylie glanced at the clock. Three fifty-five. Time for the picnic. She'd actually been looking forward to the get-together "Sure am. I even skipped lunch so I'd be hungry for dinner."

She didn't need to tell him that she'd actually skipped eating to soak in a tub of pink bubbles. Yesterday, she had shopped for outdoor clothes and came home with five bags, including three boxes of shoes. Deciding what to wear today had taken over an hour, plus she still had outfits scattered all over her bed.

Even though there was a slight chill in the air, she'd decided on khaki shorts and a navy top with a scoop neckline. Strappy navy shoes completed her outfit, along with a wooden bracelet and matching earrings. She'd even pulled back her hair to showcase her face. Even with the smile lines and crow's feet starting show, she looked good, if she did say so herself.

Taylor stood by the back door as she came around the end of the island and his eyes skimmed down her legs. Lingered. "Nice shoes."

Shoes? Ummm. His eyes weren't on her shoes.

"Really? What color are they?" she asked.

His look jerked from her legs to her shoes and then to her face. "Blue."

They both laughed…a little.

"You look nice," he said.

Her insides sparked. She liked that he'd noticed. On the other hand, he seemed uncomfortable with the vulnerable statement.

"Real nice." He gave her one of those deep, sensual looks a man can give a woman. Not the undressing kind, but the look that says I'm telling you something that's hard for me to say.

"Thank you."

From three feet away, he still seemed to invade her space. Without even moving, she felt his essence surround her, like a man she could fall into and skip a picnic for. They'd better go before he fully grasped what her own look was saying.

Her insides churned as she pushed the screen door open and stepped outside, waiting for him on the pathway as he armed the alarm and locked up. An uneasy tension sprayed the air around them as he stepped up beside her, then looked at the convertible. She glanced at the truck.

"Guess we better get a move on," she said.

"Guess so." He walked to the driver's side of the truck, climbed in, and backed down the driveway.

That hurt. Might have been her idea of the separate ways of going to the picnic, but she'd planned on him asking again. She had her whole speech ready, her sashay to the convertible planned, her tiny wave as she drove off practiced.

She plopped into her car and drove down the driveway. Evidently waiting for her, he'd stopped his truck on the street in front of the house, then headed to the stop sign when she pulled up behind him. He seemed to wait until there was time for both of them to turn before he went, then drove at a slower than snail's pace down the two-lane county road that passed through the edge of town.

Her speedometer showed he was driving twenty-one miles per hour in a fifty mile per hour zone. There wasn't even enough speed to have a breeze through her hair. Why was he driving so slow? Slow, slow, slow. They'd never get to the picnic at that rate.

The oncoming lane was clear, so she pulled over to pass him. At the same time, a dump truck exited in to the oncoming lane from a side road, and she slammed on her brakes, whipping back behind Taylor's truck. That had been close, to say the least. She blew out a quick breath of panic. Maybe she'd just stay behind him this time.

As they turned into the winding driveway at the Gregory property, she saw Taylor shoot her a very unhappy look in the outside mirror. He'd noticed what happened. She had to admit her insides still screamed from the near miss, too.

After pulling to a stop in a side parking area, Taylor jumped out of the truck with his finger pointed straight at her. "What did you think you were doing?"

"Passing." She climbed out of the car and used one of his favorite poses—hands on hips. "A turtle could have moved faster than you."

"Do you realize you nearly got hit? Head-on? Do you know what that means?" Taylor ran his hand through his hair and then went to the hand on hips mode himself.

She'd never seen him so angry. "Don't yell at me."

"Another second, and you might have been killed, Rylie. Killed."

Her hand touched the side of his arm. "But I wasn't. And I promise to be more careful the next time you decide to drive like an old man."

She smiled at the people gathered on the patio—Ashley and Mark, Dot and Lloyd, Janie and Patrick. The only person she didn't know was a man, maybe a couple years younger than her, talking to Peabody.

As she stepped to go around Taylor, he blocked her way, pulling her to him, and she tensed. What was going on? He held her as close as if she were a precious gift he'd almost dropped, but this was too much. Way too much. Why was he so upset?

Releasing her, he stepped back. "Don't ever do that again. You understand?"

"I'll try."

Never passing another car was impossible, but if it made him happy to think she wouldn't, then so be it. She figured there had to be more to this than just the drive over, but this wasn't the time or place to discuss his irrational request. Besides, whether he realized or not, he'd bared a patch of his soul to her in that embrace. She wouldn't soon forget that.

"You two plan to stand here and argue all day?" Mark asked from a few feet away.

Taylor groaned. Clearly, he and Rylie had been the afternoon's main entertainment so far. Mark welcomed them both, deftly stepping between the two of them like a referee in a boxing ring.

Janie hurried down the driveway to say hello, then pulled Rylie along with her toward the patio where Dot waited. And a guy talking to Peabody, who couldn't take his eyes off Rylie.

"You okay?" Mark asked.

"I've been better." Taylor clenched and released his jaw as he attempted to push Rylie's long legs and blonde hair out of his mind. The fear on her face as she had whipped her car back behind him had done a number on his insides. "She tried to pass me on the way over here. Almost got herself killed in that damn convertible."

Mark pointed to the open land. "Let's take a walk."

"I don't need a walk." This guy sounded just like the Major. Got a problem? Take a walk. Work it out.

"Sure you do. Otherwise, you're about to blow your chance."

"What chance?"

Mark nodded in Rylie's direction before he took off across the open land, heading toward the pines. Cocoa, his chocolate Lab, trotted alongside. "Let's see what's really bothering you."

Taylor didn't want to be psychoanalyzed, but he fell into step beside him. And the two men walked in silence for a while. Gradually, his tension eased.

"Rylie's determined to drive that damn convertible everywhere she goes," Taylor said.

"It's a nice car. I can see why she likes it." Mark led the way to a cleared glen near the back side of the property.

"One of my company trucks would get her where she needs to go just as well."

"No." Mark's tone was non-committal.

"What the hell do you mean no?" Taylor's insides tensed with being told he wasn't right. There were reasons for a truck, good reasons that could mean the difference between life and death sometimes—bigger, stronger, higher off the ground.

Mark leaned against an oak. "You can't save Rylie by sticking her in a big honking truck."

"I'm not trying to save her." Taylor paced the perimeter of pines and oaks and dogwoods.

"Aren't you?"

Taylor stopped as anger chomped at his composure and he glared at the man confronting him. "You don't know what you're talking about."

"Don't I?" Mark took up the pacing right alongside of him. "Now, don't take offense, but you might as well know I check out all the people I work with. Also, all my friends." He shot Taylor a sideways glance. "You included."

Shocked, he quickly returned the sideways glance and stared. "Well, I hope I passed your approval. Are we friends now?"

"Yeah. You wouldn't be here otherwise, because I wouldn't have invited you. And, just so you know, I don't have many friends." Mark's tone was light, matter of fact. He shrugged. "I'm not sure how much you know about what I used to do before I started working for the Parks Department, but let's just say some old CIA habits are hard to break. Don't want any surprises out in the field. Don't want any surprises on my front doorstep, either."

Taylor kept his tone friendly. "In other words, you've got your own set of flaws?"

Mark grunt-laughed. "Yeah, but I know my own flaws. Know my strong points, too. Know what I can and can't control. By the way, that's quite a dossier you've built for yourself."

What was Taylor supposed to say? He'd been more concerned with Mark seeing through his facade and had completely forgot the levels of confidential matter the man could still access. Most people would never know his personal past, and he liked it that way. Mark would be an exception to that rule. One, because the man wouldn't stop till he got answers. And two, he liked Mark.

Taylor had no doubt in his mind but that Mark walked around with a heavy load of his own to carry. The man's time spent as a CIA operative meant he didn't just go undercover in palaces with wine and caviar. There must have been times he lived in the dirt and shanties with grubs and filthy water as his meal. Not all deals were brokered with pen and paper. Some were finalized with gunpowder and steel and secrecy. He could see where Mark would have finally decided to change professions.

Taylor inhaled a good, clean breath of air. "Okay, let's talk."

"Sounds good. Let's start with the fact it's a tough thing to live with when another man gives his life for yours." Mark boomerang tossed a stick into the brush, and Cocoa rushed to retrieve it. "I'm not sure you ever completely get over something like that, but gradually, we learn to live with that gift. What do you think?"

Taylor didn't like where this conversation was headed, but he had picked up on the "we" in the conversation. So evidently, Mark had been in the same situation before. "I can live with my life."

"Never thought you wouldn't. I asked how you're doing."

Why was it so hard to answer such a simple, straightforward question? How could he make others understand his aversion to any vehicle that had an open top? The day his unit had been attacked, some of them had been in open-air light attack vehicles. They been easy targets for snipers, shrapnel, sand. He'd always wondered if there would have been less injuries, less deaths, if they'd all been in fully armored vehicles that day.

Now, Rylie insisted on driving her convertible. Putting herself out in the open. Sure, she wasn't vulnerable to the same happenings as his unit, but he couldn't get past the fact she might be hurt by a flying rock or stick or bird or—

He shook his head. That was utter nonsense. "I've moved on, if that's what you're asking?"

"Have you now?"

This man didn't let up. Always another question. Asked with an even tone. Eyes focused on more than what came out of your mouth.

Mark turned and looked him in the eye. "I read about the attack on your unit. About you saving some…losing others. Gotta say, your own physical recovery had to be agonizing. That had to be tough on a whole different level, man. I'm sorry."

"Thanks." Taylor narrowed his eyes, and his thoughts to the new issue being broached. "I was pretty torn up for a good long while, but I still got out of bed every day and focused on work. Now TRED fills my days. I've moved on."

"If you've moved on—" Mark still stared into his eyes, "—why are you trying to save Rylie by not wanting her to drive the convertible?"

Taylor leaned forward. "You're a damn son-of-a-bitch, aren't you?"

"Been called that many times. I'd rather think of myself as thorough." Mark jerked his head to the side, then walked back to lean against the tree. "Let's try this again. Why do you continue to feel responsible for everyone? Try to control the outcome? Go out of your way to have others do *exactly* what you think will keep them safe? Why do you think that is?"

"Damn good questions. I thought I had worked

through all of this till Rylie showed up." Taylor found his own tree to lean against. Talking about himself was paramount to a full-frontal attack. "Now I feel like… Hell, I'd rather have a hot poker in the eye then figure out what I feel. There. You happy? I've just admitted she's turned me into one hell of a blathering fool."

Mark shook his head, grinned as he glanced toward Ashley back on the patio. "I've heard the right woman will do that to a man."

Chuckles and silence permeated the air for a moment.

"If you're asking if I'm okay as far as the flashbacks, I'm good. Doesn't happen near as often. Besides which, I've got my coping skills down to a fine science. Try to keep my shields up as far as my personal emotions." Taylor patted Cocoa's head as she nosed her way beneath his hand. Felt good. Peaceful. Maybe he needed a dog. "As far as Rylie, I really don't know why I'm so protective about her. I'd be happy to listen to any advice you can give on that front."

"Can't help you there. I've got enough trouble keeping up with Ashley," Mark replied. "All I'm saying is…nobody can have everything under control every second of every day of every year. Not me. Not you. Nobody. Think about it. Might make life easier."

"Point taken." Taylor sighed as he nodded. "What else do you want to know?"

"Not a thing. Your word is good enough for me." Mark straightened away from the tree and held out his hand. "Friends?"

"Friends." Taylor gave him a brothers–in–arm clasp. "I don't have many, either."

Mark pulled his phone out. "I'm glad we had this talk. Let's me know I can trust you. I can work with a lot of drawbacks, but lack of trust is not one."

They traded stories of the past and walked back out into the open area before Mark punched a number on his speed dial. "Patrick, why don't you and Mitchell run on out here? Let's talk about this fishing trip I've lined up. Bring a couple beers, too."

Mark shoved the phone back in his pocket. Taylor squinted in the sun but didn't pull his sunglasses out. Looking a man in the eye was needed in this kind of scenario.

After opening the doors to an oversized metal building at the back of the property, Mark disabled the security to an inner room's doorway.

"A lot of security for planning a fishing trip," Taylor said.

"True, but sometimes this building holds more intense meetings."

Taylor stepped inside. "I know Patrick. Who's the other man?"

"Mitchell was my partner on my last mission. He's a good man." Mark glanced to the two men walking down from the house. "I trust him and his judgment."

"With your life?" Taylor asked.

"Damn sure. He's the one who saved my life." Mark reached for the beer Patrick had brought him.

Mitchell—tall, thin, and muscled—handed one off to Taylor without so much as a here you go, then the two new arrivals walked farther into the shed, and Taylor followed. Mark closed the door and set security before they moved deeper inside the air-conditioned room with no windows.

Patrick tapped his can on the counter then focused on Taylor. "Thought you should know that I was Mark's partner in the CIA. When Janie and I bought Red's Corner Market, I took an early semi-retirement. Of course, after the car accident in Washington, D.C., I had to give up the Agency for good. And that brings you up to speed on who I am." Patrick tapped his can again. "Oh, and not many know that, so don't go sharing the info."

The men all laughed.

As the four men huddled around a worktable, going over the brochures and plans for the Canadian fishing trip, Mitchell continued to glance in Taylor's direction as if evaluating the competition. Worse yet, the man's stare held that deepness that said you'd never know for sure what he was thinking, and you for damn sure better not ask.

A streak of jealousy whizzed through Taylor brighter than noon-sun on a clear day because he'd also noticed Mitchell watching Rylie as she walked to the patio. Did the man have an interest in her? Or was it the way her hips swayed and her calf muscles tightened with every step she took in those damn blue shoes.

As if a switch had been thrown, Mitchell

challenged Taylor with his stare. "So, what's the story with you and the blonde in the convertible?"

"What do you mean?" Taylor glared back.

"Looked to me like you two weren't exactly friends. So, I'm just asking if she's available or not before—"

"Back off, buddy. Don't you dare make a move on her." Clear and to the point, Taylor deepened his glare.

Where the hell had that come from? He sounded like a confused hormone-powered sixteen-year-old ready to fight for whatever the hell he was supposed to care enough about at the moment.

"Don't get your horns all tangled, buddy," Mitchell said. "I was just being friendly to her."

"You did a lot of looking for a friend, buddy. Back. Off."

Mitchell straightened as his expression hardened, nostrils flared. "Very few people get to tell me to back off. You're not one of them."

The building got deathly quiet as the four men each stood their ground. No noise, no movement, no laughter. Mark and Patrick glanced at each other, then the ground, as the air around Taylor and Mitchell heated. Time passed.

Wrong. Taylor realized he'd crossed a line with Mitchell, who was a man just like himself, someone who didn't take being talked at. Taylor eased a bit because he'd learned a long time ago that tough men could confront each other and keep respect between them.

"You two 'bout done with your little skirmish

over there?" Patrick asked.

Taylor extended his hand toward Mitchell. "No offense."

Mitchell glanced in Mark's direction, then nodded to Taylor and took his hand in a strong team player grip.

"You got nothing to worry about. My code is don't mess with another man's woman." Mitchell finished off his beer in one long gulp, tossed the long neck in the barrel.

Taylor did the same. Time to move on because the boys-will-be-boys moment had ended. Besides, he might even grow to like the stand-up man, but this being the first time they'd met, there was no camaraderie to fall back on.

"Just for the record, though. Is she your woman?" Mitchell asked.

Was she? Hell, he didn't know. "Still trying to figure that out."

"You two are so full of it." Mark straightened. "Let's get everything lined up on this guys' trip. By the way, I talked to Clayton, and since the boys will be with Jenna's parents a couple weeks then, he can come with us. Said he'd be happy to teach some of us how to catch a fish."

Patrick smiled and nodded. "That's good. Because I've decided to keep my fishing to day trips for now. Not sure I can do a week on the water in a floating house."

"We'll miss you. So that leaves me, Taylor, Clayton, Wheat, a couple guys I know in Canada..." Mark turned toward Mitchell. "What did you decide?"

"Depends if I'm back from assignment. Make it a no for now. Won't know for sure till the day before. Give my spot to someone else if you get a chance." Walking toward a chair in the corner, Mitchell glanced back over his shoulder and grinned. "Hey, Taylor."

"Yeah."

Mitchell grinned bigger. "Don't take too long deciding about Rylie. I might just change my mind while you're gone fishing."

CHAPTER TWENTY-ONE

R YLIE BEAT THE soles of her feet on the chaise cushion as she was overcome with uncontrollable giggles. Giggles that carried her to happiness and fun ten years before. She had no idea how she had suddenly found friends in Ashley, Janie, and Dot, but for the first time in a long time, she felt like one of the girls. Delighting in the sassy story Janie had just told, she roared with laughter right along with Dot just as the men walked up.

Patrick scooped his arm across Janie's shoulders. "What are you girls up to?"

"Nothing," Janie giggled.

"Looks to me like they've been telling Paddy stories," Mark said.

Patrick repositioned the cap on his head. "Now Janie Belle, what kind of nonsense have you been tellin' this time?"

His wife stood on tiptoes as he leaned his head down. She whispered in his ear a moment before his face blushed almost as red as the hat on his head, then she kissed his cheek.

"What's that all about?" Lloyd asked, as he

helped Dot to her feet from the padded rocker she'd chosen on the patio.

Her fingers entwined in his as they walked toward the door. "Janie was just telling us about blue satin and mud?"

"Oh?"

"And parking lots and trash barrels." Janie winked at her husband.

"Oh!" Mark laughed along with the others.

Standing over to the side, quiet and emotionless, Taylor and Mitchell looked like two lost boys too embarrassed to ask what was going on. Their egos seem to be the type that they'd rather stand there and play the alpha-I-don't-care game then have fun.

"By the way," Ashley said. "Wheat dropped by on his way to work. Said to tell you he'd made arrangements to take off the entire week for the fishing trip."

Mark slid his arm across her shoulders. "That's great, but he already told me that when he stopped by yesterday."

"If you ask me, I think he hoped Tracy might be in town for a visit."

Food and good conversation made the rest of the afternoon pass at warp speed. By late evening, Rylie sipped her glass of frozen lemonade, feeling herself hover just outside of wanting a nap.

Taylor rose from his chair and tossed his keys in the air, then grabbed them on the first try. "Think I'm going to head on out. Thanks for inviting me to your get-together. I haven't had this much fun in a long time."

After nodding goodbye to everyone else, he headed to his truck. Rylie was a little peeved that he hadn't at least made some smart remark about her having her own ride.

Mitchell jogged after him and extended his hand as he caught up with Taylor. From afar, Rylie watched the two men shake hands and slap each other on the shoulder before Mitchell retraced his steps to the gathering. Rylie noticed Mark had kept his eye on the two but had eased back with a contented look as it ended, might have even been a smile.

Halfway up the driveway, Mitchell yelled, "Hey, Taylor."

"Yeah?"

"Made up your mind yet?"

Taylor took a couple of exaggerated steps toward the man, then laughed. "Still thinking. Rest assured, though, you'll be the first to know."

Mitchell returned to the patio as Taylor climbed in his truck.

"You're gonna get yourself in a world of hurt one of these days," Patrick said to the younger guy.

"Nah. Me and him are good. Besides, you heard the man. He's still thinking." Mitchell walked over to Rylie and crouched down, his hand fumbling under her chair.

She shot him a what-are-you-doing look and waited. He was cuter than hell in a lanky manly way, but he wasn't her type. Still, his closeness shook her senses.

The slam of Taylor's truck door echoed through

the air, and everyone turned in his direction, then watched him walk to the front of his truck and raise the hood. Frowning, Mitchell stood up and stared in his direction.

Once Taylor glanced from beneath the hood, Rylie could swear the two men were eyeing each other like full-grown lions. In fact, Mark and Patrick appeared to be interested in the two, also.

Mitchell turned to her and crouched again. The crash of the truck's hood vibrated through the air and she jumped. What the heck was wrong with Taylor?

"Is this yours?" Mitchell held out a wooden dangle earring.

Her fingers eased under her hair she'd freed from the scrunchie hours before. "Oh my gosh. Yes. Thanks for finding it. I just bought these yesterday."

Taylor's presence back on the patio didn't go unnoticed, but he wasn't Rylie's top priority. She swung her legs over the side of the chaise and scanned the concrete for the backing to the earring.

Janie scurried over to help her search.

"There it is." Dot pointed from her rocker to a tiny gold glitter two feet from the chaise.

"Can you believe she saw that?" Janie retrieved the backing.

"Only because the glow from the fire made it shimmer."

Rylie glanced up as she slipped her earring back in place. Had something happened? Taylor, Mitchell, and Mark all stood in a loose circle. And

Patrick? Where was Patrick? He was still stretched out on his chaise, legs crossed at the ankles, red cap riding low over his forehead.

"Got a problem with your truck?" Patrick swung his legs on each side of the seat, sat up and tipped his hat back.

Taylor looked at the sky and sucked in air. "Won't start."

"Want us to take a look at it?" Mark asked. "Mitchell's known for starting things that don't have much chance of running again."

"That's okay. I'll send someone over for it in the morning."

"I can sure give it a try if you want." Mitchell's stance didn't change.

"He just found my earring," Rylie said. "If something fell off your truck, I bet he can find it, too."

Taylor jerked his head in her direction. "Your earring?"

She held her hair back. "He saw it under my chair."

"That's why you were down there?" Taylor asked Mitchell.

"That's why I was down there." The younger guy shook his head in a you-need-help-fast motion and slapped him on the back.

Taylor raked his fingers through his hair. "Man, I've become a raving fool."

"You two testosterone jocks better have this worked out before we leave for the fishing trip," Mark side whispered as he walked over to the fire pit and tossed another log on the embers. "Or I'll settle it for you."

Mitchell half-punched Taylor on the bicep then jogged toward the towering pine that surrounded the property. He seemed to disappear right before her eyes. Whatever had or hadn't happened was over.

"So, what are we gonna do about this truck?" Patrick settled back, lowering his hat again, crossing his ankles. "How you gonna get home, Taylor?"

"Thought maybe Rylie'd let me ride with her."

With her? Why couldn't one of them take him home? Of course, that wouldn't make sense. She lived in the same house, so she'd be the logical one to take him home.

"I can't believe you're willing to go in my convertible," Rylie said. "You realize you'll be taking a chance on my driving."

"You could always let me drive."

"No way." He wasn't going to pull that on her. If he wanted a ride, then it would be on her terms.

She jostled her keys out of her purse, tossed them up, and missed them on the way down. Taylor leaned in and scooped them out of the air a few inches from the concrete, then teased her as he swung them in his fingers. Her hand shot out and flipped over, palm up. After a few annoying jingles at various spots in front of her, he placed the keys in her hand and closed her fingers around them.

Too easy.

What was he up to?

"Good night everyone," Rylie said. "Thanks

for making me feel at home. It's been fun."

Janie hugged her. "Don't forget. Us three girls are going shopping in Surryfield next week. Top on our list is the Ooh-la-la Lingerie Shoppe. Who knows? Maybe you'll come back with a little blue satin of your own."

Rylie felt her face blush. "Not likely."

CHAPTER TWENTY-TWO

WALKING DOWN THE driveway to her car, Rylie kept the keys tightly gripped in her hand farthest away from Taylor. She slid into the driver's seat as Taylor grabbed a duffle bag from his truck and tossed it into the back seat of the car, then lowered himself inside. He positioned the passenger seat back to accommodate his legs and fastened his seatbelt. After propping his elbow on the top of the door, he glanced around as if she weren't even there.

Thinking they could talk on the way home, she turned down the radio. Maybe they could share a casual conversation without grumping at each other. Worth a try... After all, he had asked for a ride. Could be that was his ploy to get them in the car together. Why did that thought suddenly make her happy?

"I love evenings like these," she said.

No response except for a quick glance in her direction. No, make that a quick glance at her legs. Appearing nervous, he straightened his hands and fingers as if to distract himself. Interesting.

Once they turned off the main road, she slowed

her speed to barely twenty miles per hour going through the old part of Nature's Crossing. Not to annoy him, but to prolong the drive. "Weather like this is one of the reasons I love to have a car I can put the top down on."

His hands did that funny stretch movement right before he looked in her direction again. If she hadn't glanced to the side, she'd have missed the rapid way his look traveled up her body. Lingered on her hair tangling in the wind. She'd have missed the way his brow crinkled and his breath hitched a second before he shifted positions on his seat. Then, once more, he stared off at the roadside and she stared at the road straight ahead.

Distracted, she let her own gaze scan from his jeans to his shirt to his muscled forearms to his chiseled profile. And his hair. Hair her fingers could weave their way through without even thinking. That was her problem...she wasn't thinking. She needed to keep her focus on driving and the fast-approaching end of the trip.

Maybe she could pretend they had a flat tire. Now how the heck would she do that? Maybe she could pretend they ran out of gas. No, he'd just look at the fuel gauge and know she was lying. Maybe she could miss the turn and drive around the block a few times as if she were lost. Too late, she'd already turned on the road in front of the Victorian.

"Sure doesn't take long to get places in this little town." She sighed with the realization he really hadn't had anything else in mind except a ride home. Pulling up the driveway, she wished something had happened. A smile. A touch. Anything. Even a senseless argument.

Taylor eased out of the passenger door, and her heart emptied. Not that she was interested in him, but some notice on his part would have been nice. Maybe she didn't look as good as he'd said earlier. Might be he had a lady back in KC. He did go back there two days a week. That would explain his being all business by the time he came back to town.

"Thanks for the ride." He walked toward the back door. Paused on the steps. Stretched his hands again.

"Any time. Good night." She couldn't tear her eyes away from him, and when he glanced her direction, she felt needy.

His charisma, his shoulders, his walk, his scent, his hair, his eyes, his mouth—damn it, everything about him drew her in. Made her feel alive. She was a woman. He was a man. Nothing needed to happen, but time spent with him would make her day end on a good note.

"Would you—" they both said at once. Laughter. Silence.

"You go first," he said.

"No. You."

His walk to the driver's side tripped her switch back to the moment in the taxi with the orange. Her insides sensed that no matter what he asked, she'd agree with him.

"We've still got a couple hours till sunset," Taylor said. "I wondered if you'd like to take a drive?" He braced against the car door. "There's a place I'd like you to see."

A place? Surely, he didn't mean to take her to a teenager make-out spot. One of those places with a great view that nobody remembered the next morning. She'd been to a few in her younger days, but she was older now. Wiser. Back seats were uncomfortable. Besides, making out with Taylor Randolph was not on her agenda.

"Well?" he asked.

"Sure. Hop in."

He didn't move. "Be easier if you let me drive."

She swallowed slow and easy, then made the mistake of looking into his eyes. Butterfly flutters grabbed her insides as she opened the car door and stepped out. "Okay."

He raised his hand and index finger as if saying wait a second, then opened the back door and disappeared inside the house. She walked over to the swing at the side of the back patio and enjoyed the afternoon sounds. Less than five minutes later, he returned, carrying a wicker picnic basket, a bottle of wine, and the pink throw from her bedroom.

Setting the items in the back seat, he then slid behind the steering wheel and started the car before she made it around to the passenger's side. He leaned across, pushed the door open, and left his arm across the back of the seat for a moment. As she slid in, his fingers brushed her hair before he straightened. Or, at least she thought he had. She was a little confused at the moment.

Was it hot or was it her? What had happened to the nice cool breeze? How had she let her mind get so intertwined with thoughts of him? When had she started to notice his full lower lip?

"Where are we going?" She clicked her seatbelt a second before he started down the driveway.

"You'll see." He tuned the radio to a rock station.

Guess there'd still be no talking. Of course, that might be for the best. Every time they carried on more than a few sentences of conversation, they found a way to argue. She didn't feel like arguing this time. In fact, she felt more relaxed than she had since she left Charleston.

She felt her smile mingle with the wind, and before she thought, she trailed her fingers over his hand resting on the gear shift. He turned his fingers to intertwine with hers. At the stop sign, he moved his hand to rest on the back edge of her seat, letting his thumb lazily brush the top of her collarbone.

Turning on to the highway, he moved his hand to the steering wheel. "I do like the feel of open freedom in your car."

"Good." She reclined her seat a bit, the music soothing as silk. "We'll have to take a drive with the top down some starry night. I love that."

"What if it's cold?"

"We'll just turn the heat on."

"Heat?" He laughed. "You know… You are really something."

She flashed him her brightest smile. "You have no idea."

He pulled the car to a stop at the crossroads flashing light by Red's Corner Market. Their eyes met in a long-held gaze. Her lips parted and Taylor leaned across the console, lightly easing his palm to the side of her face before brushing his fingers gently into her hair. She wrapped her hand in his shirt, pulled herself toward him.

"No more fights?" she whispered.

"No more fights."

He closed the distance between their lips.

CHAPTER TWENTY-THREE

THE CALL OF an owl mixed with the sound of movement in the brush off to the side, made Rylie hesitant to leave the car. She still couldn't identify what to fear and what to accept as nature's enjoyment here in Missouri. Plus, the drive down a one-lane road leading into an area of Peaceful Lake Acres that hadn't been opened for development yet, had disoriented her on exactly where they were.

"Come on, I've got you." Taylor's hand closed around hers as his other opened the car door.

"What's that in the bushes?" Her fingers gripped his, still keeping her eyes on the rustling in the bushes.

He coaxed her out of the car with his movements. "Maybe a squirrel. A rabbit. Nothing to worry about. I won't let anything hurt you."

Why did just his presence calm her? Make her feel safe? She withdrew her hand from his. "I'm okay now."

"Whatever you say." He grabbed the picnic basket and walked over to a point of land before setting it down. "Come on over. Tell me what you think."

Only a few steps farther, and she was astounded by the view that greeted her. This had to be the biggest lake she'd seen in the entire Peaceful Lake Acres development. Most were small, two to five acres, this one had to be close to seventy-five, maybe more. As he stood staring out over the water, Taylor's hands weren't on his waist like usual. They were in his pockets, relaxed and casual enough to have thought he had nothing more on his mind than where he'd catch his next fish. She followed, noticing a couple of park benches here and there.

With a forever view of the water, the trees, outcroppings of rock, even an old dock on the shoreline across the way, all made for exactly what the theme for the development—peaceful. This area was fairly level with a combination of large worn-smooth rocks and a small sandy beach area which eased right into the water lapping at the shore.

Without realizing she'd done so, she found herself standing beside him at the edge of the lake. Glancing to the left was an open bay…to the right a cove that flowed back farther than she could see. A few small rocks tumbled from the rim down toward the water, and she inched back until he pulled her close.

"You're okay," he whispered without taking his eyes from the view. "I had this area cleared a couple weeks ago. The bulldozer piled the dirt off to the side, so we can use it around the properties."

"Is this some kind of park?" she asked.

"Nope. TRED owns a good hundred acres of property around this ninety-acre lake. May be another development someday. May stay as a nature preserve. But this part..." He dropped his arm and took a couple steps to the left. Swooping his hand from a surveyor's stake at the edge of the shore, around the point and back in to the cove. "All the way to the headwater is private property."

"Private as in not part of Peaceful Lake Acres?" Her business mind kicked into gear. "Shouldn't you be talking to the owner about buying the property?"

"Trust me, the owner doesn't want to sell. He's working on house plans at the moment." He crouched on the smoothest flat rock at the edge of the shoreline. Opened the basket and spread out the tablecloth from inside before sitting down to unload bread and cheese and fruit. "Now, how's this for waterfront dining?"

Shaking her head as she removed her shoes and paced back and forth through the sand. "It's so beautiful here."

He held out a bunch of grapes to her and she joined him on the rock.

"You know...you may want to keep a close eye on the plans for this plot." Slathering a dollop of honey butter on the croissant he offered, she took a bite and handed the rest to him. I'm afraid the house may be a detriment to the area if it's not under the Peaceful Lake Acres indentures."

He roared with laughter that rumbled over the

lake. "Well, you don't have to worry, Rylie. I'm the owner."

Not what she'd expected. "You?"

"Me. I personally bought the point lot when the land was first divided. But it still falls under Peaceful Lake indentures." He took a sip of wine, then rolled over on to the grassy area by the rock. Adjusting his sunglasses, he seemed to bask in the sun. "As of two weeks ago, I have first option to buy the three other lots on this lake, too."

"You've got the money to do whatever you want in the world. Live on any ocean you want. Greece, Hawaii, Monaco, Nantucket, Seattle. Heck, for all I know you might be able to buy your own personal island to jet in and out of. Yet, what do you do? You buy waterfront land on a manmade lake in the middle of Missouri." She stepped out of the car. "You never cease to amaze me."

"Not just waterfront. The point with one of the best views on the lake."

"Oh, I forgot. Only the best for Taylor Randolph. The mid-level worker down the street couldn't even imagine owning this property. But you can. Mr. KC can have anything."

"I work hard for my money." He sat up and braced his hand against the rock. Clearly upset, his wounded expression betrayed the anger in his tone. "My family works hard to keep TRED viable. You're not the only one concerned about keeping food on their employees table," he lashed out. "My family grew TRED from a piece of three-ring notebook paper years ago. My dad worked ten-hour days at his regular job and still found time to grow the business. Found time to put family first.

"Look at my charitable contributions. Donations to science. While you're at it, look how I treat my employees. Man or woman in my company, they all make equal pay for equal work. Not a one of them pays for their health benefits, and trust me, they have the finest."

For once, she wished she'd kept her mouth shut. She'd hurt him. His raw emotions were spewing forth. Emotions few others probably ever saw. Her own emotions drenched her eyes with tears, but she batted them away. Took her punishment for pushing too far.

"Back in New York and KC, no one asks me out without a motive. Money. My name. An endorsement. That's all they want. Do you think they ever stop to think about how I feel? What I want? Not hardly. Friends that care about me are hard to find. Friends like the Major." Taylor drew in a ragged breath, his face flushed with emotion, his expression weary and wounded. "There's a lot of men would just chuck everything and drive away. Never come back. But I don't! I don't. So don't you dare begrudge me my dream. If you think I give a damn about the money, you're sadly wrong."

He stopped his rant, laid back down, and stared up at the sky. "I work twenty-four-seven, three hundred and sixty-five days a year to make sure my company stays at the top. To make sure my employee's families have security when their child ends up with cancer or they lose everything in a fire or a heart attack takes them in their thirties. Twenty-four-seven. Don't I deserve something? I'm not a robot, you know. I'm a man. One that gets up and goes all out every single day of the year." His chin trembled a moment before he clenched his jaw. "Doesn't that count for anything?"

Her heart ached for the pain she'd been responsible for releasing in Taylor. She had no words. Ashamed of her insensitive remarks, all she could do was listen. She'd listen all night if he needed her to. Her words couldn't be taken back, and from all appearances, their very utterance had opened a lock deep inside him. One that evidently needed to break. She'd listen. That much she could do.

"This is the first gift I've given myself in over four years. Four years. I need this place." His voice cracked with an emotion-filled whisper as he got to his feet and stared out across the lake. "I need…to be…able…to accept my gift."

He raked his fingers through his hair. A heavy, heavy sigh rushed forth to meet the sunset edging into the night air. After grabbing a handful of pebbles, he hurled each one into the water before he finally eased and skimmed the last two along the surface. "I like Nature's Crossing. People treat me like I'm one of them. That's why I spend so much time onsite. Here, I'm just an average-Joe in jeans and work boots driving a pick-up." He looked upward. "Don't I deserve this piece of land? Would you take that from me, too?"

What were they talking about? She didn't know for sure, but her gut reaction told her that Taylor's plea was to God. To his Higher Power. The suffering in his tone gripped her as she went to stand next to him, placing her hand against the back of his shoulder.

Shoulders slumped, he slipped his arm across her shoulders and pulled her against his side. Lowering his head, he stared at the ground, swiped his palm down his face. "At least allow me to have this spot. This one solitary spot in the universe."

CHAPTER TWENTY-FOUR

RYLIE'S INSIDES CLENCHED into a tight knot, threatening her very breath, her very soul. She bit her bottom lip to stop the quiver. "I…I'm sorry. I was out of line."

She longed to take Taylor in her arms. To comfort him. Instead, the lake noises filled the silence between them. They were lost souls bound by this moment in time. The bushes rustled again but she didn't flinch. Taylor was there and she was safe. Whether he knew it or not he was safe with her, too. She'd make it a point to be his friend on this project. Truth was there were days she needed a friend, too.

By the time he raised his head his stance was back, his shoulders broad and straight. "I hope you don't—"

The gentle shake of her head felt as right as anything she'd ever done. "Your secret's safe with me."

"What secret?"

"That deep inside you're human just like everybody else. You can be broken."

"You think that's breaking?" He uttered a

guarded laugh, and in the glow of the tiki lamp he lit at edge of the shoreline, she saw his jaw clench again. "You have no idea. I'll never allow that to happen again."

She got the feeling they were talking about two different times. She the last few minutes. Him another time and place. Pressing that issue held no value to either of them, but her mind wrestled with what could have been so intense, so traumatic, that a man like Taylor broke. Maybe she didn't want to know. Memory of her own breaking point was a heavy enough load for her to carry around.

"Okay. I believe you. You'll never break." She paused for the words to sink in, then she gave one of her brightest smiles. "We'll keep that part about you being human between the two of us. The rest of the world can continue to think you're one invincible mega-man made of muscles and stone."

"Muscles and stone. I like that." A chuckle escaped his facade.

"Well, don't let it go to your head."

Taylor held his hand out to her. "Come here. I want to show you something."

Without thinking, she zeroed in on his offer and slid her hand inside his. Let her fingers close around the strength she felt envelop her own as he pulled her back to his lookout. He eased behind her, close enough for her to feel his heartbeat. His arms circled around her as he lowered his cheek next to hers. She moved to pull away.

He held her without holding. "Be still. I want

you to see this as I see it."

For some reason she didn't understand, she wanted the same thing. This evening was fast turning into one she'd remember forever. To be privy to a millionaire's imaginings was a true experience. To be privy to Taylor's was a pure gift. Easing back into his arms, she let him turn her with his turns, kept her cheek against his to focus on what he focused on.

By the time he was done, she could see the beauty in everything he saw. Could envision a home with a wall of windows to showcase the view. Could imagine walking down to the three-well dock for a glass of wine, a fishing pole, or a chance to dangle her toes in the lake.

When her mind strayed to kisses and more on that same dock, she pushed them aside—not fast, but aside just the same. They walked to the bench and settled in side-by-side with a hint of a touch, a brush of their shoulders, the bump of their thighs. He shifted to the music setting on his phone and the notes floated on the water.

"I like your property," Rylie said. "I'd like to come back again sometime."

"That can be arranged." He rested both his arms on the back of the bench. His fingers stroked the curve of her shoulder.

Nervous, Rylie eased to her feet. She walked back to the point of land they'd stood on before and raised her face to the stars making themselves known in the night sky. Eyes closed, she felt the breeze, smelled the water, heard the splash of a fish. Music from his phone lured her senses to attention. She twirled and swayed enjoying the freedom of the moment.

He hadn't touched her since she left the bench, but she knew he was close. Her insides pulsing, she opened her eyes and found him standing in front of her, arms held ready for her to slide into and dance. She could close her eyes again. Drift into his hold and pretend this was a different place, a different night, a different man, but that wasn't her way. Taylor was Taylor, and she was a woman still trapped in a world of her own making, one that shielded against the unknown. Yet, here, tonight, she craved to move forward.

The song stopped, but he didn't move. When the next song started, she raised one hand to his, and the other to his shoulder. She didn't step forward though. An arm's length away from each other should be safe. She could manage a dance with him at that distance.

They began with footsteps in a small space, then spins that covered the small patio, and finally back to footsteps in a small space. When the music ended, she realized there was no distance between them anymore. Warmth inundated her from his shoulder against her cheek, his chest, the press of his hand against her back. Her fingers inched to the nape of his neck, and she purposely stopped their caress.

If there was music playing now, she didn't notice. All she noticed was how willingly her face turned up to his. How as his head lowered, his lips parted and so did hers. Then, he kissed her with the sweet seduction of a gentle brush.

Not the testing kiss from before, but one with a touch of passion. The cool night air transformed his scent into something visceral as he kissed her cheeks, her eyes, the tip of her nose.

He returned to her lips with one that felt of hello, I'm here. She followed his lead. His next kiss arced to a firm, unfathomable, greedy need. She accepted. Nipped at his lips before she caught herself. Her palm eased to the back of his head pressing him closer as he pulled her to his body.

Yes. She wanted to surrender. She wanted to fall into his deepness. She wanted the pleasure of his touch, his scent, his taste. Heaven help her, his taste was all she could think about as his lips brushed hers, and his breath whispered against her ear.

Arms around each other, they paused. Their tight embrace was enough for a moment, then his hands moved to her cheeks. His gaze searched her face as his fingers tangled into her hair and held. Her lips parted when his kisses begged for even more, and her mouth allowed him in.

Suddenly, she wanted him. When their deep, possessive, earth-shattering kiss overtook them both, she clung to him with need. With desire. With raw emotion clawing to reach the surface, her feelings surged, and her insides skittered with sparks of what if, if only, maybe if, ifs, ifs, ifs. He pushed her top lower on her shoulder and nuzzled the tender spot of her neck.

The moment and the feel and need and the want overwhelmed her. "No...no I can't do this. I...I'm not ready. I'm sorry, I'm just..." She pushed away. "No…"

He dropped his hold and stepped away. For a moment, his face held only the heated passion she'd felt, then he turned to the lake and released a powerful sigh. She watched him watch the water, the lights, the view.

This wasn't what she had wanted for this evening. She'd simply wanted to enjoy being with him, to test the waters, to feel alive again. Her body had betrayed her mind, her emotions had stepped on lines. Lines she'd drawn for herself. Ones that allowed her to stay in her own safe cubicle of the world. The one that locked love and longing on the other side. "No…"

What had she done? She'd let him too close. His taste lingered on her tongue, and her lips burned from his hunger. Her core pulsed with moisture. She craved his arms, his mouth, his—

Why? Why had she pushed Taylor away? The other night she'd released Mathew's hold. Washed his shirt. Decided to sell her company. Find what she wanted to do with her future. Moments ago, she'd dance with Taylor. Allowed him to kiss her. Gave herself permission to kiss him back.

That was what she'd done. She'd kissed him back and surrendered. Her body had reacted. But also with something more. Something deep inside that trembled with not only animal magnetism, but with irresistible ecstasy and joy. Sensual happiness that surpassed the physical. That scared her. Down and out scared her.

As his stance reset, he seemed back in the world of Taylor Randolph, except for the fact he'd once again slid his hands in his pockets. She envied him. He'd found something on this point, this piece of land, that gave him solace and hope and his dream. No one could take that from him.

He pulled the keys from his pocket and flicked them to turn the headlights on, put out the tiki light by the shore. No toss to be caught mid-air this time. "Time to go."

"I think you have a wonderful piece of property," she said.

He nodded.

"Maybe sometime we—"

"It's time to go, Rylie. This evening's over."

She walked to the passenger side of her car and slid on to the leather. Closed the door. Locked her seatbelt in place. Grabbed a butterscotch from the console. And waited while he loaded the picnic basket and shook out the tablecloth before tossing them in the backseat.

Time to go back to the house.

Time to go back to life the way she'd made it.

Time to go back to…

She couldn't quite remember what she was going back to.

CHAPTER TWENTY-FIVE

MONDAY MORNING, TAYLOR leaned against the wall in the new building for the construction workers. He wasn't happy about the meeting, but this was Jake's show. The workers had been instructed to be there at nine, no ifs, ands, or buts. Plus, he'd also invited Mark, Patrick, Wheat, and Peabody. And told Rylie and Gwen to be there. Where were they anyhow?

Rylie had steered clear of him yesterday. Saturday night played through his mind again. He drove her out to see his lakefront property, that's all. He hadn't meant to kiss her. Then the moon's glow across the water sparkled with sexy smoothness. The night winds soothed them with their call. And when the breeze slid in from across the water along with the music's softness, Rylie's hips had swayed. Her hair had swung loose around her face, and when she'd reached for the stars, he'd lost his self-preservation.

There in the dark, they hadn't been Rylie and Taylor. They'd been a man and a woman simmering with need, willing to chance a taste of what could be. From the moment he took her in his arms, he knew the difference in the dance. Once he'd felt the tingle when he kissed her in the convertible stopped at the crossroads, he knew his world had changed. The realization felt good, and he'd needed more. Everything he dreamed of had been within his arms.

Standing on his land at the edge of a moon-touched lake with a spring wind promising renewal, she'd looked like life itself. Tasted of wine and berries. Smelled of wood smoke and musk and a scent all her own. His emotions had taken him over the edge as he kissed her deeper and deeper, trying to take in everything about her. Trying to make her his if only for a moment. He'd felt the glow all the way to his core before she quivered, flinched, and pulled back.

From the look on her face when she stepped away, she'd felt something, too. Dimmed by the darkness, her face still betrayed her. He bet she let her emotions cross an invisible line she'd set for herself, and it frightened her. It sure as hell scared him.

Of course, on the drive home, there'd been the one time she placed her fingertips to her lips with a slight caress before she lowered her hands to her lap. He wanted to take her hand in his. Feel her warmth. Give her assurance she wasn't alone in her thoughts. He hadn't.

He should never have taken her in his arms and danced with her. He should never have looked down once the song ended. He should never have kissed her and kissed her and kis—

Laughter from across the room brought Taylor

back to the present.

Jake meandered from person to person, joking, punching them on the arm, telling them what a great job they were doing. Goodbyes being said before the workers even knew he'd be leaving. Taylor's gut hurt from the thought of his friend, his brother, not being there tomorrow morning. Or any other morning for over a year.

Nothing to worry about with the crew; they'd be in good hands with Bennett—first or last name, Taylor still hadn't figured out. Everyone just called the man Bennett. Jake had chosen the right man to complete the hands-on part of the development. During the past few days, Taylor'd met with Bennett a number of times and always came away impressed.

The man had been in Desert Storm and Iraq at the war's onset but wouldn't be going back. A Purple Heart, bits of shrapnel still lodged in his back, and a limp from his crushed kneecap replacement were his badges of honor.

Today was about Jake. From around the room, the workmen's laughter lifted Taylor's darkness. They were a good lot. When he had a day where he wished he'd never agreed to run the company after his dad's heart attack and stroke, he remembered the people he worked with. Being part of a crew had been one of the few happy moments in his life. He didn't get the chance anymore. Now he had bigger fish to fry. Contracts, new developments, the environment.

Where were Rylie and Gwen?

Right on cue, Rylie walked through the door

and took her place next to Taylor. Back against the wall like him, but her hands were neatly clasped in front of her. Bright eyed, relaxed, and with just a hint of a smile on her face.

Gwen slipped in the room and turned to go grab a ringing phone in the other room. Taylor motioned her back inside, shut the door, and stepped in front of it. They were all here now. Time to get this over with. He hated goodbyes. Emotions could strain to a breaking point. "Hey, Jake, you sound like a traveling salesman revving up the crowd this morning," one of the men at the front of the room hollered. The others laughed.

"Maybe he's just setting us up for overtime all summer," another responded.

"Now guys, would I do that? Fishing season is sacred around here." Jake walked toward the back of the room.

Rylie's smile broadened when he stepped in front of her, took her hand, and kissed the back of it. "You are the fresh spunk TRED needed." He pointed at Taylor. "Don't let the boss-man say different. You've already put up with us for a whole lot of weeks, so I thought you deserve a little something special."

Jake picked up one of two boxes sitting on the table along the back wall. He pulled out a pink hard hat. TRED taped on the front. Rylie on the back. As if crowning a queen, he lowered the hat on her head. It covered half her face. The crowd howled with laughter.

A big grin filled his face after he lifted it back off. "Oops. Though I'd lost you there."

"You did that on purpose, you big lug." Rylie's eyes sparkled even more than before.

The big lug adjusted the inside straps and recrowned her.

She curtsied, and the crew's laughter lit up the room once again. "Thank you kindly, sir."

For a split-second, Taylor saw Jake's face take on a serious—way too serious—look. *Buddy, don't lose it now. You can do this.* For some reason, Jake had latched onto Rylie like a little sister from the moment she'd arrived.

Jake cleared his throat, leaned in, and hugged her. Quiet enough only Rylie and Taylor heard, he said, "You make sure Taylor eats his oatmeal while I'm gone."

Taylor pretend-jerked his brother away from her. "You're going to get TRED in trouble, hugging the help that way."

Laughter filled the hall again.

Taylor felt Rylie's questioning look. He stood firm, face straight ahead as Jake passed him by after grabbing the other box from the table. The two men had said their farewell out there in the storm that first night. Nothing left to say. Just hang on for the other so-longs and drive his friend to the airport. He focused on the United States flag hung in the corner of the building.

His peripheral vision caught Rylie turn her gaze to where his rested. A deeper questioning look filled her face. He'd already figure out she had an astute ability to pick up on things.

"Then there's this one." Jake stopped in front of Gwen. "This one wouldn't even have coffee with me after the get-together last night."

Head tilted, she stuck her tongue out and crossed her eyes in her typical sassy attitude.

"Now why is that?" Jake asked.

"You'll need to grow up first." Gwen tapped his chest with every other word.

He plopped the already tightened-strap hard hat on her head. Finger lifted her chin. "If you notice, I'm already growed up."

She playfully slapped his hand away. "What makes you think you're all growed up? Your broad shoulders or those size twelve feet?"

One of the long-time buddies of the two men glanced at Jake's feet. The man straightened and glanced at Taylor. He nodded, and then saw the man jab the one next to him and point.

The second guy squared his shoulders. "See you got some new boots there, Jake. Or should I say some old boots?"

"Don't matter if they're old or new," Gwen said. "Last night, he took me out to dinner at one of the waterfront restaurants over at the big lake. Didn't even notice my new dress."

"Oh, I noticed all right." He grinned as he waved his arms around. "What with all that spinning and twirling and flicking that skirt just so."

She gave him a little stop-it shove as she blushed. "All I know is those feet of his stepped all over my toes every time we danced."

Jake roared with the rest of the laughter in the room. "Guess I just got told." He headed back to the front of the room.

Taylor watched Rylie glance at Jake's boots, and her expression warped into that please-say-no look that women sometimes got. She'd said her dad was military, so she'd recognized the boots for what they were. Not Jake's usual work boots, but his combat boots.

Taylor held her gaze with his when she looked up at him, questioning. "Don't worry. This is just business."

Her smile reappeared, quivering a bit, but there. Her body tensed with that gentle uneasiness women got when their instincts flare with apprehension. Eyes moist, she stood beside him and lifted her chin. Face supportive and sad at the same time.

"You all know this guy." Jake motioned Bennett to the front of the room. "He's a good man. Hard worker. Knows how to read blueprints and how to kick you guys into high gear when needed."

Laughter.

"Well, he's going to be taking my place for a while."

Quiet. Murmurs.

"Where you going? Taylor finally promote you to the KC office?" a man from the side asked.

"I was promoted there years ago. They just can't keep me in the office," Jake replied. "No, I'm gonna be working for Uncle Sam again."

Quiet.

"Seems they'd like TRED to be part of some possible land development down in South America. And seeing, that I've had some experience in building and—"

"Staying alive?" one of the men yelled out.

"Something like that." Jake nodded along with a got-that-right grin. "Anyhow, my name got bounced around, and bingo, I'm heading up the group of developers laying out the entire plan. I could have hung around here for a few more weeks, but I've decided to leave this afternoon. Taylor offered to drive me to the airport, and then I'll be on my way to Fort Campbell, Kentucky, for a week or so. Then Washington, D.C., and points south."

Applause and finger whistles permeated the air in tribute to the Army camp as the crew closed ranks around Jake.

Some of the men who'd been with Taylor on other jobs, some even in combat with him or Jake, straightened and clenched their jaws. Taylor saw their faces. Hard-ass memories had kicked in for a brief moment even if they didn't have PTSD or flashbacks or dreams, which a majority of them did. He'd keep an eye on them the next few days to make sure they had someone to talk to if need be.

Gwen pushed through the crowd gathered around Jake. Tears streamed down her face as she shoved her pink hardhat in his chest again and again and again. "You can't go. You understand me? I won't let you go. I won't let you…I…I…I hate you…I hate you…I…"

Jake set the hat on the table beside them as the crew stepped back from the couple, then he engulfed her in his arms as she flailed against him, crying into his shirt with jerky little uncontrollable sobs. Resting his chin on her head, he held her tighter and tighter, and Taylor saw a look on his brother's face he'd never seen there before.

"Honey, I'm not going to war. This is strictly business. TRED business."

"But...but you're wearing the boots."

He glanced down at his feet. "These old things got me through a lot of dirt and sand during my tours. Brought me back alive. I just figured I'd let them be my good luck charm again. Understand?"

Gwen nodded, but she couldn't seem to stop the tears. And she went willingly when Jake folded his arms around her once again.

Rylie tried to slip from beneath Taylor's shoulder, but he pushed back tighter because she needed to stay beside him. Let whatever was going to play out between Gwen and Jake play out on their own terms. Taylor found Rylie's hand with his own, and she let him lace his fingers between hers. He squeezed. She squeezed in return, tight, then eased her hand away and back to her original stance.

"Maybe we should give them some space." Taylor opened the door, motioning the crew into the other part of the construction building. From the looks on the men's faces, they seemed glad to escape the raw emotions spread before them.

With one backward glance, Rylie followed the workmen.

"Bennett, why don't you get the crew organized for this afternoon?" Taylor closed the door behind him. "I'm headed to the office for now. When I get back from the airport, I'll check in with you. You've got my number if you need anything."

Bennett nodded.

Taylor found Rylie at one of the picnic tables under an ages-old oak. She had the look of someone on a vigil outside a medical center instead of enjoying a taste of springtime. He jogged back inside, grabbed a couple bottled waters from the crew's lunchroom, and joined her.

"Think we better get on over to the office?" Taylor asked.

She shook her head. "I'll wait for Gwen. She may need me."

"Let her grow up, Rylie. You can't mother-hen her forever. Besides, Jake will give her a ride back over."

Like a rocket at full throttle, Rylie jumped up and was in his face before he knew what happened. "Don't try to tell me how to treat my sister. You have no idea what Gwen's been through. How grown up she is. The memories this must have brought up for her."

"I only meant—"

"She's seen a lot of her friends go off to war and not come back. Sometimes just as bad; they come back shattered. A shell of who they used to be." She gulped a mouth of air, clenched her teeth. "There's also the ones who come back not even caring about the life they had. Willing to toss people who love them aside without a thought. Then they request front-line duty and go back again."

Her emotions caught Taylor off guard. Rylie was fighting for her sister, but more than that, he realized there must be more to the fun-loving Gwen than he knew.

"Breathe, Rylie. Just breathe," Taylor said.

Evidently, something had been tripped inside her memory bank, too. He'd let her get everything out, before he reminded her that Jake was not back in the military. Not going off to fight in some foreign land.

She gulped her water down and stared at the ground until her breathing eased and the red flush in her cheeks had dimmed to pink. "You can't imagine how hard it is to be a kid in a military family. Moving from base to base. It's hard when your dad gets on that plane to leave, but you know that's his job. Besides, he's your dad. He's invincible.

"Then you get older. Kids you've known for years—studied with, played tag football alongside of, dated—are soldiers now. They're deployed. They're wounded. They're honored with 'Taps.' My sister's younger than me, and she was right in the middle of the losses. It's been hard for her. Real hard."

Taylor nodded and turned up his bottle to cover his awkwardness. Sometimes accepting the truth was a hard taskmaster. "But Jake's not going off to war. He's going frontline at trying to rebuild something, only better. Bottom line, he's the face of TRED in this. He's everything this company is built around—help others see their dreams while helping the world be a better place to live." He glanced toward the door. "I'm proud of my brother. Proud he accepted the leadership role in this project."

Rylie fiddled with her hair, pulling it back into a fist-held ponytail, then letting it fall free. Finally, the front door to the construction building opened. Gwen and Jake stepped outside with their arms around each other as they walked to the oak tree.

Jake smiled. "I've got good news and bad news for you. Good news is you don't have to drive me to the airport."

Taylor braced for the bad news, although it couldn't be too bad, or Jake wouldn't be smiling. "And the bad news?"

"I'm gonna need a few weeks off from work." Gwen scurried to her sister's side. "We've decided to take my car and drive to Fort Campbell. Stop here and there along the way."

Taking everything in, Taylor realized Jake looked like a man who'd found paradise for a few days. Then what? Hell. This might not be such a good idea. For Jake. Or Gwen.

Rylie looked as stunned as Taylor felt.

"It's not like I can just let you off at the drop of a hat." He glared at the now arm-linked couple.

"Oh, I understand. In that case, I quit." Gwen smiled up at Jake.

Taylor grimaced. He knew his mouth was hanging open, but he couldn't seem to close it. Turning to Rylie, he said, "Tell your sister she can't quit?"

Rylie laughed out loud. "She can do whatever

she wants. Remember, I'm not her mother hen."

"Aren't you the least bit concerned about her going off with Jake? On some cross-country road trip?"

"First of all, it's from Missouri to Kentucky. Hardly cross country." She jumped in her convertible, shook her hair free in the slight breeze, and winked at Gwen. "Second, it's Jake. Trust me, Papa Taylor. My sister knows what to do with him."

CHAPTER TWENTY-SIX

SEATED AT HER desk, Rylie leaned to her left and looked down the hallway to the other end of the construction trailer into Taylor's office. It wasn't even nine o'clock, and the phone had rung incessantly for the last hour. Just like it had the past three workdays. Neither one of them bothered to answer. They let the calls go to voicemail, content to ignore the fact Gwen was gone.

Rylie had been happy when Jake and her sister left last night. They looked like a couple out to do nothing more than enjoy life. Of course, she hadn't thought about the hole left by her leaving. At least Taylor's good sense showed up before the couple left. Gwen still had a job as long as she was back within a month.

Was he crazy?

After a month of this, Rylie figured she and Taylor would have destroyed TRED with their stubborn attitudes. She remembered the turmoil she heard in the background when she'd negotiated the job for her sister in the first place.

"You need to do something about this," Rylie

shouted down the hall.

Taylor leaned to his right and zeroed in on her stare through his open doorway to hers. "Just what do you want me to do? I've got a conference call starting in ten minutes. Two contractors need approval to increase orders for materials. There's that stack of old bids to review. And still no sign of Bennett this morning."

The two of them met in front of Gwen's desk. Stared at the ringing phone.

"Don't suppose you could take on the extra work for a while, could you?" Taylor asked.

Her face must have told him her reaction to such an idea. Stupid. Inconsiderate. No way in hell.

"That's what I thought." He reached for the phone, but it clicked over to be added to the growing list of messages.

She began to take a little pity on him as he glanced at the empty coffee pot. Where caffeine was concerned, her sister had said that unlike most people, he seemed to calm down the more coffee he drank. That was why the pot was always at least half full. Usually.

He looked stressed, worn, and frustrated all at one time. Even kind of cute with his hair in disarray from the strong morning winds. Of course, his tan was already in full mode. Kind of a beach-boy tan. At least that's the way his face and arms looked.

"Where's the coffee stuff?" He crouched to look in the cabinet under the pot.

Her mind strayed. The taut stretch of his jeans

as his muscled legs filled out the thigh area along with his shoulder muscles tight against the black TRED polo grabbed her full attention. Had he said something? She felt a sting as she bit her lip, fully captivated by the endless possibilities his stance slammed through her mind.

"Rylie!"

Caught. Caught staring in the way a lady wouldn't do. Shouldn't do… Oh, heck. She was a grown woman and would stare anywhere she wanted. So why were her eyes shut now? The heat of her blush zipped clear to her core. Tingled. A slight smile quirked the corners of her mouth.

Act like nothing happened. She opened her eyes to find him staring at her. Maybe he didn't know what she'd been thinking. Not likely given the way he grinned and slid his gaze to her feet… slow and easy over every iota of her body.

"Oh, get out of the way. I'll make the coffee." She reached into the overhead cabinet for the filter and coffee packets.

With a few quick flicks, she had coffee dripping into the pot. The two of them reached for coffee cups, bumped elbows, and looked away. He might be going to calm down with the caffeine, but she needed decaf. Maybe a fan.

The phone rang. They sighed and looked back to the pot.

"We need help," Rylie said.

"So, hire a temp."

"It's your company. You hire someone."

The front door opened, and the sound of children's voices wafted through the building.

Now what?

"Hi, Rylie." The tall, slender woman with shiny-clean long brown hair held the hand of a child in each of hers. Benjamin, a toddler, on her left, and, Natalie, the nearly school age girl on the right.

"Hi, Sheila. How are you?"

Like all inquisitive children, the two surveyed the room with their dark-brown eyes.

Everyone in town knew Sheila's good-for-nothing husband had taken off with a woman barely past jail-bait age. A divorce was in the works, but like as not, any court ordered child support would be hard to come by. Still, it would be a better life for Sheila and the children than what they'd had with him.

"What's that?" Natalie pointed toward the counter.

"Shh," Sheila said, then faced Taylor. "Gwen called this morning and said you might need some help while she's gone. What with me and the kids on our own now, I try to pick up extra work. In between the bakery, thrift shop, and community college, that is."

Taylor knelt in front of the children, handing them Oreos from the cookie jar. Rylie saw a different man this time. One who would be a good father someday. One who would provide for and protect his family. One who would be a woman's man and a child's daddy at the same time.

"I didn't know you were in school," Rylie said.

"Have to finish my courses there before I

can apply for nursing at the state college over in Surryfield." Sheila waited for Taylor to stand. "Computers are easy for me. I'm honest, just ask anybody. And a fast learner. I can look at the way Gwen has things set up and follow along. As far as pay goes, I—"

"You make the same as Gwen while you're here," Taylor said.

Sheila's smile spread across her face. "I got the job?"

He nodded. "One thing, though…the children. They can't be around dangerous tools. What with the crew in and out all day, you never know when someone might leave something sharp laying around."

"That's okay. Lorna and Eloise said they'd watch them at the thrift shop. Just give me a few minutes to take them down there, and I can start today."

"By the way, we'll work around the hours you need off," Taylor said.

Rylie loved what had just happened. To know there was a rainbow's end every so often meant the world to her. "I can probably schedule time in the office, too."

Taylor grinned at her, and she smiled in return as the little group stepped out on the porch.

"Mama, does this mean there's enough money me and Benjamin don't have to share a Happy Meal anymore?" Natalie asked.

The lump in Rylie's throat formed faster than water sizzled on a hot griddle.

"Next week. Let's wait till next week."

"Yippeeee! Next week, Benjamin. Next week."
Sheila closed the door.

Taylor walked to the window and stared out.
Rylie joined him to watch the family walk down
the street.

"You did good," Rylie said.

"Thanks. Now if Bennett would just show up."

Taylor's cell phone rang as he walked toward
his office. Caller ID read Bennett. Finally. "What's
going on? Where are you?"

"This isn't Bennett, just his phone," one of the
crew said. "We found his truck lodged against a
tree. He's in pretty bad shape. I've already called
for an ambulance."

A siren blasted along the road in front of the
construction trailer verifying the emergency.

"Where are you?"

"Section three. By the creek. Looks like he hit
a deer and rolled over."

"I'm on my way." Taylor charged outside,
shoving the phone in his pocket.

Rylie ran behind him. "What's happened?"

"Wreck. Go pick up Bennett's wife. I think she
works at the school."

"Is he hurt?"

Taylor nodded. "Get her to the hospital in
Surryfield. If the ambulance passes you, I'll be
right behind. You latch on to my speed. Got it?"

"Got it. She'll want to come out to the accident
to be with hi—"

"No!" His arm shot straight out in front of him,

finger pointed at Rylie. His voice sounded harsh even to himself. "Under no circumstances are you to bring her to that scene unless I tell you different. Got it?"

Her face reflected understanding of the implications his statement made.

"Got it." Muttering what sounded like a prayer, she headed to her car parked in front of the construction trailer, then stopped to wait for Sheila, quickly running down the street, heading in their direction. Rylie motioned her near, then held out her hand. "There's been an accident on the worksite. Here's my card. My phone numbers are on it. Call me on my cell when you get inside and I'll tell you what to do."

He skidded out of the parking lot. In his rearview mirror, he saw Sheila close the office door as she went in. Rylie sped away in the direction of the schoolhouse. She'd taken charge of things so he could focus on the accident. Said a lot for her. She didn't fold like some people would have.

Dust flew behind him in sections of road not yet paved. He pulled over when the jaws of life van appeared behind him. Not a good sign. Trucks and emergency vehicles cluttered the road ahead, so he pulled onto the grassy hillside. Sprinted to the scene. As he neared, he made eye contact with one of the men who'd served with him in Iraq. The guy gave a not-sure gesture. At least it hadn't been a thumbs-down.

Taylor heard the screech of metal being peeled back. His mind jerked to another screech years ago, but he quickly recovered to the present situation. This was his life now. His employee. A silent prayer arched from his heart straight to heaven. He hated being the boss on days like this.

The paramedic motioned Taylor over. Bennett grabbed his hand, and their grips fisted around each other's. The man's family would never be the same even in the best-case scenario.

"My wife Lucy…" Bennett said.

"I sent Rylie for her. They'll be at the hospital."

"Tell her…the kids…I…I…"

"You'll tell them yourself." Taylor hoped his statement was true.

Bennett's cough gurgled. "If I…don't…you know what to say."

Taylor nodded. They'd both served. Cradled soldiers as they faded away. Spoke to their families with the words the men hadn't had time to form. He knew. Hell, yes, he knew.

Well over an hour had passed since the nurses wheeled Bennett into surgery at the Surryfield Memorial Hospital. Rylie sat with Lucy, Bennett's wife, for the first thirty minutes, then moved to the chairs along the opposite wall as the children rushed in to be with their mother. The two daughters hadn't left the woman's side since, while the two sons whispered with Peabody, Patrick, and Taylor.

"What's taking them so long?" Lucy asked.

The family's expression asked the same.

"I'm sure they'd let us know if something was

wrong." Taylor knelt in front of her. "I take it as a good sign they didn't evac him by chopper to Capitol Medical Center."

She nodded. "You're right. That's a good sign."

The girls agreed. The sons looked skeptical as Taylor rose and walked in their direction.

"Let's go talk to someone at the nurse's station," he said.

The young men followed him down the hall only to return saying the doctor said another hour. Rylie got food and drinks from the cafeteria and set them on the corner table in the waiting room. Sooner or later, someone would be hungry or just need to work off nervous energy. Eloise called to start the prayer chain in Nature's Crossing. Janie would be the link for people stopping by the market and hearing about the accident.

Another young man ran into the waiting room and grabbed Lucy in his arms, then hugged each of the family members saying a word or wiping a tear when needed. Moments later, the doctor walked in, and everyone jumped to their feet. He pulled a chair over and sat down to face Lucy, who he'd motioned to sit on the sofa. Others gathered to listen.

"Surgery went well," the doctor said. "Specialists I brought in have been working on your husband, too. We all agree he'll have a hefty recovery but see no reason he won't make a full recovery after some physical therapy."

A negligible sigh ambled from the bystanders.

Lucy sat straight and tears free. "But what?"

The doctor frowned. "I don't understand."

"What else? You still haven't told us everything."

This woman reminded her of the day the plane crashed. Keeping herself together, her mind clear, focused. Trying to evaluate the situation and make the right decisions. This woman's kids had no idea what their mother was going through right then in order to stay strong for them.

Rylie pulled back a bit. She must have paled or flinched because when her thoughts reorganized, she realized Taylor had moved to her side. His hand cupped her elbow, held her steady, steered her to a chair in the corner.

"Take a deep breath," Taylor whispered in her ear, and Rylie obeyed.

Lucy kept her composure. "What else?"

"Nothing really," the doctor said. "There shouldn't be any follow-up surgery. So recovery and physical therapy should about do it."

"How long?" Lucy asked.

"Two, three weeks, a month at most, I'd say." The doctor answered the rest of their questions, then went to check on Bennett before letting the family see him.

The family's murmurs quieted after a few minutes. Then, as the rest of the family looked on, the latest arrival walked over to where Taylor and Rylie sat.

"Mr. Randolph, I'm Dwight Bennett, the oldest son."

Taylor rose to take the extended hand. "Taylor. Just call me Taylor."

The young man made direct eye contact. "Sir, they say my dad will be okay after time to heal.

That could take some weeks, though, and we... I realize that puts you in an imposition as far as his work getting done."

Rylie glanced at Lucy who watched her oldest son with pride in her eyes.

Taylor shifted his stance. "That's not what's important right now."

"Well, actually it is, sir." Dwight glanced at his family. "You see, we need that check coming in. Mama's got us on her health insurance, but we still need every dime that comes in. So, I'd like to make a deal with you."

"I'm listening."

Dwight drew his shoulder back. "I know I don't have the experience like my Dad, but I'll work from sunrise to as long as it takes every night to get his job done. With a little guidance from the men on the site, I know I can handle whatever needs to be done. Even if it means seven days a week, sir. You won't hear a complaint out of me."

"Let's talk." Taylor sat down and slid over a chair, facing him. He leaned forward, elbows braced on his knees as the young man sat. "What do you usually do?"

"I'm going to college here in Surryfield. Work part-time at the hardware store."

"What are you studying?"

"Pre-med, sir. I got a partial-scholarship." Dwight's demeanor eased a bit, but his expression held the weight-of-the-world.

Taylor leaned back in his chair, relaxed. "That's a lofty goal. What made you choose that field?"

"A couple of things. First, my little sister in

third grade has juvenile diabetes. Maybe I can find a cure. It's not any way for a kid to have to live."

That explained needing every penny, Rylie figured. Besides tuition, there was also insulin and unplanned hospital trips in this family's life.

The young man went on, "Second, Dad talks about all the good the medics do on the front line. One day, I plan to make that trip."

Rylie watched Taylor's reaction to all this. She wasn't sure what she wanted from him, but she hoped there was more to him than business. The other night had caught her by surprise when she'd seen inside his muscles and stone facade. Now she hoped for him to be…what? She didn't know what, but it meant a lot to her. That made no sense, but lately her life wasn't making near as much sense as it had before she'd walked into TRED's office back in Kansas City.

"About that job," Dwight said.

Taylor rose and the young man followed. They stepped toward the family.

"You might as well hear this, too, Rylie," Taylor said.

She joined them. Afraid her changing attitude about him was about to be shattered, she clenched the fingers of her one hand inside the other. Don't let the stone Taylor show up was all she could think.

Lucy got to her feet. Apprehension in her eyes.

"Sounds like Bennett dodged a bullet this time," Taylor said. "Of course, he won't want to have anything to do with those therapists once they start working him. They'll make him wish he'd never seen a deer in his whole life."

Laughter through the family eased the tension.

"You all know what Dwight talked to me about?" Taylor asked.

Nods all around.

"Here's my answer." His business voice crept in. "First, any of you are welcome to work for me any time you want. With only one stipulation, it doesn't interfere with schooling. Which means, for now, Dwight should focus on what he's been doing. Hardware store and college."

The family's shoulders did a collective sag. Rylie could read their fears. She agreed with Taylor's concept, but this family needed more right now.

"Second. The company's insurance will handle Bennett's hospital and doctor bills. Rehab. Whatever it takes. Plus, there'll be a new truck waiting in your driveway tomorrow morning, compliments of TRED. Your auto insurance shouldn't get raised just because a deer jumped on the hood of the last one."

The boys smiled.

"Bennett's salary will continue to be deposited in your bank account every two weeks, just like usual. Now, you all concentrate on getting him ready to roll again and living your lives."

Lucy and the family enclosed him in thank you before Rylie and Taylor said their good-byes. The couple rode down silent in the elevator, then walked to their car and truck parked next to each other.

"Who are you going to get to take over for

Bennett for the next few weeks?" Rylie asked.

She kept pace with Taylor. The double steps she used with him at first had been replaced with long strides, and if she wasn't mistaken his had lessened just a bit. They seemed to be evening out except for when he deliberately outdistanced her just to see her skip to keep up.

Taylor took a deep breath, then grinned. "Me!"

"You? What do you know about—"

"I told you before. I helped my dad start this company." He stopped, turned to face her. "I know this company forward and back."

She felt her hands on her hips. This man irritated her to no end, and now she'd even picked up his mannerisms. "True. But when was the last time you worked onsite? What about your daily meetings and paperwork?"

Laughter. He actually filled the air with laughter as he walked to the driver's side of the truck. "If you think I can't work a crew from the break of dawn to after dark and still get my office work done, then you don't know who I am."

He jumped in the F-150 truck. As if glued to the spot, she hadn't moved. Her insides had sure as heck quavered, though. Right before her eyes, Taylor Randolph had changed. His expression had fired up, and his walk had whipped into an almost cocky jaunt. The thought of him in a hard-hat, form-fitting T-shirt, work boots, and jeans meshed together in her mind. She smiled to herself. Behind-the-desk businessman Taylor with his suits and kakis, white shirts and green ties, loafers and uncalloused hands was in for a surprise.

He powered down his truck window. "What's the smirky smile about?"

"Nothing," she lied. "I just don't see you as a hard-hat guy. That's all."

He revved the engine and grinned. "Well, baby, get ready. You ain't seen nothing yet."

CHAPTER TWENTY-SEVEN

A FEW DAYS LATER, Rylie leaned against the kitchen doorway inside the Victorian, watching Taylor barge from one cabinet to another then another then another. "What are you doing?"

"It's eight o'clock and all I've eaten today was a peanut butter and jelly sandwich. Wouldn't have had that if one of the men hadn't been nice enough to toss me one at lunch." Both doors of the side-by-side refrigerator were clutched open in his hands as he stared into the freezer, then the refrigerator and back to the freezer. "Don't we have any food in this house?"

Rylie laughed.

"I'm serious. I need something to eat." His eyes scanned her navel area, where she'd tied her shirt into a knot above her shorts. At least she had left her bra on tonight.

She pushed him from in front of the fridge, handing him an orange and banana. "You're a mess. Go take a shower. I'll have food ready when you come back down."

"I can take care of myself. I'm not a child you

know?" he grumped.

No kidding. Her body spiraled into overdrive before she could shut it down. "I know," she whispered to herself.

"Did you say something?"

She shook her head and pointed toward the stairs. "Go. Now. Should I make coffee?"

"No! I've got enough caffeine in me to keep an army on its feet all night." His footsteps echoed up the stairs.

Rylie's culinary skills were limited to the basics because she didn't like to cook. Bottom line, she didn't know how to prepare more than a few dishes, and she'd already used one of those when she made the omelets for them the night he looked over her paperwork. Besides, the more she thought about their playing house routine— him going to work and her having dinner on the table—the more it didn't seem like a good idea. She slammed the cabinet doors.

"Maybe we don't have anything to cook." Her inclination was to just go to bed, but she'd told him there'd be food, and he had looked tired, hungry, and like a typical man after a hard day of work. He'd been right, she'd underestimated him when it came to physical labor.

Finally, another glance in the cupboard produced tuna, a small quickie-bag of cheese noodles, and canned spinach. That, plus the fruit salad mold she'd bought at the market would have to do. Dessert? She tore open the bag of chocolate chip cookies and crumbled them into two small bowls, then slipped them in the freezer.

In short order, the noodles were cooked and mixed with the tuna and cheese. Pleased with herself, she nuked the spinach way too long in a way too small bowl and made a mess on the turntable in the microwave. Figuring cleanup could wait, she donned oversized potholders and transferred the bowl to the kitchen island.

"You bought stools," Taylor said as he entered the kitchen.

Rylie whirled around, bumping into his chest. Spinach splashed from the bowl she was carrying and splashed on the front of his clean shirt.

"Hot. Hot. Hot!" He ripped the T-shirt over his head and flung it to the floor. "Damn, that hurts."

"Oh, my gosh. I've burned you." Rylie grabbed ice from the freezer and rubbed it over the red marks on his chest. "I'm so sorry. This should help."

He flinched when her fingers brushed the welts but otherwise he didn't move.

She pressed on the blotches. "Hopefully, the ice will keep them from blistering. Or maybe we should go to the emergency room. What do you think? Should we go to the hospital?"

He still didn't move.

She glanced up and caught him staring at her. His hand folded around hers when she paused from dabbing the spots, and the want in his eyes brought her back to the moment. One she'd created and exacerbated even. She stepped back. Shoving the ice in his hand, she stepped even farther back as melting rivulets of water trailed down his abs.

"I think I'll survive. The ice felt good, though. Thanks." He reached past her and dropped the cold wetness in the sink, grabbed a towel from the counter, and dried the water marks. "If you don't mind, I think I'll go without a shirt for right now."

She nodded in agreement on the shirt. What else could she do? One lucky thing came to mind. The stools were next to each other at the counter which meant she wouldn't have to look at him during dinner. He might be in his late thirties, but he kept himself in shape. Oh, how she'd love to ease out of her blouse and wrap herself across his back.

Together, they cleaned up the spinach from the floor, then she filled their plates with tuna casserole and fruit. They ate amid friendly conversation about business and the community. Side by side. Bumping arms. Nudging legs.

Taylor finished his second helping and walked back to the stove. "Is there more?"

"No, but we do have dessert. Here, I'll take your plate. Sit back down."

Rylie retrieved the two bowls of cookie crumbs from the freezer and ladled cherry vanilla ice cream on top, then drizzled chocolate syrup around the sides. She grabbed the can of whipped cream from the door and removed the cap.

"Now that looks good," Taylor said. "Guess I'm gonna have to give you a five-star rating."

"You've got to be kidding. I deserve a ten just for effort." Absentmindedly, she shook the can, but her finger slipped from the rim and landed on the nozzle. Whipped cream spewed into the air. On to the counter. Splattered herself and Taylor's arm.

He laughed and reached for his napkin. "If I didn't know better, I'd think you did that on purpose."

"I didn't. Honest, I didn't." Laughing, she grabbed a fresh towel from the drawer, cleaning herself and the counter in record time.

Taylor shook the whipped topping can and performed the final touches on each of the bowls. "I like sundaes, even though they do take some work."

"Good." Rylie slid onto her stool next to him. "Oh, my gosh."

"What now?"

"You've got whipped cream in your hair." She wiped it away with her napkin, then stood. "And your forehead."

He swiped at his cheek on the other side. "I think there may be some over here, too."

"Let me see." She turned his face and wiped the finger-dab size of cream away with her fingertips. "I think that's everything."

"Whatever you say, baby."

The feel of his skin against her palm, his breath mingling with her own, the intensity of his look, all combined and heated her thoughts. He hadn't moved, hadn't reached out for her, but her lips parted, her breath hitched, and she leaned toward him.

She stroked the pad of her finger over his bottom lip a second before she kissed him.

His lips felt warm beneath hers, and when she nipped them, he opened for her, but he still didn't reach out. Their mouths eased into place as she teased and tasted and took. More and more, deeper and deeper, until her fingers twisted his hair. He slightly shifted on the stool, but still didn't reach for her. Instead, he took everything she offered and in return he gave everything she wanted.

Her palms slid across his shoulders, and his muscles tightened, his forearms forced against the counter as if fighting not to break free. Tender and light, she edged closer as her kisses changed to sensual sweetness and enticed them both with the promise of ecstasy. A slow, easy dance of tongues and the overwhelming need to be with him felt like the lure of a glowing fireplace after a downhill run on the slopes.

Yes, this she wanted. This man with muscles of stone, tenderness hidden from the world, and a body she'd love to feel spooned around her. This man warm and willing beneath her touch. This man she was devouring with every passing moment. She wanted all of this. All of him. Now. Right now.

Hot and sexy and more…more…more—

Rylie jumped back to the end of the island counter. What the heck had she done?

Flushed and quivering inside. Flushed and quivering outside. She gasped for air as her body pulsed. Reacting. Releasing. Responding. Good lord, where had she taken herself? Taken them?

Backward, she stepped toward the doorway

needing to get away. Far, far away.

"You didn't finish your ice cream." His voice was ragged, his eyes languid.

Still, he didn't reach for her, but his inhales were deep and the exhales heavy. She knew he wanted her. But she also knew he'd made her have to decide. Made her have to take the first step. Made her have to realize what she wanted and realize what she lost if she pulled back.

And she had pulled back. Damn it to blazes, she had pulled back.

"I'm not hungry." Her only hope to regain her self-control was to leave the kitchen. Leave Taylor and his scent and her want. This evening had turned into more than she'd bargained for, and she had no one to blame but herself.

"Don't you like sundaes, Rylie?"

"Yes, but I'm… I… I'll see you at work tomorrow. Good night." On the way to her room, she pulled the kitchen pocket door closed behind her, then kept walking.

He opened the door. "You left the whipped cream on the counter."

"Put it in the fridge." She kept walking.

"The Jell-O?"

"Let it melt." She kept walking.

"What about some ointment for my burns?"

She stopped at the French doors to her bedroom and turned to face him. He had to be one of the most frustrating men she'd ever met. Her breasts tight against her bra, she wanted him so darn bad she could barely put one foot in front of the other. "Listen, I'm only going to say this once. You need to get in your truck. Drive to the grocery. Find your own ointment. Then. Dab. It. On the red spots."

Taylor grinned. "You did such a good job with the ice, I thought maybe you could rub the ointment on for me."

Rub it on? Her hands itched to do a lot of things, but applying burn ointment to his chest was not one of them. Maybe massage oil, but that was another whole situation she couldn't contemplate with him standing in front of her. "Well, you thought wrong. And while we're at it, there's one more thing."

Hands in his pockets, ankles crossed as he leaned against the doorjamb, he grinned. Nothing said, but the world of unspoken said enough because those hip-riding jeans of his were stealing her thoughts. Never mind his muscled abs and the play of hair on his chest.

She inhaled deep. "I will no longer be fixing your meals. Not tomorrow. Or the next day. Or the next."

"Whatever you say, ba—"

"And stop with the baby. Stop, stop, stop!"

She hated his self-assuredness, and her own insecurities, but most she hated the overpowering taste of desire in the room.

"Good night, Taylor Randolph."

"Good night, Bridgette Rylie Crawford. Sweet dreams."

CHAPTER TWENTY-EIGHT

IN THE FEW weeks since Bennett's accident, Rylie hadn't seen much of Taylor. Since the whipped-cream incident, he'd been up and out the door before she made her way to the kitchen each morning. By the time he appeared in the evening, the sun was long gone. She knew he spent hours in his office after the work outside was done. Probably ignored eating most of the time.

Each night, the old pipes in the Victorian house relayed when his shower was finished. The quiet afterward made her think he crawled straight into bed to get some rest. In good shape to start, his body still probably ached from the physical workout of lift-haul-up-down construction labor he'd been doing the past couple weeks. Not one to complain, he worked till he dropped and then got up again. That's who he was. That's what drove his company. That's why he was the CEO—Nature's Crossing, Kansas City, or New York.

She'd been wrong about him not being a hard-hat type. The times she had run into him lately had been mildly earth shattering to say the least, what with the black T-shirt that hugged his muscles like a glove, the work boots that gave him more of a hero edge when he walked, and the jeans. What could she say about the jeans? They were damn snug in all the right places.

One thing for sure, though. Taylor was Taylor, and no one would change him. She'd figured that out for herself, too. He didn't ask for help, and now that Jake was out of the picture, there was no one to see what he needed and make it happen.

For the past three nights, she'd seen Taylor drag himself up the stairs. No food, nothing to drink. Not even his usual can of soda each evening. At that rate, he'd exhaust all his reserves and make himself sick. She could at least take a couple of ham sandwiches, veggies, chips and salsa up to him. If he ate would be up to him.

Besides, she'd noticed he had included azalea bushes for landscaping at various places throughout Peaceful Lake Acres and even in front of the Victorian they shared. When she'd asked him why he chose azaleas, he muttered something about her thinking he didn't pay attention. That had made her feel good. Meant he'd actually listened when she talked about how much azaleas meant to her.

He gave her azaleas. She made him dinner. Seemed like a fair exchange.

Rylie climbed the kitchen-to-second floor steps, clutching the loaded tray in both hands. She'd never been upstairs before. The weekly cleaning lady took care of the entire house. Now, she could feel the change the moment she made the final step on to the upstairs landing. A glow at the end of the hall told her that must be the master suite.

There was no answer when she tapped on the door, but it eased open slightly, and a muffled sound of water emanated from somewhere inside. Pushing the door open farther, she hoped there'd be time to set the tray down and leave before he finished his shower. Question was, where to leave it.

If she set the tray on the table by the window, he might not see the food. Maybe the nightstand, nothing much there except the lamp and clock radio. She balanced the tray on the edge and slid it backward, moving items as it made its own space.

Glancing around the room drew her in even more. His keys and wallet were on the top of the chest, iPhone on the other nightstand. The small computer desk, nooked into the bay window facing the backyard, held his briefcase plus a stack of paperwork topped by a pair of broken-in work gloves. Splashing sounds came from behind a closed six-panel door next to one that stood open to reveal a walk-in closet bigger than her dayroom downstairs.

She didn't step inside, but she could see the closet's layout from where she stood. One side held a row of hangers filled with shirts, pants, jackets, and a couple of suits. Appropriate shoes were shelved below the clothing. The other end held jeans and work shirts, a couple of hard hats on the shelf above and work boots on the floor below.

As she turned away, the other side caught her attention. There hung a set of desert and jungle fatigues, plus a full-dress Army uniform. Name tag read Captain Taylor Randolph. Her eyes focused on the jump wings pinned above rows of campaign ribbons and medals. She'd seen the same in her parents' closet years ago, and as far as she knew, they hung there still.

The floor below held shined dress Army shoes. Next to them, a pair of broken-down combat and jump boots. Exactly who was Taylor Randolph? Where had he been in life? One thing she knew from the looks of things, he had to have been more than a New York CEO all his life. Was he still?

When she turned away, the sight of his tousled covers from where he'd rolled out of bed that morning stirred her heart.

Her hands moved across the bed, smoothing the soft navy-blue sheets, straightened the cream-colored comforter. Except for one, all the pillows were scattered by the side of the bed, and she plumped them one by one before she tossed them against the headboard. She eyed the scrunched and battered pillow originally on the bed, then pulled it against her and let her cheek rest against the end as a mixture of soap and him seeped into her mind, replacing the smell of his cologne.

What would it be like to wake up to that scent each morning? To turn over and—

"What are you doing, Rylie?" Taylor said.

She jerked around. Flustered. Caught. Speechless.

Arms crossed, jean-clad Taylor leaned against the door facing of the bathroom, towel tossed over one of his bare shoulders, his slight grin was unreadable, but she had a feeling her own face was transparent. The heat in her cheeks. How long had he been watching her?

"You've had a long day, so I brought your dinner up." She pointed to the tray beside the bed as the pillow slipped from her grasp on to the floor.

He stood away from the doorframe and toweled his hair but never took his eyes off her as she bent to retrieve the soft cotton bundle. She needed to…ummm…fluff the pillow…to…get herself away from temptation.

"Thanks for the food." After tossing the towel behind him, he plowed his fingers through his damp hair and took a couple steps forward. "Why are you still here?"

Those low-riding jeans of his were going to be her downfall. Jeans and skin and muscle. She knew it deep inside, and from the look on his face, he knew it, too. But she'd be damned if anything happened between them tonight. Just because it crossed her mind didn't make it real. A lot of things crossed her mind. He was right, though. Why was she still there?

Fluff the damn pillow and leave.

He took a couple more steps, slow and easy, almost like someone trying to calm a scared puppy or child or woman. She turned away and placed the pillow against the headboard, and when she straightened, he was behind her. Her self-will still couldn't tell her why she didn't leave.

Gentle and soothing, his fingers skimmed upward from her hands to her arms to her shoulders to her neck. Her body tensed with the lean of her head as he swept her hair aside of her neck. As she tilted her head, he wound his fingers through her hair, twirling it into strands and sliding them down her back.

"Your hair's like spun gold." Taylor's husky tone was barely hearable. "Silky like those pajamas you wear."

No. This can't happen. Why am I still here?

His palms slid to her shoulders and over the curve, then the touch of his kiss against her neck created an involuntary arch against his lips. Her emotions soared on her intake of breath.

"Turn around, Rylie."

Slow and unsure, she shook her head. This was too much. If she turned, nothing would ever be the same again. If she turned around, Mathew would be gone. If she turned around, Taylor would stand in his place. Did she really want that? Maybe… No. Too much. First the business. Now this. Too much.

His fingers twisted through her hair again. "Turn around and face me."

"No."

"Why?"

"I'm afraid."

His hands stilled. "Of me?"

"No."

"Then what?"

She shook her head again. How could she explain what she didn't understand herself? "I don't know. I really don't know."

The touch of his hands left her. Then, the sound of his footsteps crossed to the window.

"I'm sorry," she said as she crossed to the door.

"Nothing to be sorry for. That was my mistake. Please forgive me."

Her hand trembled on the doorknob.

"Rylie," Taylor said, although he didn't turn to face her.

"Yes."

"I won't make the first move again. If you ever come to me it'll be of your own free will. I don't want you any other way."

"I—"

He picked up a stack of papers from the side table. "And don't come back in my bedroom just to bring me a tray of food."

Her heart jerked like a fist had pounded through. Nausea rose, and she couldn't breathe. Go back. Go back. No, she couldn't. What had she done?

"Good…good night…Taylor."

He didn't answer, but from the corner of her eye she saw him walk over and shove the pillows from the bed. The muscles across his shoulders tensed as he picked up the last malingering one and threw it into the corner.

She stepped out of the room and closed the door behind her. Halfway down the hall, she stopped at an oval mirror positioned above a polished to perfection table. Her hands moved to her hair and then slid down her neck with the moments-ago memory. She'd only been thinking of his hunger from the long workday when she brought the tray of food. Right? If so, why had she stayed? Why had she felt the need to straighten his bed? To notice the closet. To hold his pillow close. Why?

Just the look of him in those jeans had taken her places long forgotten, and his touch had… For a moment, her eyes closed with the remembrance. When they opened again, her reflection in the mirror finished her thought. There on her face was a softness and smile that warmed her insides, but she'd refused the man her heart was crashing forward to encompass.

Why? Betrayal? No, her till death do us part with Mathew had come and gone. She knew that now.

Maybe this was just like high school when her first date leaned in for a kiss, and her nerves filled her lips with tiny twitches. Except this wasn't high school. They were both adults…experienced adults. And what lay behind that door was a lot more than just a kiss.

Her cell phone chirped with Gwen's ringtone.

"Hi," Rylie said.

"Hi, yourself. I'm back from my road trip with Jake."

"Good."

"Thought you might like to come over. We could order pizza in."

Rylie glanced down the hall to Taylor's door.

"I'm kind of busy right now. At least I think I am."

"Oooooookay. There better be a good reason I'm getting the brush-off."

"There is. Trust me. I think I'm ready, Gwen. We'll talk tomorrow."

Rylie ended the call and turned her phone off. Her sister had been right about one thing. This better be good. Scurrying down the front stairs to her room, she knew what she needed to do. Maybe her purchase from the Ooh-la-la Lingerie Shoppe during the girl's day out with Ashley and Janie had been a good idea after all. The rest would be up to him.

CHAPTER TWENTY-NINE

TAYLOR BLEW HIS cheeks out with a long sigh. Throwing the damn pillow hadn't helped matters, and he was way too hungry to pitch the plate of food, so he carried the tray to his desk. The past few days he'd subsisted on a donut here and there, plus coffee. Lots of strong damn coffee. Occasionally, one of the men would toss him an apple or the extra sandwich they didn't want, but for the most part, they'd just looked at him like he didn't belong out there beside them.

Too bad. It was his company, and if he wanted to be out there in the mud and the muck, he'd be there. Bennett would be back on the job within a few more weeks. By then, Taylor's blisters might be healed.

There was also the fact he needed to get back on his fitness routine. Even if it meant running by himself. Everyone would laugh at him running in work boots, but nothing built your leg muscles like picking-up and putting-down boots on the hard, hard ground. Otherwise, without Jake around, no one would goad him to push through the pain and stay ready.

He set the tray and dishes in the bathroom after he finished eating. No way was he taking them downstairs tonight. Standing by the windows he blew out a sigh, then grabbed a handful of papers from the stack on his desk. Damn, he was tired. Maybe he could sleep for a while and get up early for the paperwork. No, he'd said that the night before.

A soft tap on the door caught his attention.

"Taylor?"

"Go away, Rylie."

Women! They always wanted to talk about why they did something. Feelings. Turn it around until it was your fault. Not going to happen tonight. Or ever. He'd made a decision. She wouldn't be allowed into his life.

"Can I come in?"

Hadn't he just told her to go away? Irritating, that's what she was. And bullheaded. "Taylor?"

"Go away, Rylie. I'm busy."

He heard the knob turn, then a couple of footsteps before the door closed. Had she left or stayed? He figured the latter. Well, she could stand there for an hour for all he cared. In fact, he didn't care if she stood there all night.

"I'll wait." Her voice was soft, but something else, too.

"I'm busy."

"I'll wait."

Patience at an end, he turned around. Heat flushed through him like water through a fireman's hose. He felt the moment his adrenaline jumped to attention right along with his body.

Rylie looked like a starlet from a remake of a 1940s movie, leaning back against the door with her blonde hair brushed to a sheen falling to her shoulders, soft and inviting. The pale-blue satin gown shimmered over every curve of her body, and a slit from the floor to her thigh revealed one long, tempting leg. The touch of shine to her lips was the only thing on her face's fresh, clean look.

Nonchalant, he placed the papers in his hand back on the table behind him. "What are you doing, Rylie?"

"You're busy, so I'm waiting. Of course, you did lay the papers down. Are you finished with your business for tonight?" She pushed away from the wall.

Was he finished with business? Hell, yes. "Are you sure about this? Real sure?"

She took a couple steps toward him. "Very sure."

He watched her, barefoot and leggy. With every step, the slit in the gown swished back and forth, back and forth, back and forth. Rylie had changed the game, and he needed to catch up. Yet her slow seduction felt good. He'd have all night to pay her back. By morning, he planned to have met all her wants and needs—even the ones she didn't know she had. Right now, though, he had a few wants and needs of his own that were in full force.

Her fingers slid along his bare skin when she eased in front of him, and his breath caught then released with a groan. The feel of cool satin caressed his bare chest, and a furnace-hot shiver shot through him as she leaned against him.

On tiptoes, she reached up and pulled his head toward hers. He volunteered easily. Fingers caressed his neck. Her lips teased his, nipped like the night in the kitchen when she'd slipped her way into ecstasy and scrambled to back out. If she changed her mind and ran this time, he might implode. Then, almost shyly, she tilted her forehead against his chest. Damn, she felt good.

"I don't know what you like," she whispered.

He released the breath he realized he'd been holding. She wasn't leaving this time, and that hit him like an oasis in the desert. Then, another shot hit him even deeper. He didn't want her to leave. If she sat down right now and said all they would do tonight was talk, he'd accept the gift with open arms. His body might go into permanent what-the-hell mode, but he'd be okay. Better than okay.

"And I don't know what you like, either." He raised her chin with his fingers, gazing into her look of surrender and apprehension. "Is this your first time since the plane crash?"

"Yes." She didn't flinch. Didn't pull away. Didn't blink away a tear.

The reality of what that meant exploded inside him. He might not be the smartest when it came to women, but he wasn't stupid, either. She'd chosen him to bring her back to life, and he wouldn't disappoint her. Wouldn't rush her. This moment would be about her. He'd make sure of that.

"Why don't we see what we like together?" Full and deep, he kissed her until she relaxed into his kisses.

Her fingers slid down his chest to rest at the top of his jeans, fumbling with the button, but he moved them away.

"Not yet, Rylie. You and me got a long way to go tonight. A long, long way."

Her lips followed every peak and valley of his muscles, and he savored her reactions to his touch. Gently, her toes skimmed to rest on the top of his bare feet as he slid one of the gown's satin straps from her shoulder.

Action and reaction built. Highs and lows. The highs higher with each passing moment, each movement. His fingers stroked her breasts, feeling the change in them as she gave herself up. And he loved how her fingers tangled in his hair. Tighter and tighter and tighter. She might not even realize she trembled, but she did. She trembled beneath his touch and he liked that. Liked it a lot.

With the abandonment of insecurities, her body arched into his as he slid the satin gown to the floor, along with his jeans. Then, she stretched her arms upward, swaying just like she had that night at the lake when the music took her. He realized this time she swayed for him, and he embraced her roundness and lowered his mouth. Slow and easy, little by little, he took her where she needed to go.

"Taylor…oh, Taylor."

No matter what else happened in his life, he'd never forget that she called out his name.

"Now…" she whispered as he laid her across the bed. "Now…"

Rylie woke to find herself hooked inside Taylor's arm, snug against his side. Content to lie that way all day, she listened to his night sounds and watched him sleep. Last night had been more than she'd dreamed it would be, and now in the light of day, she had no regrets.

Her body ached. Partly physical. Partly with need for more of the man who yelled out her name last night. More of this man who'd taken her places long forgotten. Even places she'd never been before. Memories of the past hours played through her mind and brought her body awake. She snuggled closer and slid her hand through his chest hair, wanting to follow her fingers through the coarseness across his abdomen. Unsure, she stopped.

She'd wait. His words and actions in the light of the morning sun would tell her if she'd been right about last night. Had it been as wonderful as she remembered? Had he felt their spark, or was it only her imagination? Had the world finally moved on for her? Yes.

No matter what the other answers turned out to be, her world had moved on.

Life had snuck in during the past few weeks, building her self-worth that she deserved to live again, that it was okay to be herself again. A woman with needs and wants. She giggled to herself and smiled. Needs and wants had certainly been met last night. She'd made love, and she was okay. Very, very okay.

"Good morning, baby." Taylor's words brought

her back to the moment.

"Ummmm, good morning yourself. You overslept. It's almost ten." Her fingers tangled through the coarseness again.

"Do you think the boss will fire me?"

"If he does, he'll have to deal with me." She stroked the side of his face, teased his lips with her fingers. "Do you want me to make you some breakfast?"

Taylor pulled her closer as his hands traveled familiar paths from last night, stroking her skin, nuzzling her neck. Then, in one quick, smooth motion, he reached out and eased her on top. Guiding her hips to his, he settled them as one. "I've got everything I need right here."

An hour later, Rylie shoved a couple of protein bars in Taylor's hand. His hair still wet from his quick shower, she pushed him out the kitchen door. It had been a long time since she'd had such a beautiful start to a morning. The tinge of what she'd done flashed through her mind, and a tiny sense of betrayal battered her emotions. Betrayal of Mathew, their love. She pushed the unfaithful thought aside. She'd passed one hurdle, now on to the next.

Her first appointment wasn't till one, which left her time to rework some ideas with her company's finances. Time to review the offers that had come in to buy Crawford Enterprises.

CHAPTER THIRTY

TAYLOR WALKED IN the main door of the new clubhouse building. He couldn't remember the last time he'd been so happy. Flat out happy. Maybe never.

Although still being furnished in the common area, the new surroundings felt good. TRED finally had a showcase presentation area to welcome clients. Next week, the landscaping would be completed and the pool filled. Finally, Peaceful Lake Acres would be a premier home destination in the Midwest. And Nature's Crossing would have a new addition to their community.

Gwen greeted him with a smile on her first day back at work since her road-trip with Jake. The vase of daffodils and daisies Taylor had ordered delivered on her return, decorated the corner of her new polished cherry desk. A photo of her and Jake at the leg of the Gateway Arch adorned the other.

"About time you got back," Taylor said, smiling. "Jake get settled in okay?"

"As settled as he can. Him and a few other businessmen are flying to Washington for some meetings this morning. Then they head overseas tomorrow. He said to tell you thanks for holding my job." She jumped up and gave him a hug. "I thank you, too."

Taylor awkwardly gave her a small hug in return. His gaze fell to a zipped insulated bag on the file cabinet in the corner. "What's this?"

"That is what's known as a lunch box nowadays." Gwen twirled her hands in a Vanna impersonation of presenting the questioned item.

"I know that. Why's my name on it?" Frowning, he peered inside and was surprised to see it filled with fruit, a pre-packaged salad, and deli sandwich. His stomach gurgled with hunger. A thermos and refillable bottle of water occupied the additional pocket with what felt like frozen ice packets lining the bottom and sides.

"A few of the work crew brought it by this morning. They informed me it was my job to make sure there was food and drink packed inside every day."

He could only imagine what she'd said back to them. Might have even garnered one of her trash can banging sessions, although the new ones weren't really to be banged around.

Gwen twirled her pen and sighed. "You know that's not in my job description, so you better remember that at my evaluation time."

"Yes, ma'am. But, why'd they—"

"Evidently, they like you out working with them. But when lunch time comes, you just sit there like an outsider. Like you've forgot what lunches are about. They're tired of sharing their own food with you, so they took up a collection, bought the lunch box and gave me my instructions."

Taylor smiled. "They like me hanging around?"

"I had that same reaction." Gwen gave an eyebrow-lift smirk.

They liked him. Good. He liked them, too. "Guess this wasn't the right day to be late on the job, huh?"

"Probably not. Where were you anyhow? You didn't even pick up your cell phone when I called."

"Busy. Come in my office and we'll go over a few things before I head out to the site." He gripped the navy satchel, held it at eye level, and grinned before depositing his lunch bag on the side table in his office. The men liked him. Gwen seemed to like him, too. And Rylie absolutely, without a doubt, definitely liked him. Life was good.

Gwen followed, taking the seat across the desk from him. Suddenly, she scrunched her nose as if trying to place something. Then, her eyebrows shot up, eyes lit on him, and she leaned back in her chair.

"Is that a new cologne?" Gwen asked.

So that's what had his office manager's attention. She smelled Rylie's shower gel. On him. All over him, in fact. Gwen had noticed, which meant the men would notice. Then they'd rib him or shoot him a look that said "we know." So what? He was old enough to do what he wanted, when he wanted, and so was Rylie. Two consenting adults who needed each other for a while. Nothing wrong with that. Need…pure and simple.

Gwen leaned back, pen and pad in hand. "About time."

He ignored the comment, and for the next hour, brought her up to date on happenings around the development. Truth be told, he'd missed her smile and sassy comebacks around the office. Sheila had learned quickly, and he'd be keeping her on part-time as she finished her nursing school.

"Hey, how about lunch, sis?" Rylie said, walking into the office.

"Damn." He'd almost forgot lunch. Like a man on a mission, he grabbed the new lunch box and charged through the atrium to the front door. "I have some personal business at the County Court House over in Henton. But first, I'm going to have lunch with the guys working out on the development site. Call my cell if you need anything."

He deliberately made eye contact with Rylie as he passed by. Made sure to touch her hand with his fingers. "I'll see you later."

CHAPTER THIRTY-ONE

BACK IN KC or New York, being dressed up in a suit and tie was second nature to Taylor. Here in Nature's Crossing, he felt like shucking the jacket and tie requirement that Mark and Ashley's wedding invitation had suggested. They'd wanted their day to be special, complete with the outdoor wedding at the edge of the pines and the dinner held in a huge reception tent with a danceable floor throughout. The sparkling lights and fold-down sides with clear windows along the side, in case of rain, were only the beginning of the transformation of the property's back acreage.

When Rylie got a glance at who all might be on the guest list, she'd insisted they dress for the occasion. Taylor had made sure he looked every bit of what he knew she'd want. He liked this community and didn't really mind the obligations his business persona entailed, but today the tie and cuff links were constricting.

Glancing at Rylie, he couldn't believe how professional, classy, and sexy she looked all at the same time. He doubted she even knew how good she looked today. Of course, if she asked him what she had on, all he'd be able to say was something kind of sheer and green.

But the way her hair fluttered in the breeze and her shoulders peeked from the extended neckline, plus the pendant that hung just at the hint of the curve of her breasts…those were etched in his soul. He figured she was his to lose and considering the way fate treated him, he was sure he could screw everything up.

Taylor grabbed Rylie's elbow and steered her across the patio toward the dance floor. "Come on, I'll show you how to tango."

She came to an abrupt stop. "You tango?"

He slipped around her to the rhythm of the beat, his hand never leaving her body. "What do you think?"

"Pretty darn good for a construction guy." She laughed. "How many more secrets have you got in store for me?"

A jerk reaction powered through his body, and tension raced through his soul. He stopped and faced her. "Not many. I promise. Not many."

Her expression told him she'd picked up on his unease. Apprehension took root in her face, and she did that little lip-biting thing she did whenever she wasn't sure of something important to her. Rylie stayed at the edge of the dance floor.

"Come on. We can do this." Even he heard the unease in his voice.

Peabody chuckled into the pair's conversation. "You know, besides the bride and groom, I think you two are the classiest couple out here."

Taylor stepped to the side, and Rylie pasted a fake smile on her face.

"Did I interrupt something?" the elderly gentleman asked.

"Nope. We were just discussing tangos." Taylor pasted his smile on, too.

"And secrets." Her look seemed to crawl inside him, looking for answers.

The momentary quiet between the three stretched like an eternity.

Rylie slipped her hand into the crook of Peabody's elbow. "Now, I think you're the most dapper guy here. What say we go for a spin around the dance floor?"

Peabody smiled. "What about your fella here?"

"Don't worry about me." Taylor took a few steps toward the edge of the crowd. "Enjoy the dance, Mr. Peabody."

Taylor's insides quaked at what had transpired in the last few seconds. A catch had floated between him and Rylie, one he needed to fix. One he should have already explained weeks ago.

His PTSD had raised its head the day he'd interviewed Rylie. The same day he'd fired Chase. Of course, that had also been the anniversary of his unit being assaulted. Since then, the only time there'd been a moment of panic had been after he and the Major had talked after he'd settled in here in Nature's Crossing.

But just because he had better control of situations now didn't mean everything would stay fine forever. Rylie deserved to know everything about him. He needed to explain the assault and physical recovery. The connection between Chase and the man who saved his life. The deal he'd made with God and the universe.

The pines whooshed in a welcome breeze as dusk dropped in, and an early owl relayed his call across the band's music. Melodic. Lonely. Captivating. He needed to talk to Rylie.

Rylie blended in with the crowd of local people she knew best. From the dance floor, she watched Taylor set off across the grass. What had just happened with Taylor? What secret? No, she was being paranoid. They'd already shared their pasts. Their secrets…emotions. Just now, she and Taylor had been joking, and his statement about not many more surprises had been part of the joke. She let her unease go. Time to enjoy the reception.

For the next hour, she laughed and ate and danced. Danced with Peabody and Chadwick, Patrick and Mitchell, and Clayton Reynolds. She'd asked the last two when she saw them each by themselves. Something about Clayton's expression reminded her of the first time she'd been at a wedding after Mathew had died. Feeling alone and lost and having a boatload of memories crash into your heart.

She moved with each of the men's gentle dance lead, but no one's hold would ever be like Taylor's had been earlier in the day when they glided around the floor. He'd made her feel like the luckiest woman in the world. Loved and treasured all in one moment. "Thanks for dancing with me, Clayton. I seem to have lost my original partner."

The man seemed shy. "First time I've danced since my wife passed on. Feels kinda nice."

His honesty caught her attention. "I hear you've got some mighty fine boys. Imagine they keep you pretty busy."

"They're a handful some days, but I wouldn't know what to do without them. Tim, my oldest, he may just get himself a soccer scholarship to college. He's an ace at scoring goals. Best at the high school." Clayton spun her around and even smiled in enjoyment as the song ended.

Taylor walked up beside her and slipped his hand in hers. And for a few moments, the three of them discussed how happy Mark and Ashley looked. Even their dog Cocoa had a carnation in her collar.

"Well, I'd better go catch up with my boys. See how much cake they've managed to eat." Clayton turned toward her. "Thank you, Ms. Crawford. I appreciate the dance."

"Why don't you ask Sheila?" Rylie pointed to the woman, where their part-time office assistant sat bouncing her son on her lap. "This is a special day. A wedding day. And I know all I want is happiness today. Sheila looks like she could use some, too.

Taylor's insides warmed with Rylie's comment. Only happiness today? If that's all she wanted, that's what he'd give her. No talk of business. No explanations about his past. No conditions on their future. Today, only happy would be on their agenda. Tomorrow, they'd talk.

Shaking his head, Clayton glanced at Sheila then back at Rylie. "Doubt if she'd dance with me. She's busy with her children."

"Then help her watch the children. Or get one of your boys to watch the children while you dance. Maybe your football prospect could teach the little ones to kick the soccer ball around." Rylie nudged his bicep with the palm of her hand. "All she can say is no."

"Thank you for the dance, Ms. Crawford." Clayton smiled and took a step in Sheila's direction. "And the encouragement."

She smiled, then turned into Taylor's arms, stroking his cheek with her fingers. Her smile ignited his insides. And her trust completed him. A trust he needed to make sure stayed in place… tomorrow.

He grabbed Rylie's arm and steered her toward the dance floor. "Now how about I steal a dance with the most beautiful woman at the wedding?"

CHAPTER THIRTY-TWO

THE DAY HAD been touching and happy, but Rylie was glad to finally walk into the kitchen at the Victorian. She slipped out of her strappy heels and twirled them on the tips of her fingers. "I'm thinking about a shower before bed."

Taylor's all-male look clicked on. She loved that look. If she wasn't careful, that wouldn't be all she loved. He'd already crept into her soul and battered the door to her heart more than she ever thought possible again.

She dropped her shoes and backed him against the center island as her fingers made their way down the front of his shirt. Each undone button was one step closer to the end of a perfect day. When she tugged the shirttail out, he finished the row and then shucked the shirt to the floor. His fingers tangled through her hair, fanning it like butterfly wings till light and airy strands fell back to frame her face. She felt herself arch into him, letting her hands make their own pathway across his chest.

No kissing tonight, only touching. Sensual, exploring touches that each of them seemed to need. His thumbs teased even through her dress, and her breath came in tiny, ragged gasps. The rasp of his day-old beard against her skin as he suckled the sensitive spot in the crook of her neck was pure seduction. Pure exquisite seduction. Seduction she never wanted to stop, now or ten, twenty, thirty years from now.

A corner of her mind whispered to let go and accept whatever Taylor had to offer. No matter his secrets. Give what you can and accept what he can give you. Today and tomorrow and always. She realized no one else saw this part of him—his tenderness, his consideration, his need and want. This wasn't casual, this was a gift. A gift only for her...only her.

"You looked beautiful today. All I could think about was how lucky I am to be the one coming home with you." His fingers lowered the zipper down the back of her dress and pushed the green sheerness from her body. He groaned as he watched the material glide to the floor.

She felt the coolness of the room on her bare skin. "The dress has a built-in bra."

He grinned. "In that case, you need to buy more of those dresses."

His fingers returned to their teasing spots, and she wilted more and more with each stroke. She strained to pull against him, her nails biting into the back of his shoulders, but his hands kept her at bay as he watched her dissolve with pleasure, and his heavy open-mouthed breaths rose and fell in sync with her own. When his mouth nipped and whispered in place of his fingers, she closed her eyes, floating in her emotions.

And when she reached the rise of the moment's sensation, she shook her hair free, tickling her fingers through the silkiness and into her overhead stretch, aching for more. Then Taylor stopped. The responsive flash opening of her eyes found the look on his face possessive, eyes half-hooded. He was in the throes of her need, her want, yet he waited. She grasped to pull him close again, but he wouldn't bend to her. Instead, he grinned, waited, and waited as she sagged into a senseless body held up only by the power of his arms as she nuzzled against his chest.

Then his breath began to cover her hair in an is-it-really-there sliver of cooling heat. She straightened enough to look into his eyes. The stream of air through his lips caressed her face, then her shoulders. and she blew him sighs in return.

Only her green silk panties remained, and she expected him to make quick work of those. Instead, Taylor dimmed the lights, skimmed his thumbs across her in one slow, triggering move, then slipped his arms beneath her. She folded against him, skin to skin, heat to heat. He'd made sure her day was happy. Even though something else had troubled his mind at times. He'd still given her a perfect day. What more could she ask of a man?

Love?

"Maybe I should take you to the dining room table." His breath tickled her neck with his whisper. "Would you like that, baby? Or maybe the gazebo in the backyard." Nuzzling behind her ear, he finished with a nip of her lobe. "Or maybe the master Jacuzzi?"

She giggled. "Whatever's your pleasure."

"My pleasure. Now that's another story. We may need to grab the whipped cream, in that case."

"Can't…you left the can out the other night and the cream spoiled." Her finger teased its way across his shoulder, made hearts on his neck before pulsing inside his ear until she felt his muscles tense.

A low rumble escaped his control. "Guess we'll just have to pretend."

"Ummmmm…"

Should she tell him she loved him or wait? She didn't want to spoil this delicate, delicious moment. He moved through the living room to the main double staircase and carried her up with ease. As her cheek rested against his shoulder, the vague remembrance of the night he'd carried her from the recliner to her bedroom flickered through her thoughts. This time would be different, though. He was taking her to his bed or his bath or any of a zillion other places he wanted to go. She was thankful to be in his arms. So very, very, very thankful.

Someday, she'd tell him she loved him. That she was sure of. When she did, would he turn away? A silent prayer shied through her essence, she hoped not. Her arms tightened around his neck as if she were holding on for dear life. Now that she accepted how much he meant to her, she wanted more, needed more. Needed his love, his commitment, his words. Oh, how she longed to hear "I love you" from a man again. And not just any man—from Taylor. Only Taylor.

Her world…their world…wouldn't be complete until she heard those words.

CHAPTER THIRTY-THREE

A WEEK LATER, EVERYTHING was falling back into place in Taylor's life. Weather was good. Suppliers were on schedule. Bennett was back at the job. Gwen was happy with her long-distance affair with Jake. Sheila kept up with everything Gwen didn't like to do.

Most important, though, was Taylor's time with Rylie. She brought bits and pieces of him back to life with a touch, a look, a laugh. Even that damn scent of hers lifted the weight he'd burdened himself with for years. He realized there was no turning back. No rebuilding those barriers. Life had found him again, and he planned to do everything in his power to hold onto it.

And he definitely planned to hold onto Rylie, the woman he cared more about than himself or his company. She was his future, and even though he still hadn't told her of the promises he'd made to himself after rehab, he would. There just hadn't been a good time yet. No, that wasn't right. There had been times, but he wanted things to stay just like they were between them—happy and alive and safe. Safe from the past.

Besides, she knew how he felt. He'd already showed her that part and would continue to forever. Together, they'd build the house on the point. Picnic on the rock. Boat on the lake. Enjoy each other. Enjoy their friends. Enjoy the life they'd make together. She'd understand he couldn't break his promise to himself. After all, what were words, just a bunch of letters— iloveyou—strung together to say what could be shown in other ways.

Besides, he liked the way she was making the Victorian feel like a home. Like their home. The four azalea bushes had already bloomed, but they'd been beautiful. Ripe with buds and promise of more blooms in future years. He jotted a note to call the Major later. Let him know about Rylie. Plan a time they could all get together.

Happy to finally have his onsite company offices settled in the development's clubhouse, Taylor leaned over the plans spread across the worktable. Rylie and Gwen stood ready to answer questions from Mr. Peabody and Chadwick Andrews. Even the sometimes enemies had temporarily settled their feud and appointed themselves guardian angels of the new development and Nature's Crossing. Taylor took them with a grain of salt and a smile. After all, they'd lived here most of their lives. Taylor was just a newcomer, as Chadwick liked to point out.

Today the two townsmen stopped by to walk around the hole starting to take shape for the pool. Not that either one of them would ever step foot in the sparkling water, but they wanted to see the hole.

"When will the Peaceful Lake Acres and Nature's Crossing scale model be installed in the lobby?" Peabody asked.

"Should be by the end of the week. The manufacturer's running a little behind." Taylor placed a paperweight on one corner of the blueprint.

Chadwick rolled an unlit cigar between his fingers. Looked around the room as if he'd built it with his own money. "I want the people in Nature's Crossing to be able to walk in that front door to get a look at what we're planning. Not everyone can envision the future like me and Peabody here."

Rylie rested her notebook on the edge of the drawing beginning to curl, Gwen held the other.

"That's very true. Once it's in and set up, we can hold a grand opening," Taylor offered. "We want to make sure the community and our buyers are pleased with their investment."

Peabody and Chadwick nodded.

"Gwen, bring me the folder with the park outlines, please." Taylor walked to a collection of pictures hung on the north wall. To the right, windows overlooked the pool on the east side of the reception area. "Gentlemen, the sketches will show a few of the parks I've designed to be placed around the town and the development."

The two elderly men followed.

"As you'll be able to see, I blend the parks in with the surroundings yet make sure safety and security options are in place. Lights. Water fountains. Shelter from the elements. Emergency phones linked to our office and also 911," Taylor said.

Gwen headed to Taylor's office, but detoured to a ringing phone.

Rylie followed her. "I'll get the folder, Gwen. Where is it?"

"In Taylor's desk. Check the desk drawers."

Rylie made her way to Taylor's office and eased into his chair. His scent floated on the air as the leather enveloped her. Others wouldn't have noticed the essence, but she'd stored it in her memory. The aroma made her feel safe and secure.

She reached in the bottom left drawer, pulled a stack of folders out and placed them on the desk. No need to take all of them. She opened the burgundy file. Figures on lighting. Next the green one. Prints of plumbing fixtures. Next, beige. A checklist for the opening day celebration. Her hand reached back in the drawer and retrieved another folder. Black.

"Where's the file, Gwen?" Taylor asked from the hallway.

"I'm on the phone. Rylie's getting it from your office," Gwen said.

Rylie opened the file. A yellowing newspaper article stared up at her in return. Her gaze raced to the headline above the photo of mangled wreckage—*Catastrophe for Well Known Real Estate Developer's Ranger Unit*. Air in the room charged into her lungs on a gasp. Her eyes blinked in disbelief, upper lip tingled. Deep inside her lungs jerked. Her mind fought the words.

They'd talked about his military experiences, but the photos told what had happened in vivid detail. She lifted the newspaper article and stared at a glossy eight-by-ten photo of Taylor and other men dressed in fatigues. Standing in dirt and sand, they looked strong and fit and happy, just a casual photo of a group of soldiers enjoying a drink and a laugh.

She flipped it over and recognized Taylor's writing. At the top was the date and then all the names of men. Men she figured had been in his final battle. She felt the tears burn in her eyes but brushed them away. Putting the photo back in the file, she noticed another name near the bottom—*Photo taken by my commander, Major Charles Dodd*. She checked the next couple of photos and laid the last one on the desk in front of her.

"The right drawer!" Taylor's footsteps came fast and heavy to his office. "The right—

"All this time, I knew Mathew's friendship was one of the reasons I may have gotten the interview." Her head raised to face him. Pointed to the photo on the top of the desk. "But is this the real reason you hired me?"

"What?" The only sound in the room was of Taylor as he eased into the chair and stared at the photo. "That's the Major. I've told you about the Major and me."

"My last name may be Crawford now, but my maiden name is Dodd."

"Gwen's last name isn't Dodd."

"Gwen is divorced. Her married name is Prescott." Rylie tapped the photo emphatically. "That's. My. Dad."

Shaking his head, he leaned back in his chair. "You've got to believe me, Rylie. I'm as confused as you. It's not—"

"Then how is it, Taylor? You let me spill my soul out to you about Mathew. Help me move on with my life. Got me into your arms. Into your bed. Even let me fall in love with you." Rylie's breath hitched. "And even then, you didn't have the courtesy to tell me about the plan you and my dad concocted for you to help me?"

"I'm just as confused as you, but you don't hear me going off about how the Major must have sent you to check up on me." Taylor slid his fingers through his hair. "How about a little pity for me in this situation."

"Is that what you gave me? Pity?" She jerked her hand away. "Am I just a pitiful widow you've taken in for a while? Kissed and made love to out of sympathy? But you had no faith in me. You didn't even trust me enough to tell me you knew my dad. Why?" Her face felt like paste beneath the tears that flowed with a will of their own.

He didn't trust her…and any chance of love had to be built on trust. She dashed her tears away as the reality set in. Her eyes darted with panic, as if running from the truth. She was crushed to her core with the realization. He'd. Lied. To her.

"How little you must think of me," she whispered. "Of us. Why?"

His jaw clenched as he shook his head. He walked to her side and took her hand in his.

"You have no answer, do you?" At least not one he'd share with her, she realized. That was even worse. Her back tingled with the straightening of her shoulders. A new type of emptiness filled her inside as numbness crept in. She had no emotions left to give. To share. To feel.

"Please let go of me." She tugged to free herself. His hold wasn't tight, but he didn't open his hand.

"Now," she said.

He dropped his hold.

Wiping her face on her sleeve, Rylie fled to her office and grabbed her purse before she calmly walked back to the worktable holding the blueprints. "Peabody. Chadwick. I'm sorry but I just remembered an appointment. I need to...to go."

A tear slid from the corner of her eye. She wouldn't wipe it away. Maybe the men wouldn't notice she'd been crying. Peabody patted her on the shoulder. Chadwick offered his handkerchief. They seemed like grandfathers she'd never known.

Chadwick frowned at Taylor. "Is there a problem?"

"No," Rylie hurried toward the door.

"Yes. If you'll excuse me, I need to speak with Rylie," Taylor said.

After tossing her purse inside the car, she slid into the seat and turned the ignition.

"The way I feel right now, I don't want to talk

to you." She revved the engine. "Maybe never."

She sped away, but in the rearview mirror, she saw him run his hand through his hair. At the intersection, she looked back. He stood braced against the side of his truck, head bowed.

What just happened? Everything had been going so well. Her life had come back, her laughter, her happiness—all because of Taylor. Now this.

Time to think. That's what she needed. He'd lied. No, he never lied. He just evaded. Sidestepped the issue. She needed a man to trust her. To give his all and let them share the ups and downs of life together no matter what.

For a couple of hours, Rylie drove the backroads of the county. Paved or gravel, she kept going. Dust in the rearview mirror buffered her emotions. Distanced her. Slowly, she realized the miles wouldn't keep her from the ache churning inside. Nothing would.

Finally, she retraced her steps, drove past the office, and made her way to the Victorian. Taylor's truck sat by the side of the house.

Her heart ached like before she met him. Before he'd made that ache go away. Now it was back. Even worse. She couldn't go inside. Not yet. Who could she talk to? Not her sister. Not this time.

Rylie backed out of the driveway and drove the streets again. She needed a friend. Someone who'd listen and tell her when she was right. Tell her when she was wrong. Share a glass of wine with her and make her forget how serious she took herself.

Her childhood had been filled with moves, and friends left behind. Even now, her life was a continuous movement with her company. Maybe it was time she reached out and trusted someone enough to call them a friend.

She turned off the highway onto a side road. Within a quarter mile, the sight of tall pines eased her mind. The winding driveway welcomed her. Ashley…Ashley would listen.

CHAPTER THIRTY-FOUR

TAYLOR PUSHED THE answer button on his ringing phone before the sound even finished. "Are you okay?"

"This is Mark."

"Oh." Taylor sighed and plowed his hand through his hair.

"I've had more enthusiastic receptions from enemies."

"I thought you were someone else."

Mark laughed. "Rylie?"

"Yeah."

"She's here. Pulled in the driveway about fifteen minutes ago."

Taylor's insides eased just a bit. At least she hadn't left town. Left him. "She okay?"

"Depends on what you mean. Her face was flushed, and she tried to make chit-chat. The second I saw her chin start to quiver, I got the hell out of there." Mark cleared his throat. "Her and Ashley are sitting on the patio ripping somebody to shreds with their words and finger pointing."

The vision wormed its way into Taylor's mind. Part of him smiled. Part of him cringed. "Okay then."

"That all you got to say?" Mark said.

"What do you want me to say?"

"Well, from the looks of it, one of us is in trouble. I know it's not me. I'm telling you right now, if I end up taking the blame for anything, I'm going to rip your friggin' head off," Mark jabbed the last few words with emphasis.

Taylor chuckled at the thought of the two men coming to blows. Felt good to jerk each other around. He missed that camaraderie since Jake was gone. "Bring it on. We'll see who rips who and what."

For a few minutes, Mark and Taylor tossed around the bull, laughter and bravado. Then, as if on cue, the two men went quiet. The quiet of an early morning patrol looking for signs left in the dark of night.

Taylor cleared his throat. "Is Rylie still there?"

"Yeah. Hey, the reason I called is to finalize arrangements for this fishing trip," Mark said. "Everything on your list has been ordered. Should be in place when we get there. Anything else you need?"

"Not that I can think of."

"Okay then. I'll pick you up at eight Wednesday morning. That gives us plenty of time to get to the airport in St. Louis. Once we land in Chicago, we'll meet up with the other two guys I told you were going along. My friends in Canada have everything arranged on that end, including the puddle jumper to get us as far up-country as we can before driving is all that's left."

Taylor's throat tightened. He didn't like going away right now. He and Rylie needed some time to work things out. Things? Future. Work their future out. If there was still even a chance of one.

"Sounds like this should be relaxing. Guys. Houseboat. Fishing. What's not to like?" Taylor said.

"I do this every few years," Mark said. "Beautiful scenery up there. And some great Northern Pike!"

Taylor got up from the kitchen counter stool, and as if in slow motion, he saw the vase he bumped with his elbow slide off the side. His grab wasn't fast enough. Water splashed him and the floor, flowers scattered from the container as his fist closed around the crystal. He stretched to catch the stems, slipped on the wetness, and went down hard.

"Damn it all," Taylor muttered.

"What was that?" Mark asked.

"A vase of flowers I'd bought for the counter. Now they're all over the floor." Taylor wasn't about to tell his friend he was sitting on over half the broken stems.

"You must really be in trouble. Hey, I better hang up. Rylie's getting in her car." Mark laughed. "From the look on her face, you might need to find a white flag. Show no fear, Taylor. No fear."

Mark ended the call.

Taylor yanked a handful of flowers from beneath him and cringed when a thorn from one of the roses jabbed his palm. Then another. And another. First the thing with Rylie. Next, wet pants from sitting in the water that spilled from the vase. Now blood. What next? Fate sure had it in for him today.

As far as fear went, he might as well admit he had one more. One he hoped she'd understand when he explained everything to her.

Rylie entered the Victorian through the front door, planning to go straight to her bedroom on the first floor. Instead, she found Taylor sitting on one end of the three-cushion sofa in the living room. Forearms braced on his thighs, he held a mug of coffee with both hands. The table at the other end of the divan held another cup of coffee with cream, and she bet sugar, just the way she liked. Looked steaming hot, which meant he'd been watching for her.

She could ignore him, ignore the gesture, ignore everything they'd been to each other during the past couple months. Would serve him right. She watched and waited, but he didn't make eye contact. He just kept his eyes lowered, staring at the mug as if the weight of his lifetime had pressed him to the ground and the cup's warmth was the only thing keeping him afloat.

The longer he stared into nothingness, the more confused her heart became. Her mind knew exactly how upset she felt, how betrayed.

If he couldn't face her, though, she needed to be strong enough to walk away. To save them both the pain of the unspoken. She took a step toward the alcove. The place she'd slept and cried before Taylor happened in her life. Could she go back to that time? No, but she could give herself the respect to move forward if they weren't to be.

"Please don't, Rylie." Taylor's voice sounded ragged. Worse than he looked at the moment. "Please don't sleep in there."

"It's the middle of the afternoon, I'm not going to sleep," she lied.

His face turned to hers, then looked away. "You know what I mean."

She knew what he meant.

To flee to the alcove would be to hide. She was stronger than that. The coffee looked inviting, so she took the seat at the end of the sofa. Tried to tell herself she was staying only for the coffee, not for him. Time passed, her coffee grew cold as she sipped every so often. Still there was only the sounds of chirping birds and a distant mower through the open windows. The smell of freshly cut grass wafted through on a slight breeze.

Taylor opened the laptop on the coffee table in front of them. "I had no idea the Major was your dad. None whatsoever. But the more I got to thinking about this while you've been gone, it occurred to me that maybe he sent you to check up on my wellbeing.

"No, no, no." She shook her head. "I did all of this on my own."

"I figure as much, because when the Major wants something from me, he's more direct. He flat out asks how I am, what's going on. Will you, can you, why, why not. So that's why it wouldn't occur to me to be upset that we all know each other."

"When I talked to Ashley, she brought up that exact same point. I guess I overreacted without knowing the whole story." She started to stand.

"You'll want to sit back down for this." He tapped a Zoom link. "When I saw you turn in the driveway, I texted the Major—"

"My dad?"

"Yes, your dad. Anyhow, I sent him a Zoom link and told him to wait until I got there. I figure we both need answers." Taylor pushed the final button. "So here we go."

Instantly, they were all on the screen.

"Well, this is a surprise," the Major said.

"There are a lot of surprises today," Rylie said, then introduced her mom to Taylor.

Her mom stood in the background, smiling, as first Rylie and then Taylor questioned just when and how the Major had been involved in any of this.

Finally, her dad pointed his finger at them. "This is a bunch of..." He scratched his ear. Shook his head. Then started making his point while embellishing his words with hand gestures. "I'm only going to say this one time. I had nothing to do with this situation. I was in Europe when Rylie applied to TRED without my knowledge. Taylor, you're the one who gave her the contract. Bottom line—" he slashed his hand out in front of himself, "—I am completely out of the picture on this. End of story!"

"Why didn't you say anything once you knew who had hired me?" Rylie asked. "Wait a minute.

That afternoon when Mom said tell her about the Captain…was that about me and Taylor?"

From the background, her mom nodded. Taylor stood up, but Rylie tugged him to sit back down in front of the laptop.

"You already had the job, what was I supposed to say?"

"Then why didn't you let me know she was your daughter?" Taylor grumped. "That you'd rather she didn't work for me? That—"

"You wait right there, Taylor Randolph." Again, with the embellishments along with the statement. "I never said she shouldn't work for you. I never said anything, anytime, anywhere in that regard. You're a great businessman with a great company. She's a great businesswoman. Why shouldn't you two work together?"

"You are so full of it, Dad." Rylie embellished her statement in return. "I'm not letting you off that easy."

"I've only got one more thing to say on this matter. And that's…whatever else is going on between you two is your own business." He got up. Nodded quick and to the point. Walked away.

"It was good talking to you, Rylie…Taylor. We'll chat more later." Mom leaned in front of the screen, fluffed her purple-streaked hair, and winked. Then shrugged her shoulders, blew a kiss, and ended the call.

CHAPTER THIRTY-FIVE

TAYLOR RETURNED FROM the kitchen with two fresh cups of coffee, then silently took the spot beside Rylie on the sofa, setting one of the cups in front of her. He prayed she wouldn't get up. Wouldn't walk away. Wouldn't leave him alone in his darkness.

She cupped his cheeks and brushed his lips with her kiss, then whispered in his ear. "I love you, Taylor Randolph. I love you."

A light went on inside his heart, yet he flinched. She'd said the words he longed to hear. The ones that gave him hope and made his soul swell with the warmth his coldness craved. The words he'd never say in return. Lightly, he kissed her in return.

"I know we just faced our first argument, and there's still lots to think about on that front. But there's something else we need to talk about, too. Something important. Something I kept meaning to share with you." He set his mug on the end table and turned to face her. "There'd always be a phone call or one of us would have a meeting or... None of that sounds so important right now. I guess I really don't know why this is so hard to say."

"Just say what you feel. I'm listening," she said.

He shook his head, slow and defeated. "Because you were happy. We were happy. Do you know how long it had been since I felt alive? Since there was a reason to get up every day? To smile and not even know I was smiling." Taylor fidgeted with a piece of lint on the sofa. "Maybe it sounds selfish, but I couldn't bear the thought of going back to the darkness my life had become. You were the only light I had. You were my future."

She clutched the cup in her fingers. Sipped lightly. Didn't look away from him.

He leaned forward, elbows braced on his knees, hands clasped in front of him. "I need to tell you about the war. About the day I thought it was safe enough to put the sides up on the all-terrains, to get some sun, feel the wind from the forward movement. The day my unit was assaulted. The day Chase's stepbrother stepped in front of a bullet to save my life."

Slow…and quiet…Rylie set her cup down and pulled a throw pillow against her stomach. She lightly placed her finger on his arm. "You can tell me anything, Taylor. Anything you want. I'm here to listen…now…and forever."

Taylor rose from the sofa and paced around the room. Seconds turned into minutes, minutes turned into almost an hour. He told her everything, just as he remembered, only this time there was no PTSD hammering his soul, only the recounting of the past.

Rylie could only sit where she was, watching the man she cared about face his wounds. Watch him suffer as she suffered right along with him. He braced his hand against the doorjamb, voice trembled, chin quivered as his jaw worked against the pain.

Finally, Taylor eased into a chair by the door, leaning forward once again. Her own face covered in wetness, Rylie moved to his side and knelt, unsure if he even realized she was there. The man who'd enclosed himself in his business world in order not to feel had just now faced the dark and walked right through it. She laid her cheek against his knee, and after a while, he straightened in the chair. Wiped his face with the back of his hands.

Rylie jerked with an inward emotion. If she hadn't taken a well-deserved day off for some pampering at the spa, she'd have been on the airplane with Mathew the day it crashed. She always figured they'd both have perished. Maybe not. Maybe life wasn't that simple after all. Maybe there wasn't rhyme or reason for the end, for accidents. One thing she did know was the why-not-me feeling.

He pulled Rylie upward, and she eased onto his lap. His arms folded around her, and together they rocked with their emotions. Slow and easy and peaceful. He shared what he went through in recovery. The deal he made with the universe, with God, that had kept him going ever since. The oath he took upon himself to work for the good of TRED and the world as repayment for his life. The promise he made to never allow himself to love too deeply. Never say the words for fear destiny would jab him once again. And about the PTSD that grew less and less all the time.

Now she understood his aversion to her driving a convertible. She understood his quiet moments. She understood why the point of land he'd bought as a gift for himself meant so much. She understood…so many, many things she understood.

He pushed her hair back and bent his forehead to hers. "I'm sorry, Rylie. I never meant to keep things from you, but I did. There's nothing I can do to make it up except say I'm sorry. It won't happen again. You mean more to me than anything in this world."

They cuddled together in the chair until the sun was only a silent glow left in the sky. And when the room darkened, they gently kissed once again.

"I love you, Taylor," she whispered. "I love you for sharing your past with me. For trusting me with your emotions. For everything you've ever done for me. I love you."

"From that moment in the taxi back in KC, all I've ever wanted was for you to love me," he whispered in return. "Not for my money or my power or because you feel sorry for me. I need you to love me for who I am. Just a man. A man who cares more for you than anything in the world. That's all I need. I hope that's all you need, too. That's all I can give you, Rylie. I hope that's enough."

Hours later, Rylie snuggled deep into the safety of Taylor's arms wrapped secure yet loosely around her. Their spoon position included a layering of legs as if they'd shared the same space for years. His even breaths assured her with their sound, their closeness.

Easing the sheet over her shoulder, he braced on his elbow and stroked her hair. His look beyond tender, he placed soft kisses across her brow.

His hands smoothed down her body, his fingers gentle as they pulsed in tiny pendulum movements. So soft, she thought maybe she was dreaming until his touch caressed her core. As she caught her breath, she knew she was awake. Awake and alive. He eased over her, arms braced by the sides of her head.

The rhythm of his love was slow and giving, and she took him completely. "I love you, Taylor. I love you more than you'll ever know."

His love didn't stop, and his lips took her kiss with the one he gave in full to her.

Later, as they slipped back into nestled spoons, Rylie realized once again he hadn't said the words. Why? Maybe Gwen was right, maybe he just didn't understand their importance to her.

"Taylor?"

"Yes, Rylie."

"Why haven't you told me you love me?" She felt a tiny flinch of his body. She wished she hadn't asked. She wanted to go back to a few minutes ago, when everything was perfect.

"We'll talk about it another time."

She'd gone too far, to turn back. "I need to know now."

His jaw worked as it rested against her shoulder, and the deep sighs relayed his agitation. His discomfort with the subject. "We'll talk tomorrow."

"Now." She tried to turn over, to face him, but his hold gently kept her where she lay. "Now, or else let me go."

"You know how I feel about you. How much I care. You're more important to me than anything in the world." His arms loosened as if he offered her freedom. "I'll do everything within my power to keep you happy, but I swore to never say those words, and I won't. I told you about my deal with the universe, with God. I survived. I recovered. I keep deals. I keep promises."

His fingers twirled her hair into twisted ribbons, sliding them down her neck. "Baby, don't you know how much I care?"

"Yes. Yes, I know."

Taylor kissed her shoulder. "Then that should be enough. Let's get some sleep."

For a brief moment, his voice had held that TRED persona he'd hidden behind when she first met him. His way or no way. That side of him hadn't raised its ugly head with her since the night he'd carried her to the daybed. Her heart struggled to hold on to what she'd found with him since then.

At what cost, though? Rylie stared at the red numbers on the digital clock as the minutes flipped by. Ten long, long minutes. She knew he hadn't gone to sleep. His night sounds were hiding, waiting for her final request.

She knew the question. Did she want the answer? Maybe not, but she needed the answer. "Why? Why did you swear to never say them?"

"Because fate and destiny are a pair of first-rate hell-in-the-world taskmasters." He huffed and rolled to his back. His arm still lay beneath her head. "They're lying in wait for me and anyone important to me. Just like they were the day of the attack. The day the other soldier gave his life for me. Well, this time I'm in charge. I'll show the damn future who's the boss this go-round."

Rylie turned over, resting on her elbow to look at him in the dim glow from the night light in the bathroom. "You can't control fate. Or destiny. Do you really think you can?"

"Why can't you let this go?" He jumped from bed and jerked his pants on. "You've got to understand. I will not say the words even if it means losing you. Not now. Not ever. Because to say the words means I might lose you. Fate might kick me again. And I can't let that happen. Not to you. Not to me. Never!"

After grabbing a shirt from the closet, he headed for the door.

She couldn't believe what was happening. This could be the end of them. An end she didn't want to visualize or even think about. Maybe she could live without the words. Maybe… "Taylor…"

He opened the bedroom door before he looked back. Even in the dimness of the room, she could see the pain in his expression. "I'm not going to talk about this anymore."

She didn't know what to say. What to do. The future was just that—the future. A place to dream of and hope for and take as it came. Sometimes hard and demanding. Sometimes happy and optimistic. What could possibly make Taylor think he was in charge? No one was in charge.

Fate, destiny, the future, whatever it might be called, had a set of rules to play by, and no one could figure them out because no one saw them until the moment was at hand. Not even serious, I'm-in-charge Taylor Randolph. Not even him.

He shook his head, ran his fingers through his hair. "Even if it means losing…"

After stepping into the hall, he closed the door behind him.

Not loud. Not soft. Just closed.

And her mind filled with doubts as the seconds ticked by.

CHAPTER THIRTY-SIX

READY TO LEAVE for the fishing trip in Canada, Taylor headed to the front porch to wait for Mark to pick him up. He was really looking forward to the trip, and all the men's fishing equipment had already been shipped to the houseboat company's departure location. Mitchell had even sent word that he'd meet them when they landed in Chicago.

Two days and two nights had passed since the photo incident. Since he told her about his fate and destiny idea. Since he'd refused to say I love you and stormed out of the bedroom in the middle of the night. Later that night, he'd found her downstairs in the alcove bedroom, and he'd let her stay.

The two days since had seemed the same as usual. Work. Dinner. Conversation. At some point every day she said "I love you." Not an in-your-face statement, but more of a factual offering, and he had to admit he liked the sound of the words.

In turn, he made sure she knew how much he cared in everything they did. They'd made sure to share something about their past each day.

Sometimes more than a few personal memories—some happy, some sad, some funny. Some for no possible reason except to say this happened to me and I remember.

She'd gone to Gwen's the first night after their argument. Last night, she'd come back and went to the alcove. In the end, they'd made love, but she'd slept in the alcove. And he thought he'd heard her crying. So far, this morning seemed like any other day…yet somehow different. He didn't want to leave with anything left unsaid, except what he wouldn't say.

Curled up on the swing, Rylie looked beautiful in a fresh way. Cute little shorts adorned her barefoot legs, brushed hair wisped around her face in the gentle air, and a T-shirt caressed her body. He sat beside her, and she leaned into his hold, her head resting against his chest. Her fingers clutched the front of his shirt for a moment, and he covered them with his own.

"I'll be okay," he whispered in her hair.

She released her hold. "I know you will. I have no doubt about that."

"If you need me, call Patrick. He'll get in touch with Mark."

"Don't worry, I'll be fine. If there's anything I need, I'll find it somehow. Some place. I don't think you realize just how strong I am." She slipped from his hold and walked to the edge of the steps, hands palmed into her two back pockets.

Her tone triggered a warning deep inside him. His gut jerked. Why? What had he heard?

Nothing. This was just a typical good-bye when two people cared for each other. His emotions were playing games with him. Mark pulled into the driveway with Wheat and Clayton in the backseat of the SUV. Best for both of them to make the goodbye quick. Besides, they wouldn't be apart long, just a week.

He stepped down the stairs in front of her, turned, and pulled her into him and his kiss. She didn't kiss back. Her hands stayed in their pockets. Easing away, her expressionless face filled his view. What he saw in her look he didn't like. Didn't understand and didn't like. He kissed her again as if his entire life depended on it. Her lips responded, then her body, and at last, her arms wrapped around his neck. Their kiss broke, but they held each other in a deep and strong cheek-to-cheek hug for more than a moment before she shifted her forehead to his chest.

Taking her heat with him, he turned to leave until her hand gripped his arm and tugged him around. Her hand cupped the side of his face, then she placed a warm and tender kiss on his mouth. One he'd remember till the end of time. As she nuzzled his ear, her whisper of breath floated between them.

"Don't ever forget I love you. Ever." She dropped her hand and moved backward. "I will love you forever."

Once again, his gut flashed a warning. Ask what's wrong. Why? Nothing was wrong. Just his imagination. He stepped away, tripping over an empty garden container and shovel. Three newly filled containers lined the flowerbed. "Why are you digging up the azaleas I bought you?"

"They don't belong here."

Azaleas lined up on the backseat of her convertible, Rylie drove to Peabody's and left one for him and one to give his sister Eloise. Next, she left one for Ashley and one for Janie. A note tied to each one told them how thankful she was for their friendship, along with her cell phone number.

Back at the Victorian, she showered and packed, loaded the car. In the master bedroom, she made the bed, crying as she tossed the pillows against the headboard. Pushing the pull of his essence from her mind, she walked to the front porch and locked the door behind her.

She loved Taylor more than she could put into words, but she had to take care of herself. If she stayed and he never said I love you, then she'd turn into a woman with concrete barriers. Into second-best for herself. Into a cold entity that might lose the love she had for him. Become bitter. She didn't want to be that woman. Bitter was not an option for her love. Better to walk away now and let him live his life the only way he could survive. It wasn't for her to tell him how to live.

She hoped he kept at least part of their time together, at least a laugh or a smile to remember her by. Maybe he'd find someone who could take his love the only way he would allow himself to give—actions and gifts. Yet always holding back anything that might make him a man so enveloped by love he couldn't help but shout the words to the world.

Her insides jerked, felt raw and soggy. Maybe she should stay. He might change his mind. Maybe if she tried hard, she could learn to ignore… No, this was best for both of them. She could love him forever if she left now.

Numbness crept into her core, but she straightened and pushed it aside. No more emptiness allowed. She'd found life again and planned to hold onto it with both hands.

The TRED office would be her last stop before heading away from Nature's Crossing. She pulled up in front of the new clubhouse with the memory of the first time she parked at the old construction trailer. No music this time.

"Gwen? Where are you?" Rylie strolled through the sunshine-filled atrium, then spotted her by the pool and went outside. Her sister looked like she didn't have a care in the world besides making sure her tan had no strap marks. "Aren't you supposed to be working?"

"I'm on a break." Lounging on a chaise, wet hair tousled and shiny, bikini glistening with water droplets, Gwen lifted her sunglasses. She jumped to her feet. "What's wrong?"

"Nothing." Rylie laid her stack of paperwork on a patio table. "Here's the file on the final sale of plots. Everything signed, sealed, and delivered. Get Taylor's approval first, then send it to Mrs. Parker. And there's my final payment request.

Crawford Enterprises' contract with TRED is officially complete."

Gwen flung a lacy cotton poncho over her suit. "You seem to forget I'm your sister. I can read you like a book. Don't give me that nothing answer. What's wrong?"

Rylie's chin quivered, she bit it back. "Taylor left on his trip this morning. My car's loaded, and I'm heading out also, that's all."

"Uh-huh. Does he know that was good-bye?"

"No, and don't you tell him I'm gone. Don't tell him where I'm at, either." She waggled her finger at Gwen. "I mean it."

"Has this got anything to do with what you told me about him refusing to say I love you?"

Rylie nodded quick and to the point. "I don't want to talk about it."

The sisters hugged, then slung their arms around each other and walked to the convertible.

"I'm sorry he doesn't love you, Rylie. I really thought he'd change and—"

"Oh, he loves me. At least I think he does. But he can't say the words." Rylie slid into the car seat. What if he really didn't love her? She couldn't, wouldn't, let herself believe that. "I deserve a man who not only gives me his body, but gives me his heart and soul as well. And the words."

"Are the words that important?"

Rylie bit her lip and nodded.

Gwen leaned against the door. "Maybe I'll quit and move on, too."

"Why? You like your job, right?"

Her sister's glowing smile answered.

"So, stay. Taylor and I have nothing to do with you or your work. Besides, you like the connection with Jake that you get from the men here. Right?"

Lots of nods and a smile greeted that question as Gwen fairly glowed.

"By the way, I faxed off papers finalizing the sale of Crawford Enterprises this morning. You're looking at an unemployed woman."

"I'm proud of you, Rylie." Gwen leaned down and hugged her once again. "Won't take you long to find something you like. Sooner or later, you always land on your feet."

"You're right. I've already been working on a business plan for another venture. One that's all mine and something I'll enjoy. But first, I need time to relax before I commit to a new idea. Time to think." Rylie buckled her seatbelt and started the car.

"Just so I know. Where are you going?" Gwen stepped back from the driver's door.

"I'm headed home." Rylie popped her sunglasses on and clicked the radio to a low volume. "Where the beach is close and the She Crab Soup is waiting. Charleston. Charleston, South Carolina."

CHAPTER THIRTY-SEVEN

THE PAST WEEK on the houseboat had been fun, relaxing, and lonely. Taylor had enjoyed the comradery of the men, but he'd missed Rylie. By tomorrow night, he'd be back in her arms. That thought alone made him smile.

"Hey, who's up for one more round of fishing?" Mark shouted.

Clayton nodded. Taylor headed in their direction. Mitchell and Wheat said they were all fished out. And the other two men offered to cook dinner for everyone.

The individual fishing boats had already been stowed alongside the houseboat, so the men agreed they'd just cast some lines off the side. At this point of the trip, they weren't trying to catch any more fish. Now was about enjoying the sunset and practicing their casting skills. Each of them seemed to be lost in their own thoughts, not even talking much, just taking in the final evening.

"Here's my last cast of the trip." Mark let the line fly. Missed the angle and watched it sail across Clayton's line. He jerked back on the rod, but the momentum and sinker and bait caught the other line tangled.

"You remind me of Jenna." Clayton shook his head. "At least once every time we went fishing, she'd cross my line. Would take us a good ten-twenty minutes to untangle the mess. We'd…" His chin quivered. He bit his lip. "We'd finally get to laughing so hard we couldn't…" His voice took on an emotion-filled huskiness. "Well, half the time, one of us would just end up cutting the line and…" He swiped his palm down his face, wiped his fingers across the tears left on his cheeks.

Mark patted the man on the back. "You've got some good memories there."

"Lots of good memories, but…" Clayton nodded, bit his lip again. "I'd give the world to have her standing by me again…oh, how I miss her…" Sighing slowly, he regained his composure and slightly laughed. "Only thing Jenna didn't like about fishing was the cleaning of the fish. She'd always scrunch up her nose. Make the cutest little pouty face." He slightly laughed. "So I'd do that part, and she'd fry up the catch. Made the best hush puppies I've ever eat." He bit his lip one more time.

The three men were quiet for a while. The fishing was done.

"I'm sorry reliving all those memories of your wife is so hard." Taylor stared out at the water. "That why I can't tell Rylie I love her."

Clayton glanced in his direction. "What?"

Mark took a couple steps back and leaned

against the cabin side of the houseboat.

"I've already faced a lot of loss in my life. Don't think I could face losing someone I love," Taylor said. "So I've decided to never say I love you."

"Excuse me, but that's not how life works." Clayton moved closer. "Do you love Rylie?"

"Yes. Very much."

"Then how is not saying the words going to ever save you from the pain if something happens to her?"

The question shot to Taylor's mind. To his heart. To his soul. He'd never thought of that. Never let himself imagine there not being Rylie in his life. He glanced at Mark then back at Clayton. Never contemplated that he really didn't have any control over anything life decided to throw at him.

"I...uh..." Taylor had no answer. None at all.

"Sorry if I stepped over a line, but just consider how many memories you may miss by not saying what you feel." Clayton cleared his throat. "Sure, there's times the memories make me cry. Sometimes laugh. Sometimes get me through the night. But no matter how hard it is to remember what I've lost, I wouldn't give up one moment we ever spent together. Not one. She was my life. And I still tell her I love her even now."

The boat's dinner bell rang, and the sound of Wheat and Mitchell's footsteps sounded on the deck, heading to the dining room.

"Good luck, Taylor. Life can be tough. But you'll find the answer..." Clayton tapped his chest. "It's in there just waiting to get out." He walked toward the dining room. "Time to eat."

Taylor stared at the unmoving Mark. "You were right. I have no control over life. No matter what I do, life's just going to happen."

"When I first met Ashley, I had no desire to be anything more than a man doing his job. And I sure didn't plan to let a woman ever be in danger because of me. But before I knew what had happened, I couldn't live without her." Stepping up beside him, Mark motioned they should head to dinner. "Trust your gut, Taylor. That's one thing I've learned in life. Always trust your gut."

Early the next morning, the shuttle boat from the departure dock picked them up and deposited them back on dry land. Felt good to have the ground beneath his feet again. Felt even better to have cell service once again.

Taylor powered on his phone and started through his messages. A few from Gwen, all very professional and business related. A couple from Mrs. Parker in KC's main office. A call from Bennett that ended with a lot of static and what sounded like "everything was a lot better when Rylie was here." What the heck did that mean?

There were no messages from Rylie.

All the other calls could wait, but Taylor needed to hear her voice. Needed to call her baby. The other guys were each in their own area, probably making the same calls. Even Mark had walked away from the group as he talked on the phone to Ashley.

Taylor dialed Rylie's number, and it went to voicemail. "Hey, Mark."

"Yeah?" The man shot him a this-better-be-good expression.

"Ask Ashley if she knows where Rylie might be? She's not answering her phone."

Mark relayed the message, then listened with his hand stretched out to keep Taylor from walking away. "You want me to tell him? Okay, I will."

The expression on his friend's face as he ended his call and walked in his direction, was serious. Taylor didn't like that look. Something was wrong. He braced for the worst.

"Rylie's not in town." Mark looked at the horizon. "Ashley said there'd been a note and azalea sitting by our back door the day we left."

Taylor forced a grin. "Guess she didn't want them. She was digging them up when I left that morning."

"The note said she was leaving Nature's Crossing."

"Probably went to stay with Gwen while I'm gone."

"That's not what the note said. And that's not what Rylie told Ashley when they talked on the phone yesterday." Mark looked him in the eye and shook his head. "She left you. Figured you'd know why."

"Yeah. Well…I have to get her back."

"You might want to work on your tact before you face her."

Taylor nodded. "True. Very true. Guess it's time to make what's wrong right."

No need to try Rylie's number again. Instead, he dialed the office at Peaceful Lake Acres in

Nature's Crossing.

"Hello, this is—" Gwen answered.

"Where is she?"

"Taylor. Nice to hear from you. Did you have a good time with your buddies?" She said in an exaggerated Western accent.

"Don't play games. Where's Rylie?" If Gwen didn't tell him, he'd fire her. No, he wouldn't do that. She was the only one who could keep everything in the office in working condition. But she'd better tell him…and fast. "If you don't tell me, I won't give you a raise for five years."

Gwen giggled. "Don't try to intimidate me, because you don't stand a chance. I'm more afraid of Rylie than you. She told me not to tell you, so I won't."

Exasperation filled his sigh as he exhaled. The men seated around him looked on with just as much interest as he had, or at least close.

"I have to find her," Taylor said. "There's something I have to tell her."

"Well…" Gwen produced her own sigh. "I bet there might be someone else in TRED, say in KC, that might know where Rylie is. Say someone who's my counterpart who's probably not sworn to secrecy. Maybe if you asked the right question."

"Thanks. You're the best." Taylor shot the guys a thumbs-up.

He dialed Mrs. Parker and waited patiently for her answering spiel. Then made chit-chat with her until she quieted to attention. "Where's Rylie? Rylie Crawford."

"If she's not in Nature's Crossing, I'd have no

idea. As far as I know, she's not here in Kansas City or New York."

He was back to square one because Mrs. Parker was not one to lie. She genuinely didn't know. A question. Gwen had said something about a question. What question?

"Hold on, Mrs. Parker. I need to think for a minute. I need to—" He snapped his fingers hard and fast. "Where did you mail the contract between TRED and Crawford Enterprises when this all began?"

"Charleston, sir. Charleston, South Carolina."

CHAPTER THIRTY-EIGHT

TAYLOR UNFOLDED FROM the more-than-compact rental car, the only one he'd been able to get on walk-up notice at the Charleston Airport when he landed. Rylie had reduced him to an idiot who hadn't taken time to shave or shower or change clothes before boarding the flight from Chicago to South Carolina. Like a fool, he'd bought three tickets in coach and requested the last row of seats, just so no one would be put-off by his looks or smell.

He loved her, plain and simple. And didn't plan to go home without her.

Why else would he be standing in front of a beautiful Charleston single house looking like a transient? Any other time, the shutters in Charleston Green, gabled roof, and white columned piazzas on two levels would have made him smile in appreciation of the beauty—not today. Today, all he wanted to appreciate was Rylie.

Hopefully, no one called the police to pick him up for loitering. At least the end door to the main piazza was open with a welcome sign. From his historical architectural studies, he knew that meant he could go directly to the main door at the side of the elongated-style house. He'd have gone there anyhow, even if the end door had been bolted closed. He'd have climbed the railing.

The curtains at one of the windows on the second floor dropped close the moment he glanced upward. His guess? Rylie was watching him. Of course, that meant she'd thought he'd come…or at least she'd hope he would. Maybe that would be a plus in his favor. Groveling would probably be an even bigger plus.

Would serve her right if he got back in the car and waited until she came out. No, it was damn hot in Charleston this time of year, and he wasn't sure if he'd eaten in the last twenty-four hours. Heat and starvation were beginning to take a toll on his body.

Of course, it could be Rylie who was taking a toll on his body, mind, and emotions. He waved in the curtain's direction, motioned her down, and then placed his hands on his waist in an exaggerated fashion.

She raised the window. "Go home, Taylor."

"No. Not without you."

"Never." She shoved the window closed. Lowered the shade.

He combed his fingers through his less-than-clean hair, straightened his wrinkled, dirt-laden clothes best as possible, and then ran his hand across the beginning-to-soften beard on his face. He'd need to shave before he kissed her. And, yes, he intended to kiss her before this day was out.

Or at least before he left Charleston.

He stomped onto the porch and rang the doorbell. Footsteps on the other side sounded heavy and forceful. Definitely not female. Rylie yelled something about not opening the door.

Taylor leaned his finger on the bell and held. The door opened. "Major."

"Captain. 'Bout time you got here."

Rylie came halfway down the stairs before leaning over the rail. "Tell him I don't wish to talk."

He deserved that jab. Wonder what else she had planned. Taylor stepped through the open door and nodded to the Major's wife, then turned toward the stairs.

"First, why don't you get cleaned up, Taylor. You look like hell." Dad nodded to Rylie. "Show him the guestroom and the extra clothes in the closet. We'll all meet in the dining room in an hour."

When she complained, her parents walked away. Rylie started up the steps, and it was all Taylor could do to keep his hands to himself. He could hardly wait to kiss the woman pulling him up the stairs just by the sway of her hips.

She whipped her head to the side, eyed him with annoyance. "This doesn't change anything between us. I'm not going back with you."

"We'll talk about that later." Taylor grinned. He considered the fact she'd come down the stairs to be a good sign. "I caught some fish. Some walleye. Northern pike and—"

Rylie stopped on the step, turned and glared at

him. "That's what you want to talk about? Fish? You came all this way to find me, and you want to talk about walleye and pike?" She turned back around and continued up the stairs. "You have so much to learn about apologies."

"Okay." He really needed some carbs or protein because this felt like the longest flight of stairs he'd ever climbed.

"And you can't make me." She stepped onto the polished hardwood of the upstairs hall like a woman making a point. Then, she turned to face him again.

"Make you what?" Taylor asked.

His head hurt, and all he wanted was to rest his cheek against Rylie. Let her loop her arms around him and skim her lips across his forehead. But from the look on her face, he was supposed to be paying attention to something he couldn't make her do. Hell, he figured he couldn't *make* her do anything…at least not anything she didn't already want to do.

"You can't make me go home with you." Her voice softened with that statement.

Home. She'd said home. There was hope for him yet. Should he dare touch her hair, her cheek? He did. She jerked away. He shouldn't have.

"Have I ever forced you to do anything, Rylie?" She shook her head.

"And I never will." He touched her fingers with his. After a few seconds, she turned away and took her warmth with her.

Halfway across the second-floor landing, Rylie pointed to a room. "That's where you'll be staying. There's a shared bath between yours and the next room."

He figured this was as good a time as any to begin his plan of attack on her senses, so he grinned. A grin he knew she liked. One that usually caught her in a web of desire. "So, there's a bath connecting our two rooms?"

Her mouth dropped open, eyes squinted their aroused displeasure.

"That'll make it easy to conserve water." He braced his elbow against the doorframe. "You know…me, you, one shower."

"Oh, thank you so much for the offer to be environmentally conservative." She pushed his arm from the doorframe, and brushed dirt from the wood. "Thank you very kindly, but I have my *own* room with my *own* bath."

"Are you going to show me the clothes?" He grinned again. If he could just get her in the room, she'd never want to come out.

"No."

"Scrub my back?"

"No."

"Give me a kiss?"

Her eyes rounded with the tilt of her head. "You've got to be kidding. Have you looked at yourself lately?"

She marched to her room and opened the door. He caught a flash of pink right before she stepped inside and slammed the door behind her. He dragged himself in front of the full-length mirror on the door of the guest room bath.

"Aw, hell." He looked like it, too.

By the time he showered, shaved, and went downstairs, there was food waiting on the table. Rylie had already been down and ate. She'd already gone back to her room, also. Taylor nodded when her mother offered him another helping of herb baked chicken.

"If you'll excuse me, I've got a cake to ice in the kitchen. The Major will get you anything else you need." Her hand brushed her husband's shoulder as she left the room.

"Thank you." Once she'd left the room, Taylor pushed away from the table and turned to the Major. Like a man on a prolonged mission, the body was tired, the brain was fried, yet adrenaline still fueled the will to keep going. "You said you didn't know Rylie applied for the TRED contract, but I find it a little coincidental that you happened to call while I was interviewing her. Just between you and me, I want an answer now."

The Major sat down at the side of the table. Twiddled a half-empty coffee cup in his hands. "I called you the minute I found out Rylie was presenting Crawford Enterprises proposal to TRED. You didn't answer the phone. So I left a message to call me back."

Taylor figured that had to be the call he'd sent to voicemail. The one that had caught Rylie's attention with the "Airborne Cadence" ring. "You never told me not to hire her."

"By the time you called me back, you'd already given her the contract. What was I supposed to do, say you couldn't? Say she couldn't take it?" Rylie's dad set the cup down with a thud. "Let me tell you, I was none too happy about this at the beginning. None too happy. But it had nothing to do with either one of you personally. I just didn't want either of you to ever think I had a hand in the outcome. Besides, I figured what was done, was done."

Taylor laughed. "How's that working out for you, sir?"

"Not worth a darn." The Major leaned back in his chair. "Besides, how'd I know you two would fall for each other?"

Taylor realized fate might or might not have had a hand in his and Rylie's meeting, but he was tired of worrying about the inevitable. Time to just let life happen. Face each moment. Face it and move on. "I'm glad I didn't answer your call that day."

"Really?"

"I'm glad Rylie came into my life." Taylor walked to the window and glanced to the back yard. A swing, a gazebo, and azaleas filled the scene. Time to win her back and take her home to Nature's Crossing where she had the same yard, plus him. "You won't ever be sorry she found me because I plan to take care of her forever."

"Well, if you don't mind me saying so, how do you plan to get her to agree?" the Major asked.

Taylor walked to the bottom of the stairwell and began his climb. "I plan to sleep right outside her door till she comes out."

Her mother had come back in the room at just that moment and her eyes rounded just like Rylie's sometimes did. "Don't lay across the doorway, she might come out and trip over you."

The Major pulled his wife against his side and looked up to Taylor. Grinned. "Getting kicked in the back as she trips over you won't feel too good, either, son."

Didn't take much for Taylor to figure out that Rylie learned the door locking from her mother. He made a mental note to make extra keys for all the doors they had in their house. After lowering himself to the floor long-ways in front of her bedroom door, he grabbed a throw pillow from the closest chair.

The last few night of fishing, he'd slept on a boat on the water. Now the floor. What next? At least he was clean and shaved and in the same house as Rylie.

Still awake at two in the morning, Rylie slipped from her bed and cracked the door open. There lay Taylor, huddled on the floor with a throw pillow, from the hall chair, scrunched under his head.

He'd come for her. Dirty and tired, he'd come for her. That had to count for something. She loved him more than life itself, and just this once she'd settle for knowing he cared enough to come for her. Loved her enough to lose her if he thought it meant protecting her from fate.

She grabbed a blanket from her bed, opened the door, and knelt beside him. Her fingers stroked his hair, forehead, his firm jaw. How had she been so lucky? Destiny or heaven-sent? Or maybe they were just one and the same. Fluffing the cover over his body, she made her decision.

"I don't need the words," she whispered, then kissed her fingertips and placed them on his cheek.

His fingers folded around hers, and his eyes opened wide awake.

Her clinched reaction to pull away caught her, but she eased instead. "I thought you were asleep."

"No. I've just been dozing. Waiting for you."

"Oh…" Had he heard?

"I'll never forget what you said just then. Made me realize what a very lucky man I am to have someone love me unconditionally." He braced on his elbow and reached the other hand to her hair, tangling his fingers into a hold while his thumb smoothed lazy circles on her temple. "Made why I followed you here that much better."

He pulled her to his lips. And she went willingly. Before their kiss broke, he sat and pulled her on his lap. When she tried to burrow her way into the crook of his neck, he held her back. When she leaned to go to him once again, he still held her back. When she closed her eyes for fear this moment wasn't real, he tilted her face to his.

"Open your eyes, baby. Look at me." He stroked her lips with his finger. "This is important."

Her insides fluttered as she gazed into his eyes. She felt like a butterfly fighting to reach a light that had no end, only the warmth of forever.

"I came here to say…" Taylor's lips caressed

hers slow and gentle, then he leaned away to where she could see his expression. "I love you, Bridgette Rylie Crawford. I love you."

EPILOGUE

SIX MONTHS LATER, standing on their point of land by the lake, Rylie couldn't imagine a more wonderful place to be than next to the man she loved. He might be a tough Type A businessman to the rest of the world, but to her he was loving and gentle and everything she ever wanted. He was the love of her life.

Last week, he'd asked her to marry him. Given her an engagement ring. Presented her with the first draft of floor plans he'd had drawn up for the property. Told her she could make any changes she wanted, and he'd already had her name put on the property title. Today, they'd walked the property looking for differing views for different windows and rooms.

They kissed once again before she walked toward the car, putting a little extra sashay in her swing. Silently, he spun her around, then slid her to her feet, her back to his front. He pulled her close as his fingers danced across the low neckline of her dress, his thumbs making lazy circles on her skin.

"Baby, we need to stop on the way back to

town." Taylor's voice was husky and low as his hands played their game of seduction.

She slipped her shoes off, teasing as she caressed his calf with her arch. From the expression on his face, she had his full attention. He sure as heck had hers. "Ummmmm…why?"

After tossing the convertible keys into the air, he grabbed them mid-fall and grinned. "We need to buy some whipped cream."

THE END

Thank you for reading
TIME TO GROW

**TO BE NOTIFIED OF FUTURE BOOK RELEASES
JOIN MY NEWSLETTER**
http://claudiasheltonauthor.com/

COMING SOON!

COMING NOVEMBER 2, 2021

COCOA FOR TWO

(An Awesome Christmas Book)

The second Friday in December officially begins the Holidays on the Square festival in Awesome, Missouri. During this time, most everyone in a five-mile radius will come to enjoy the sights, scents and sounds of the Christmas activities.

He's got a limited amount of time to spend on handyman work. She's running low on patience for repairs to the property she inherited. And *Holidays on the Square* is being inundated with five times the usual festival visitors. What had her Aunt done now?

PRE-ORDER NOW at
https://tinyurl.com/353eufsx

AVAILABLE 2022

Nature's Crossing, Book 3

Return to Nature's Crossing, where the town festival is becoming a reality. Bed and breakfast permits have been requested. Land has been optioned. Grapes have been planted. And, differing opinions on a family farm are throwing roadblocks in the path to romance.

TO BE NOTIFIED OF FUTURE BOOK
RELEASES
JOIN MY NEWSLETTER
http://claudiasheltonauthor.com/

ACKNOWLEDGEMENTS

A story takes hold in my mind. A hero and heroine appear with plot lines. A setting emerges. And suddenly, months later, I've written the first draft of my manuscript. Finally, the story expands, growing better with reworks and edits, until the book comes together for you to read.

Here are some people I'd like to thank for being involved in making TIME TO GROW a story I hope you enjoy. First, always, is my family! Their love and laughter, energy and excitement, make every day special. My life is a million times better because of them. Love you all forever!

Next, my critique group The Cosmos (Linda Gilman, Michelle Sharp, Suzie T. Roos) can always be counted on for catching mistakes and offering suggestions. Plus, my writing accountability buddies, Lisa Wells and Barb Bettis, make sure I'm doing something with my writing Monday-Friday.

A big thank you to the people who help me actually put the book into print/digital— content/copy editor Tera Cuskaden, proofreader Susan Panak, book cover designer Jeff Shelton (Fan Favorite Digital), and formatter Jennifer Jakes (The Killion Group, Inc.) who always answers my numerous questions with a smile.

Others include my beta and ARC readers. And

the fabulous Skye Warren, who shares so much business info in her Romance Author Mastermind and Author Ads Intensive workshops.

And thank you to everyone who buys my books, follows me on my various social media sites or subscribes to my newsletter—you are the reason for my stories! Hope you enjoy the Nature's Crossing series with its small-town setting and everyday characters. Maybe this story, and others I'm working on, will call to you as much as they have to me.

Smiles,

Claudia Shelton

Books by CLAUDIA SHELTON

CONTEMPORARY ROMANCE

Nature's Crossing Series
A Week at Most
Time to Grow

An Awesome Christmas Book
Cocoa for Two

ROMANTIC SUSPENSE

Shades of Leverage Series
Slater's Revenge
Dangerous Lies

Risk Series
Risk of a Lifetime

ABOUT THE AUTHOR

Award winning author Claudia Shelton had already proven herself a contender in romantic suspense novels that cross over into the mystery-suspense-thriller genre. Now, with her Nature's Crossing series, she has entered the contemporary romance and women's fiction market. Whether writing emotion filled small-town settings or action-packed sexy protector agents, her stories give the reader what they want—considerate alpha heroes and confident heroines strong enough to love them.

Claudia is a two-time finalist in the Daphne du Maurier (unpublished) Award for Excellence in mystery and suspense. Her debut book release, Risk of a Lifetime, was voted one of Ebooks Galore's top reads for 2014.

On a personal note, Claudia considers herself a music lover and water person, plus she enjoys anything to do with nature. In fact, the Nature's Crossing series allows her to bring all of those things closer. Her main priority, though, is spending time with family, friends and her two sweet, conniving rescue dogs, Gidget and Daisy.

She enjoys hearing from readers, so stop by her website and drop her a note. While there, sign up for her newsletter or some of the other sites where she keeps everyone informed on her writing shenanigans.

Newsletter Sign-up: -
http://claudiasheltonauthor.com/
Website: -
http://claudiasheltonauthor.com/
FB -
https://www.facebook.com/ClaudiaSheltonWriter
Twitter -
https://twitter.com/ClaudiaShelton1
Pinterest -
https://www.pinterest.com/claudiashelton1/
BookBub -
https://www.bookbub.com/profile/claudia-shelton/
Instagram -
https://www.instagram.com/claudiasheltonauthor/

THANK YOU IN ADVANCE FOR
LEAVING A REVIEW
ON THE BOOKSELLER'S SITE—
IT'S TRULY APPRECIATED

Made in the USA
Coppell, TX
16 May 2021

55803474R00218